Other Books from Emily O'Beirne

A Story of Now Series

A Story of Now
(Book #1)

The Sum of These Things
(Book #2)

Points of Departure

by Emily O'Beirne

Dedication

For all the girls out there who like girls and who deserve their happy endings, too.

Acknowledgments

Thank you to Astrid at Ylva for giving me a home for my stories, and thank you to Michelle for such a lovely editing experience.

Characters

Liza

After realising that being an athlete might not be for her, Liza's just broken it to her parents that she wants to quit running. And that she's pretty sure she's gay. And now she's leaving the country. On this trip, Liza's hoping to figure out what her new life without running could be like. And maybe she'd like to meet a girl who actually likes her for a change. She just didn't plan on doing any of this without Kit by her side.

Kit

It was Kit's idea to take this trip. But hapless, charming, and a known walking disaster sometimes, Kit has yet again failed to follow through on one of her plans. Now, instead of going on this dream holiday with her friends, Kit's forced to stay home and work through her summer holidays in Melbourne. Then there's that small problem of finding a life plan...

Olivia

Olivia always thought she had her life mapped out. There's the plan to study law, there's the friends she's taking to uni with her, and there's a relationship with a guy who is as much like a best friend as a boyfriend. But after a disastrous break-up and an exam meltdown, Olivia's forced to confront the fact that maybe she's been mindlessly following the paths that she thought she was supposed to, not the ones she really wants.

Tam

Tam's had a rough year trying to get through Year 12 and her father's illness. Her desire to be a chef takes her on this trip to learn more about food and to see the world, but can she do that when homesickness and worry about her father are making it hard to enjoy herself? Then there's also the added complication of what happened with Matt before she left.

CHAPTER 1

Liza, Melbourne

She stops at the lights and fights to catch her breath. Cars, trams, and cyclists speed past, fighting it out for space in the busy intersection. Liza shakes her legs to loosen her calves. She could feel their tightness as she ran down the street, flinching each time her feet slapped the hot concrete. Just a few days off training, and she's already lost fitness. How does it happen so fast?

The sun beats hotly on her shoulders, the first proper summery day of the year. There's not even time for the sweat to settle on the surface of her skin before it evaporates under the glare. And it's only late November. If she weren't about to leave, she'd have to start putting on sunscreen before she runs. And she'd still come out of summer an even darker burnished brown.

As she waits for the lights to go her way, she gazes idly along the street. The tables outside cafes are full of people delaying the inevitable, pretending with coffee and leftover news from the weekend that it isn't Monday. And it hits her all over again. She's no longer required to care if it's Monday. School is done. A thrill shoots through her. VCE, her taskmaster, the fire-breathing beast that made her stomach ache and her breath catch every time she thought about the pile of study in front of her for the last eight months, is slain. Now she's free for three whole months until uni begins. It's surreal.

Lunging, she eases her legs into a stronger stretch. The pedestrians around her have made their Monday effort, and perfume and aftershave form a fragrant cloud around the haircuts and self-conscious styled-to-casual outfits. Liza is suddenly hyperaware of her uniform of sloppy singlet and shorts. She can't remember a day in the last six years that hasn't started with her dressed like this. And she can't imagine a day that doesn't start without the head-clearing ritual of a run.

Finally, it's their turn. She steps out onto the road with a light jog, breaking ahead of the crowds. Once she's cleared them, she slows back to a walk, passing a line of tiny single terrace houses in varying shades of decrepit and gentrified. There's no sign of life at Kit's house, a flaking pastel pink place. The gate's shut, for once, and an electric blue piece of fabric shrouds the dusty glass of the darkened front room.

The house next door, the better-looking twin, is equally quiet. Its manicured garden and fresh paint job seem to mock the fetid wheelie bins and straggling hedge outside Kit's. A poster boy for gentrification.

There's something different about the posh house today, though. It takes her a moment to work it out. Then it hits her. The cherub statue in the front yard, a chubby nude boy with a grimace of a smile, is gone. He's usually balanced creepily astride the rim of the stone birdbath. How many times have they mocked that stupid, kitschy thing? Now only some stubby stone legs remain, planted stubbornly on the chipped bowl. Maybe Kit will know what happened.

As instructed by the text message, she doesn't stop at Kit's. Instead, she continues to the pub two doors down, a dark blue brick heap on the corner. There's no sign of life there either. She peers through the glass doors, but all she can see in the light that manages to penetrate the filthy windows is the shadowy outlines of bar stools and a pool table. She stands back and contemplates the place, dubious. Why can't they just meet at Kit's house? Or at a café, like normal people? Nope, Kit wants to meet at the pub. At what could only be considered brunch time, at a push.

She tentatively tests the door. It's open. It falls closed behind her with a clatter. She's instantly assaulted by the reek of beer and sweat and something else that manages to be both sweet *and* sour. And definitely alcoholic. It's the kind of smell you could probably get a contact hangover from if you're not careful.

A male voice yells from somewhere. "I'll be out in a sec!"

The good news is that the air conditioning is on. As she crosses to the bar, she can feel the slight stickiness of the tiled floor under her runners. She tentatively hauls herself onto a bar stool, takes out her phone, and types the standard daily *where the hell are you* message.

Cooled now, she unties her hair and lets the curls explode around her face. Then, resigning herself to the inevitable Wait for Kit Time, she leans her elbows on the bar. But, feeling that same sticky sensation as on the floor, she removes them just as quickly. She folds her hands primly in her lap instead and wonders just how many hours of her life she has spent waiting for her best friend to show up.

As if Kit knows exactly what she's thinking, her phone buzzes with a message. *Two mins. Promise!*

Liza sighs. The quiet in the pub is suddenly broken by a loud bang and the rattle of glass coming close to breaking but not, followed by a string of curses. A tall boy emerges from a door behind the bar, rubbing his hands on his jeans.

"Hey, can I...help you?" he asks. But he already sounds doubtful about it. He combs his fingers through his greasy hair and frowns. "Sorry for the wait. I was expecting you to be the beer delivery guy."

"Uh, no, I'm just waiting for...Kit." She points in the vague direction of Kit's house.

"Oh, sure." He picks up a cloth and vigorously wipes the bar in front of her. "She usually surfaces around now. You want coffee?"

"Uh, yeah, that would be great."

"Alright. I'll just wait for Kit too. She's bound to need it," he says. He disappears again.

Ten minutes later, the pub door finally opens. The roar of traffic pours in along with Kit. She's dressed in a pair of jeans that clearly aren't hers, given the way they hang off her hips. The upper half of her small frame is wrapped in a huge hoodie despite the gathering heat outside. Her long, bleached-blonde hair hangs down her back.

She launches herself across the room and throws her arms around Liza, nearly knocking her from her stool. "Hi! I *missed* you."

"I missed you too." Liza returns the squeeze and smiles. She can smell Kit's perfume and second hand cigarettes and something else that she can't quite pick.

"How was training camp?"

"It was okay." And that's all it was. Okay. The whole time, Liza had kept trying to make it special by reminding herself that it might be her last. But it didn't work. It just continued to be the same as it had always been, with the added complication of avoiding Alika, of course. But she doesn't want to talk about any of that right now. "Nice spot you've picked for a morning coffee."

Kit grins and shrugs. She takes one of the spare elastic bands wrapped around Liza's wrist and wraps her hair into a messy ponytail.

There's still a panda swipe of yesterday's make-up under her eyes. Liza automatically reaches out and swipes it away.

Flinching, Kit submits. "The coffee is *good*, though. And it's usually free," she whispers. "And believe me, I need free."

"Hey Kit Kat." The guy behind the bar is back.

"Hey, Ollie. Meet Liza, my best friend in the entire world." Kit kneels on her stool and kisses him exuberantly on the cheek before settling back into her seat.

Liza smiles her greeting, but she's really smiling at Kit. Because Kit's been announcing her in that same proud, possessive way since Grade 3, when they first met and consolidated their relationship on the edge of the netball courts. It was a friendship born from a mutual hatred of a sport. And it's a friendship that's lasted them a decade.

"Coffee?" Ollie pats the machine.

"Yes, please." Kit mumbles through an emphatic yawn. "Two flat whites, please."

He nods and pulls a carton of milk from the bottom of the beer fridge. "You working tonight?"

"Yep."

"What? Here?" Liza asks.

Kit nods and runs her fingers in small circles on the bar.

"When did you start working here?"

"Friday."

"But why? When there are only a couple of weeks before we go?"

Kit doesn't answer straight away. Just keeps making relentless, useless circles on the sticky wood. Finally, she looks up. "That's why I needed to see you."

"*What?*" Liza is instantly wary. Because Kit's got her shame face on. And when Kit's got that face on, it means she's usually made some kind of mess of something. "What's going on?"

"Oh, Lize." Kit drops her head onto her arms on the bar and lets out a loud moan. "I messed up."

"How?"

Ollie slides two coffees and a jar of sugar over to them and makes a rapid exit.

"Kit, what's happened?" Liza pulls at Kit's sleeve. "Tell me."

Kit finally lifts her head an inch to say, "I can't come overseas."

"What? What do you mean?"

She shakes her head and mumbles. "I've got no money."

"Yes you do. You've got all your savings from the café."

"I don't anymore."

Liza's so slack-jawed from this new bit of information, it takes her a minute to muster the question. "What happened?"

Kit turns and rests her cheek on her arms. "Well, first, Liam and I broke up. He's moved back to his parents' and left me with all the rent for this month and next."

"So he continues to be a selfish prick, then."

"Uh-huh." Kit sighs loudly. "Who said it was a good idea to move in with him?"

"Definitely not me. But that can't be all your savings?"

"No. But that's not all. You know how we had that party for the end of exams?"

Liza nods. She missed it because of training camp. Just like she's missed everything. "Yeah?"

"Well, the place got kind of trashed, and we also have to pay for some damage to the neighbour's yard."

"Not that creepy cherub fountain?"

Kit lifts her head. "How'd you know?"

If Liza didn't want to cry, she'd probably laugh. "Saw it when I came past. It's demolished." Nope, she has to laugh.

Kit buries her face in her arms again. "Don't laugh. That freaking monstrosity is worth thousands of bucks, apparently. Thousands that me and the boys now have to pay, and pay now or sooner because that stuck-up couple that live there are like, second cousins of our landlord or something. And there goes my savings."

This is a lot of new information to compute, and Liza quickly gives up trying to make sense of it. All she knows is that Kit is saying she can't come overseas any more. Trust Kit to drop a bomb like this only a week or two before their trip. "You *really* can't afford it?" she asks.

"I *really* can't afford it."

Liza sighs. "How do you always find yourself in the middle of these shit storms?"

"I have no idea." Kit drops her chin on her arms again and moans. "So now I'm going to be moving into Mum and Darren's and working my ass off until I can pay back the rest of the money instead."

"But you already have a ticket." Liza refuses to believe this happening, despite that sick feeling in her stomach telling her otherwise.

"Yeah, but I have no money for anything else, like food, accommodation, getting around. I'm going to see if I can refund it and put it on the debt."

Liza only committed to this trip because it was Kit's idea. Now what?

She stares at Kit as she slowly stirs her coffee, looking morose and ashamed. She feels terrible for her, but she also can't help feel a prickle of resentment at Kit's typical shambolic life. Why did she ever believe Kit could actually follow through with this? It goes against everything she's ever known about her best friend. Six years of high school, and Kit barely managed to make it to a class on time. How was she ever going to get on a plane to Europe? To the airport, even?

"Our trip," she says mournfully.

"I know. I'm so sorry, Lize."

Liza doesn't reply. She can't. Because she's still not sure if she's going to cry or get really, really angry. And she doesn't really want to do either.

"You'll still have an amazing time with the others," Kit says hopefully.

"I can't go on this trip without you. I barely know those girls."

"You went to school with Olivia and Mai."

"Yeah, and I said more to them those couple of times we had coffee to plan the trip than I have in six years of school."

"You know Tam."

"I haven't seen your cousin in, like, three years, Kit." She sighs and knots her fingers together. "This is going to be *so* awkward."

"It'll be totally fine once you get to know everyone," Kit tells her. "Olivia's awesome, and Mai's hilarious." She nudges Liza. "You're always super shy until you get to know people. You would have felt that way even if I *was* there, you know."

That's supposed to make her feel better? Liza sips her coffee instead of speaking. Because it's getting harder and harder not to get mad.

Kit clutches the edge of the bar and moans softly again. "Oh God, I'm so depressed now. I cannot believe I can't go."

"Me either," Liza says, bitter.

"I'm *so* sorry I really am. I'm a giant fucking idiot."

"It's okay," Liza replies. It's not really. But it's not as if Kit's going to be having a great time, either. She's going to have it just as bad, stuck in Melbourne in the heat, working in this stinking bar. It's not the summer either of them envisioned.

They sit there in silence, each locked in their individual post-Kit-trauma misery. Liza wonders for a second if she could find a way to get out of this trip. Because does she really want to do this without Kit? But then she thinks of all the work, school, and training she's missed for this. All those Sundays she spent working at the shop so she could take this holiday.

And she has to do this anyway. Because she promised herself this trip would be all part of her grand getting-a-life plan before she starts uni.

"I'm sorry," Kit says again, clearly taking Liza's silence for anger.

"I know," she says slowly and wraps an arm around her friend's shoulder. "So did you tell the others?"

"I called Tam last night. And I'm seeing Olivia later."

"How did Tam take it?"

"Kind of furious at first."

Liza's not surprised. She remembers Tam as nice, but kind of stern and forthright, too—so different than her scatty, sociable cousin.

"So, how are the parentals holding up?"

"They're okay. They're being kind of quiet about it all."

"They're just taking their time. You did drop two bombs on them at once."

Liza nods. She kind of did. And now they're being quiet and careful with her. It's weird.

"And now you're fleeing the country. Classy, Lize. Who gets to do that?" She grins.

"Lucky me, huh?"

"Lucky you." Kit frowns and drops her chin on her hands again.

"They want you to come over soon. They miss you."

"Of course they do. I'm not working tomorrow?"

"Cool. Come for lunch. No, dinner."

Kit narrows her eyes at her. "You don't trust me to make it by lunchtime, do you?"

"Maybe." Liza grins at her.

Ollie comes out from the backroom, hugging a small ginger cat to his chest. "Hey Kit, meet Otis, the new pub cat. He's been hanging out in the back lane all hungry and sad. So we started feeding him."

Kit just stares at the cat. Then she drops her face onto her arms again and lets out a long loud moan.

"What's up?" Ollie asks as he rubs the cat's face with his own.

"That's *our* cat," Kit mumbles despondently as she looks up at it. "That's Pip. I haven't seen him for a week."

Leaning in closer, Liza does recognise the scrawny thing from Kit's crazy share house.

Kit lifts her head and drops it back on her arms. "Oh God, what is wrong with me? Of *course* I can't get my shit together to go on a holiday. I can't even keep a freaking cat!"

"Oh, Kit." Liza rubs her friend's back and tries not to laugh. "I have got to go." She slips off the stool, pulls a note from her pocket, and holds it out to Ollie. He just continues to croon at the cat like it's a child and waves the money away. Liza smiles her thanks and runs her hand over Kit's tangle of blonde ponytail. "Sunday dinner, okay? Promise you'll be there?"

"I'll be there." Kit turns and wraps her arms around her briefly. "Promise. Tell your dad to record the cricket for me."

"Okay, weirdo." Liza laughs. "Bye."

CHAPTER 2

Tam, Tasmania

She steps onto the porch, the wind catching her hair immediately, blowing it over her face. Her father is out there already, pulling on his boots.

"Hey." She leans on a post and watches him drive his feet into the embattled leather.

"Hi there." He stamps a few times on the dusty wood. "How's the preparations?"

Tam shrugs. They bought her backpack yesterday from one of the camping stores in town. Now she has to figure out what to put in it. Packing's still a bit of a mystery. After a couple of pairs of jeans, some tops, a jacket, toiletries and her new super-small travel laptop, there's going to be a lot of space left. What else, she wonders?

"Can't help you there, Tamo," He takes a hat from the hook and pulls it over the stubble of regrowth on his scalp. The sun is burning fiercely. It's hard to believe it was raining sideways an hour ago. "Ask one of the aunts." His soles grind against the gravel as he steps off the porch. "One of them'll be able to tell you."

"Yeah." She'll ask Anita.

"Not long now."

"Yep." That's all Tam can think of to say to that. She suspects she's supposed to be more excited.

A few weeks ago that feeling she'd get when she thought about this trip was just a small tingle, a bubbling sensation in her chest—like swallowing a huge mouthful of cheap champagne. Like her blood seeming to hesitate for a moment in its journey around her body. But now, so close to leaving, the feeling has become a stiff bristled brush, scouring out the insides of her chest. It's as if her entire being balks at the prospect of being absent from this place for so long. She knows it's fear. How can she leave her dad? It feels way too soon, no matter what the doctors say.

He picks up the shovel and a bucket and straightens his back slowly as if it hurts a little.

"You okay?" she immediately asks, scrutinising him.

"Matt's coming," he replies instead. With a nod in the direction of the road, he begins his slow march down to the sheds.

Tam squints up the hill. Yep, there he is, loping down the road, hands jammed in his pockets. And although she can't make it out from here, she can picture the thin, white cord of Matt's headphones under his hoodie, winding from his ear to wherever it is he secretes that device so that no one ever knows he's always only ever half-present. The other half of him is always, inexorably, given to sound.

She yanks on her boots, not bothering to tie the laces. Dodging past the sweep of prickly grevillea, she parks herself on one of the flat rocks that border the driveway, and waits.

She watches him weave around the ever-expanding potholes on the surface of the road. The whole road needs grading, but the council doesn't care about a road that is populated by a handful of houses. No tourists ever come this way. Why should they care about this private, green valley—one of the few places on this whole peninsula tucked so far inland that you can't even feel the proximity of the coast?

He takes his time getting to her. She's only ever seen him move faster than a walk twice. The first time was a school sports day, when the PE teacher threatened to fail any kid who didn't take part in at least one event. Tam chose the 100-metre sprint. Short and sweet. From her position at the starting line, she watched him jog slowly towards the high jump mat, gathering a little speed before taking off, attempting a Frosbee flop like a professional athlete. But weighed down by his boots, he hit the pole on the way over. Still, he clambered to his feet and raised his fist in a victory salute, as if he'd just wiped out an Olympic record, the headphones still jammed in his ears. She stood there on the other side of the oval in her ancient sneakers and laughed, almost missing the start of her own race.

The second time was after he moved here. He'd been living with his mum in one of the rough, elemental towns out west. But, worried that the tiny school in the nearest town over there wasn't getting him anywhere, she'd sent him here to do his final year of high school. He moved in with his uncle, a grizzled, silent logger who lived up the hill from Tam in an ornate gingerbread wooden cottage he'd built himself.

It was late, and darkness had fallen in that utterly complete way it does in this part of the world. They were driving back from an afternoon of fishing, bundled in Nick's truck, sharing a steaming bag of potato cakes, crisp and golden from the deep fryer. That's when they heard the thunk against the car tire and saw the dark shape skitter onto the shoulder of the road.

"Stop." It was one of the first things Matt had said all day.

"Nah. Just a wallaby," Nick said, and kept his foot on the pedal. Tam didn't react either. Road kill is a fact of life in this part of the world where, after sunset, roads are just long stretches of impossible darkness, lit up only by the high beams of the occasional passing car. The endless parade of wildlife coming and going across the highway can make it feel like peak hour, though. And no kid who lives around here even blinks at the bloodied animal corpses that litter the road or at the fetid smell of rotting flesh that washes through car windows in summer.

But Matt did. "Stop," he said again. "Wombat."

Nick clicked his tongue but stopped. Kicking the car into reverse, he took it part way up the hill again.

Matt already had his hand on the door handle. "Torch?"

"Under the seat."

Matt jumped out of the car. Intrigued by this tall interloper who had performed the miracle that is getting Nick to do anything he doesn't want to do, Tam stared out the back window. His dark outline tramped up the short stretch of road, the beam of the torch leading the zigzagging way. A moment later, he was jogging back to the car with that same loping run. Saying nothing to Nick, he lifted the canvas cover of the ute, rooted around until he pulled out the rifle, and ran back up the road. The shot fired out into the darkness. Tam blinked. Claire jumped and then giggled in the front seat. Nick just clicked his tongue again.

Nobody said a word as they drove the last kilometres back to the intersection, and Nick and Claire let them out at the bottom of the road.

As they trudged back up through the mud to their houses, Tam asked him why he did it. He told her what he knew about wombats, about their bone-tough hides, built for protecting them against predators attacking from behind in their burrows. About how because of this toughness, if you hit them from behind in their car, they took ages to die, sometimes with young in their pouches. Every now and then Tam took her eyes from the treacherous, potted road and watched him talk under the weak moonlight. She wondered why he didn't mind being seen caring about another dead animal on the road. Most guys around here wouldn't dare.

He finally makes it to her. Tam stands and smiles into the cold breeze that whips down the hill. His return smile is crooked and casual. Wordlessly, they trudge back down the driveway and up the hill, pushing between the damp clumps of salvia bushes, to the small ridge above the orchard. Her father had planned a rock garden there, but then they found the lump, so he never got further than hauling rocks from the back paddock and dumping them in a haphazard pile. Now the only thing growing around them is the long grass that pushes cheekily out of crevices where the mower can't reach.

They settle on the rocks, facing the sweep of green hillside specked with cattle and patches of mud. Sometimes, on good days when they've got time to spare, they climb right up the big hill behind Matt's place. In good weather, they can see the relentless beat of waves pounding along the craggy, shipwrecking cliffs, and the way the coast bears down on them from all sides of this peninsula.

Tam can feel the damp under her backside, but she doesn't care. It's just part of living here. Fat drops of water plunge from the giant pines from the rain earlier. Drops so big, Tam can hear them hit the grass below.

Matt pulls the buds from his ears. Tam can never help feeling a little bit honoured that she's one of the few people he'll take them out for.

"So, when do you go?"

"Next week." Why doesn't he know that?

"You ready?"

She sighs. "If by ready you mean packed, then no. If you mean ready to leave Dad, then no."

With a grin, he leans against a rock and slides his tobacco pouch from his pocket.

She snaps a twig from the bay tree, breaking it into tiny pieces. "If you mean ready to travel with three people I barely know now that Kit has bailed, then no." She tucks her chin onto her knees. "Bloody Kit."

"Right then." He chuckles. "Not ready."

"Have you figured out what you're going to do for the summer?" she asks, just to get them off the subject of her own plans. She can't think about it too much, because that panicked, scouring feeling comes back.

He shrugs lazily, his fingers deftly rolling up a skinny cigarette. "I thought about doing the mines for the summer. Mum's boyfriend said he can get me a job driving the trucks. Eight-hour shifts driving 30 k per hour in and out the mine all day."

"Sounds thrilling."

"It does when you hear the pay." He lights the cigarette. "Enough to get up north."

She nods. Matt wants to see the desert. He craves the dry, utter opposite of here. Wants to replace the cool, green greys of eucalypts and the restless ocean with the violent red palette of the desert. Just for a while.

"But then your Dad said I could probably work with him in the orchards, so I don't know."

Tam feels a small bubble of hope in her chest. If he stayed, he could tell her if anything was wrong. If Dad started to look sick again. She knows her father won't tell her anything. Especially not after he worked so hard to convince her to go on this trip in the first place. "Which do you think you'll do?"

"Dunno. Probably stay here. The mines are better for the cash, but there's shit-all else to do out there."

"You'll tell me if Dad's all right?" She doesn't look at him. "While I'm gone?"

"Of course." He turns and smiles his slow, lopsided smile, his shoulder-length brown hair whipping around his ears in the wind. He leans back on his elbows and stares up at the endless sky.

A small rush of relief floods through her as her gaze follows his up to the clouds torn ragged by the wild winds. "Thanks," she mumbles.

CHAPTER 3

Olivia, Melbourne

Her phone lights up on the table. It's Mai again. Olivia doesn't pick it up. It'll be yet another excited question about what to take, or how they're going to organise everything. Olivia's misery can't deal with Mai's excitement right now. She tucks her phone into her pocket, where she can't see it, and rests her chin on her hands.

She watches her mother push the last few mouthfuls of food around her plate, finally sated. Her mother has always eaten the same way, hungrily and rapidly, not stopping to savour flavours. It's like taste has no bearing on the meal at all.

Which is probably why she likes this buzzing hippie co-op with its colourless, monkish, organic, biodynamic, gluten-free, sugar-free, fun-free meals. The food might be unsullied from the evils of capitalist mass food production, but it's also completely flavourless. Olivia has barely touched hers. Not that she's in the mood to eat.

Even last night's meal didn't tempt her. It's hard to believe only sixteen hours ago she was eating at some ridiculous yuppie restaurant in The Rocks in Sydney, where one tiny artful entree probably cost her father more than her and her mother's meals added together. An expensive dinner to soften the blow of telling her he's moving to Shanghai to marry his girlfriend. The marriage she is happy about. The Shanghai part not so much. And now she is here eating half-cooked grains in this hippie den with her mother. Even though her mother could easily afford to eat in upscale restaurants for every meal if she wanted to. Such is Olivia's world, spread between the discordant lives of her parents. She cannot imagine what it would have been like when they actually used to share a life. That happened before her memories start.

Her mother drops her fork onto her empty plate, done, and brushes her newly bobbed hair behind her ears. Attracted to serviceable knits and wary of make-up, her mother has never cared how she looked. Not in Olivia's memory, anyway. There's proof she did once, though. Olivia thinks of that ancient promotional photo of her mother with her scruffy blonde Stevie Nicks hair and that floaty black dress. The one the papers always use when they reminisced about the bohemian *Lowlands* days. But if there wasn't photographic evidence, Olivia could never have imagined her mother once dressed like that.

Ruth folds her arms on the table in front of her plate, scrutinising her. "Are you sure your exams went that badly?"

Olivia blinks at the instant prick of tears. "I'm positive. I completely choked on the last two." She really did. She just sat there, muddled and panicked, and wrote barely formed answers to things she knew only weeks ago. And now there is no way she's getting into law. Not at the uni she wants, anyway.

"So what are you going to do about it?"

"I don't know." Olivia rests her cheek on her hands and stares out the window. This is such a typical question from her mother. Never has it occurred to her to actually play her role and perhaps offer a solution or advice. That's not her style.

But she's never been that kind of mother. Ever since they were young, Ruth has always treated her two daughters like these autonomous little beings. Olivia and Anna were expected to make up their own minds about what they wanted to do, to eat, to wear. They told *her* when they were hungry or needed a nap, not the other way around. Olivia was the only girl in her grade who didn't have a bedtime in primary school.

It is less a parenting philosophy and more the result of her mother's perennial mental absence. Ruth has always been tucked too far into her own mind to produce the kind of overbearing parenting Olivia has seen inflicted on some of her friends by their parents. Like Mai, for example, who is treating this upcoming trip overseas as some kind of a freedom ride away from a parental dictatorship. Ruth has always acted more like a curiously inquiring neighbour than a parent with a vested interest.

Sometimes she wishes her mother were more of a mother. Especially now. Because Olivia has no idea what to do. Because in those hellish two weeks of the exam period, Olivia's carefully laid life plans have gone out the window, and she has no clue how to get them back. And the worst part of it is, one of the few people who actually knows about it is her mother. What world does she live in where she's too afraid to tell her friends of her failure, but feels completely safe telling her own mother?

She's spent the weekend avoiding her friends. But that can't last forever. There's goodbye drinks this weekend and then there's the trip. She chews on her lip. How the hell is she going to avoid telling Mai? Mai, who somehow straddles the miraculous line of ditz and genius, who probably got the highest marks in the school in Legal Studies and English? Olivia has no idea how to break it to her that they probably won't be studying at uni together next year. She couldn't tell Will if she wanted to either. Because he won't even speak to her.

The only friend she could stomach telling is Kit, because Kit doesn't care about stuff like that. And Kit's as much as a disaster area as Olivia right now, anyway. She stabs at the clump of brown rice dominating her plate and frowns. Is there anything else that can go wrong? She always thought this period between finishing school and starting uni would be amazing. She'd be high off a successful VCE campaign, and then she'd get to take this holiday, collect up the study score she needs to get into this course, and then enjoy the summer until it's time to start. But no.

Now, instead of going on this holiday, all she wants to do is burrow down in the lounge room at her mother's, watch movies, and ignore all phone calls and social media. Possibly for the rest of her life.

Ruth picks up her purse. "I have to get going. You've got your keys?"

Olivia nods. "What are you doing now?"

"Interview." Ruth grimaces. She hates doing media. "You?"

Olivia shrugs.

Ruth pats her arm. "Don't agonise over it Livs. Law's not the only option. This trip might open your world a little. You never know." She stands and pulls on her jacket. "I'll see you in a couple of hours."

Olivia doesn't reply. Because as far as she is concerned, law has always been the option. She and her friends have been planning on it for years. It's the only thing she has ever been able to think of that she might want to do. And when you have two ridiculously successful parents and a sister who can only be described as a quiet overachiever, you've got to have your own life plan.

They pay and leave the café. Olivia watches her mother turn for the tram stop and slinks down a laneway back to the house as another wave of misery overwhelms her. Time to hide.

* * *

Liza, Melbourne

She locks the shop door behind her and tries to forget work immediately. The pre-Christmas period has to be the worst time in the world to be a retail slave. Liza likes to think of herself as an accommodating, pleasant person, which is why she's kept this job since she was sixteen. But some of the customers today were seriously getting on her nerves.

She's trying to decide whether to catch the tram home or not when the traffic lights decide it for her. The green light flashes on the pedestrian crossing leading to the leafy street that will take her through the gardens and back to her house. Enticed by the cool breeze that coasts up the tree-lined avenue, she takes off across the road.

She paces through gardens, taking the wide path that cuts between the cricket field and dog park, breathing in the smell of the grassy air. She can't believe she's about to trade in this dream weather for far colder places. She frowns. The thought of this holiday makes her stomach clench now. And not in the good way. How is she going to do this without Kit? The excitement she felt when she left the house to meet Kit yesterday has been swiftly replaced with dread. Does she even want to go on this trip anymore? Not that she has a choice. She's paid up and ready to go.

How does Kit manage to be so magnificently hopeless all the time? She's the sweetest, most awesome person Liza knows, but she's also the most delightfully shambolic too sometimes, limping from minor crisis to minor crisis. Most of them are usually fallout from yet another poorly executed life plan. And most times, Liza could have warned her.

When Kit told her halfway through Year 12 that she'd decided to move in with Liam, Liza thought it was a terrible idea. A terrible idea because, as per Kit's sometimes questionable taste, this guy is a dickhead. And how is moving out on your own during the final months of high school ever a good idea?

She accelerates, trying to quench all doubts with the mind-numbing physicality of a sprint. And she doesn't let up until she's home again.

The television echoes down the narrow passage the moment she opens the door.

Her father is in the living room, watching the cricket.

"Hey Dad. Aren't you supposed to be building a new compost bin?"

He dodges that with a question of his own. Instead he asks, "How was work?"

"Fine."

"And how's Kit?"

"The same. No, wait. Worse."

He chortles into his tea. "What's our walking disaster done now?"

"I'll tell you about it later." Liza doesn't want to get into it right now. What if her parents freak out about her travelling without Kit? They've got enough to freak out about right now.

"And you? You okay, kiddo?"

"I'm fine," she tells him, wishing they'd both stop asking her that. It's getting annoying.

But she shouldn't complain. She *did* just mess with their world in some pretty important ways. In just one conversation, she told them the two things she needs them to know before she leaves for this trip. Things they maybe never expected to hear.

First, she broke it to them that she doesn't know if she wants to race any more, even though Patrick sat both her parents down a few months back and informed them that with her current times, Liza has every chance of making the Comm Games selection squad. And then she told them that she's pretty sure she's gay.

Considering these grenades she's launched—things that she's sure made their picture of her fracture into little pieces and reform again—she should probably let them keep asking if she's okay. Maybe she should ask them if *they're* okay.

Instead of going to the shower to slough off the sweaty run, she flops down in the chair under the window and stares at the brand new backpack sitting on the floor. Besides, she might as well let them worry, because in a couple of weeks she'll be on the other side of the world and they won't be able to ask her every five minutes. She'll just have to figure it out for herself.

There's so much she wants from this trip. Maybe too much. She wants to know if she knows how to live without training in her life. She wants to know if she'll miss it. She also wants to figure out who'll she'll be if she's not that girl who runs, which is pretty much how everyone knew her at school. And it's true. She's never done much more than train and study and sleep. And now she feels shy and awkward around new people, like she never learned the rules. And this is even more daunting because next week she's going to be travelling with three strangers. She kicks her legs up onto the bed and stares out the window.

And maybe she'd like to meet someone. Someone *not* like Alika. A girl who actually likes her. Who can look her in the eye. But that part can probably wait. For now, she'd just like to begin to figure out who this new version of her is going to be. She just never thought she'd have to start doing that without her best friend at her side.

CHAPTER 4

Kit, Melbourne

Pedalling hard across the intersection, she leaves the busy streets behind, replacing it with the leafy tunnel of tree-lined Moore Street. She pulls the air in through her nose—air suddenly cleaner and cooler than the exhaust-ridden fug of her block. When the descent begins, she stops pedalling and lets gravity draw her down the hill. The air rushes over her bare arms and shoulders, making her smile.

Turning a hard left, she coasts past the wire enclosure on the north side of the local pool. Sunlight glances off the bleached concrete of the stands and bounces over the blue tiles. She can hear calls and laughter from the shallow end as kids begin their summer early. Breathing in that chemical—but somehow sweetly nostalgic—chlorine stink, she brakes hard and climbs down from the worn saddle of the bike.

How many days of their lives have she and Liza spent laid out on the blue tiles of that pool? Hundreds at least, she knows. They lazed through so many summer afternoons under those achingly familiar black-lettered warnings to swimmers: *Danger, aqua profunda.* As she secures her bike to the freckled trunk of a tree, she wonders if she had exchanged all those hours of lying around for study, would she have done better at VCE? Would she have come out of her final year of high school with a chance at university or a job like the rest of her more ambitious, together friends?

The smell of burnished wood and eucalyptus replaces the chlorine as she pushes the door open. Again, she breathes in deep. She loves the smell of this house.

"Hello?" she calls down the narrow hallway.

A voice calls back from somewhere in the belly of the house. "Hi there!"

She kicks off her shoes and pads along the polished concrete floor until she emerges into the vast wood and windowed chamber that is the living and kitchen area. Sunlight glints through the high windows, beaming down on the leafy, green plants pressed up against the glass.

Muted chatter streams from the television as commentators try to wring a story from the lack of action in the five-day cricket test. The same story that she left at her house, watched by the handful of sleepy boys scattered around the lounge room, already exchanging coffee for beer even though it's only late morning.

"Shouldn't you be architecting something?" she asks the back of Geoff's head as she skates her feet across the smooth floor, the same way she has done since she was a kid. "Is that even a word?"

"Katherine," Liza's dad booms, ignoring her tease *and* her question. "You sound exactly like Liza. So, tell me something."

She leans over the back of the seat. "Australia's going to lose."

"Well, we both know that."

"Lize here?"

A shimmer of a pause hangs in the air before he replies. "Yep. In her room, I think."

Kit squeezes his shoulder. Liza really has thrown her parents for a loop. "I'm going up to see her. Don't strain yourself there."

He chuckles again. "I'll do my best."

Upstairs, she flops across Liza's dark blue doona, pulls a pillow into the shaft of sunlight sprawling across the bed, and lies on her back. She watches Liza unpack her training bag. "So what exactly did you say to them about it?"

"Which one?" Liza smiles ruefully as she tosses a pair of runners into the depths of her wardrobe.

"The running thing."

"Just that I don't know if I wanted to devote all my time to something I'm not sure I love."

Kit nods. She's never really understood the whole running thing anyway, no matter how much Liza has explained it to her and how many times she has watched Liza do it and win. She just knows it's something her best friend is great at. She never thought about whether Liza loved it. It was never talked about in those terms.

She tucks her hands behind her head and stares up at the walls. She loves Liza's room. It's so lovely, with its wooden beams and its purposefully haphazard shelves. "Where's your new backpack?"

"I moved it onto your bed." Liza points up at the loft bed, built like a small cave into the space above the built-in cupboards. "Until it's time."

Kit smiles. It *is* her bed. Since the year they became friends, it feels like Kit has woken up in that bed as much as she has woken up in her own, a much-abused old single futon tossed down in corners of rooms in a long line of rentals. When her mum and dad were splitting up, she practically lived here for a while. And Liza's parents, angels that they are, pretended not to notice they'd suddenly adopted another daughter. Geoff just popped Kit into the draw for Friday night movie pick rights, and Pam started making an extra school lunch. Kit will never stop being grateful for those few months she hid out here.

Liza finishes sorting her washing and climbs onto the bed. She leans against the wall and kicks her long brown legs over Kit's. Kit runs her hands along Liza's sharp, brown shinbones, feeling that familiar bubbling of envy at her friend's ridiculously great legs. Why can't she have a body like that, instead of this short, scrawny one?

"You have to help me pack," Liza says. "Promise?"

"Of course." Kit pouts. "And you have to promise you won't have too much fun without me."

"Highly doubtful." Liza inspects the ends of her hair, pulling the wiry coils straight.

"And you won't find a new best friend?"

Liza just looks at her. "I'll be gone four weeks, Kit. Four weeks. I'm just hoping I can manage a conversation with these girls, let alone make friends with them."

"You'll be fine," Kit tells her for the thousandth time. "Mai's fun. Tam's a sweetheart, even if she seems tough. And Olivia's awesome."

Kit frowns as she thinks of Olivia yesterday. Kit's never seen her friend so miserable. Olivia's usually so assured and self-sufficient. But she's *so* messed up over her exams and Will. Poor thing. She wants to tell Liza to look out for her while they're away, but Olivia begged Kit not to tell anyone about exams. So instead, she just says, "Hey, Olivia might seem kind of, I don't know, distant or whatever, but she's going through some stuff, that's all. Give her a chance. You'll like her."

Liza shrugs, like she's only half listening, and continues to inspect her split ends.

Kit taps her fingers on Liza's leg. "Anyway, who knows? Maybe you'll meet someone on this trip. Have an exotic one-night stand with some Mediterranean hottie."

"Maybe." She stares out the window, her eyes closing against the sunlight streaming through the window. "Doubt it."

Kit watches the pink staining her best friend's cheeks fade slowly.

Liza's cheeks were even pinker the night of the end-of-school party, when she dragged Kit out to sit on the kerb, an uncharacteristic bottle clutched in her hand, and told her about this Alika girl.

The fact that her best friend was telling her that she had spent the last couple of months in some fraught, unspoken thing with a *girl* didn't surprise her, exactly. But that Liza was finally saying anything to her about it did.

The fact that Liza might be gay had crossed Kit's mind a couple of times over the years. It would explain why she's so damn shy around guys. And it would explain why, at eighteen, she's never had a boyfriend despite some of the incredible talent Kit has spotted at those athletics comps. But Liza never even talked about those guys, let alone seemed that interested.

But even though she'd thought about it, Kit never said anything—in case it hadn't actually occurred to Liza yet. And Kit had known that her best friend would tell her if and when she had anything to tell her.

And that turned out to be the night of their final classes. Liza was so drunk and fevered with her need to tell Kit about this mess she had gotten herself in, she kind of skated right past the liking-girls news. Instead, she went straight to the part where she had started some clandestine, unspoken thing with a girl in her training squad, an impossibly withdrawn, beautiful nineteen-year-old who was apparently barely willing to admit she was a lesbian to herself, let alone to someone else.

Kit kept her arm wrapped tightly around Liza's waist as she told Kit about this girl. Liza swiped tears from her eyes, telling her how the only time this girl seemed to acknowledge Liza was when she was jumping her in the car after competitions or climbing into her bed at night at the training institute. Not that Liza didn't want to be doing that, she said. She just didn't want it like that. And Kit just held on and let her cry it out. And when the tears were done, Kit wiped the tears from her friend's face and told her to dump her.

It wasn't until a few weeks later that they even broached the topic of Liza being gay in general, when Liza admitted how nervous she was about coming out to her parents, about dropping two big revelations on them at once. But by then her coming out to Kit just didn't seem like a thing. So why make it one? At that point, the fact that Liza had stopped talking to this girl who kept treating her like crap seemed way more important than workshopping Liza's sexuality. That kind of seemed like a done deal at this point.

"Hey, does Alika know you're leaving next week?" she asks.

Liza shrugs. "Don't know, don't care."

"Good," Kit tells her, even if she doesn't one hundred per cent believe her.

She looks over at her friend. She's gazing out the window, a small frown on her face. Kit hopes Liza does meet someone. Someone who likes her out loud and who makes her feel like the awesome, beautiful person she is. She deserves it. Maybe even needs it a little. She's the sweetest, most quietly funny and wickedly insightful person Kit has ever met in her life. And she thought that about Liza when they were eight. Now Liza and the rest of the world need to know it.

"I wish you were coming with us," Liza suddenly moans.

"So do I." Who wouldn't choose four weeks of travelling in Europe over four weeks of working double shifts all week to pay off one party? Not even a good party. A party where she found Liam lying in the bath fully dressed with that stupidly hot Rachel perched on the end with her perfect pixie hair and MAC red lips. And even though they weren't doing anything but talking, Kit spent the whole night drinking too much and wondering if she was going to have to worry. Yes, she did, it turned out. Because every form of social media has informed her that Liam and Rachel are now hooking up.

Liza shifts across the bed so she's lying next to Kit. She wraps her hands around Kit's arm and squeezes it. "You were, like, the social glue."

"I *know*," she says again, resting her head against her friend's shoulder. Kit's already keenly aware Liza's terrified she won't get along with the others. What she doesn't know is that everyone feels like that. Her cousin was furious when Kit broke the news. Olivia was even more depressed, and Mai told her outright that she was a stupid, freaking idiot.

She sighs. She will get her shit together this summer. She *will.* She grabs her friend's hand and shakes it. "I'm so sorry, Lize," she says for the zillionth time.

"It's okay," Liza says softly.

They lie there in a shaft of muted late afternoon sun. Kit listens to Liza breathe slowly next to her. She's going to miss her so much.

"I'll miss you," Liza whispers, as if she's heard her thoughts.

Kit snuggles up to her friend and smiles. "I'll miss you, too."

CHAPTER 5

Liza, Melbourne

They traipse away from the track in a loose pack. Liza lifts her heavy ponytail from her sweaty neck and takes a long sip of water.

The girls are silent as they enter the dank concrete change room. Tracy lays her towel on one of the concrete benches, kicks her legs up against a set of lockers and groans. "God, what's up his butt today? That was evil."

Manda cackles as she yanks her bag out of her locker. "A serious bug, that's what."

Shae shrugs. "He's pissed because it might be Lizey's last training and he's lost his only good 800-metre runner in the whole club."

Tracy flings her empty water bottle at Shae's head. "Excuse me? Who beat her PB at camp the other week?"

Shae shrugs again and pulls off her tank top. "You did it *once*. So, Lize, how does it feel?"

Liza wraps her hair into a tight bun and shrugs. "I don't know." She really doesn't. It's weird. She kept trying to say it to herself all through the session. *You may never do this again.* But the sense of finality just wouldn't come.

"How did Patrick react when you told him? Was he *completely* gutted?" Tracy asks.

"I couldn't really tell," Liza admits, sneaking a glance at Alika, wondering if she's listening. "He just said it was my decision and that he hoped I would come back."

"Bet that's not what he was thinking."

"I don't know. I don't want to think about it." She hates the thought of disappointing Patrick. She started training with him when she was thirteen. And now she feels like she is dumping him.

Shae grabs her bag and steps over to Liza. She pulls her into a fierce hug. "Well, *we're* going to miss you like hell, lady."

"We are," Tracy grumbles, coming over and hugging them both. "Even if it does mean I've got a better chance of making state."

Liza giggles as Manda joins them, and she's squashed into their collective, clammy embrace. How many times has she laughed and hugged with these girls, sweaty and jubilant on the side of a track after relays and meets? She has no idea if she'll miss running yet, but she knows she'll miss *them*. A lot.

"I gotta go." Shae pushes a loud kiss into the side of Liza's cheek. "Post lots of photos so we can feel jealous, okay?"

"Yeah, and bring me back a present," Tracy orders. "A hot Portuguese dude will do." She bolts out the door after Shae.

Manda gives her one final squeeze and jogs out the door. "Hey, you're giving me a lift, remember?" she calls.

And then there were two.

Not that Alika even registers her presence. She just keeps packing her bag, her back to Liza. Liza kicks off her sneakers, replaces them with some sandals and watches the willowy girl retie her hair. She wishes she could speak to her, but she has no idea what she'd say.

Eventually Alika pulls her pack onto her muscular shoulders and turns. She gives Liza a quick smile. "Have fun on your trip." And she's gone.

Liza watches her transform from person to shadow as she heads out into the bright sunlight. That's all she gets? *Of course it is,* she tells herself, feeling stupid. Alika barely gave her more than that when they were sort of together. Why would she change now?

Still, it hurts.

* * *

Tam, Tasmania

"That was *delicious*, my girl," Anita says, dropping her plate by the sink and giving Tam a giant smacking kiss on the cheek. "I'll do the washing up."

Tam grins as she stretches plastic wrap over a salad bowl. "Thanks on both counts."

"I'll help." Linda comes over and starts stacking plates. "Great meal, Tam. Where'd you get the salmon?"

"Bill got it from that guy who works at the orchards."

"Good work, Bill," Anita tells him as he puts a stack of bowls on the counter and grins at Tam. It's that baffled grin he gets when all the aunts are here. His oestrogen-overload grin.

Tam just shrugs and grins back.

They spent the whole afternoon cooking this meal together, cleaning the fish, working the sauce, and making the dressings for the salads. Tam savoured every second of it, knowing it's the last time she's going to get to cook in her own kitchen for a long time.

She loves making meals with Bill. Even though he cooks by the seat of his pants, she's learned more from him than she has ever learned working in the café or in Food Tech class. But then, he's been everywhere, cooked everywhere. He's earned his living the last decade travelling around Australia, working different jobs on farms or in hospitality. And when Tam's father offered him a spring and summer helping with the cherry crops, he took over the shack up the hill and settled in. And while he was at it, he's taught Tam everything he knows about food.

It was his idea for her to stay away longer on this trip, to go to the cooking schools in Chiang Mai and Hanoi. She can't wait for that part. She pauses again, the cork only halfway back in a bottle of cooking wine. There's that feeling in her chest again. She's flying in less than forty-eight hours. No matter how excited she is about the idea of travelling, she can't shake this feeling of dread at leaving.

Her father and Matt are standing talking, with their backs to the fireplace even though there's no fire. Her father is still skinny. Some people puff up on chemo, but her dad went to bone. He definitely looks better than he did, but sometimes she just wants to force feed him, to flood his body with strength. Caloric insurance against the next months she'll be away.

Matt catches her staring at them and gives her a brief lip curl of a smile. She returns it and turns back to her aunts' conversation at the sink.

She doesn't really want to leave him behind either.

Later they stand out on the porch, putting off their goodbye. The wind is tearing down the hill, pushing at the house. Tam listens to the deep complaining creaks of the frame. She's so used to it that still nights used to keep her awake when she was little.

He tucks his hair behind his ear and shuffles his feet. "So what time do you leave?"

"Mid-morning. Dad's got his appointment in the afternoon."

"When do you fly?"

"The night after. We're staying with Anita in Hobart."

He nods, staring at the ground. "It's going to be boring without you."

She feels a small flicker in her belly. He'll miss her. "You should come for a holiday. Meet me in Vietnam. There are heaps of cheap flights."

He just shrugs and zips up his jacket. "Maybe." He sounds unconvinced. "Anyway, I better go. I've got to be at the orchards at six."

She nods. "Okay."

He lurches forward, wraps one arm around her neck, and pulls her into an awkward hug. They've never hugged before. For the first time, she smells him, dusky and surprisingly familiar. As she steps into the embrace, he takes a proper hold of her, and it becomes more than cursory. When he pulls back, he gives her one of his funny half-mouth smiles. She smiles back, surprised at his vehemence.

The smiles fade, but they don't stop looking at each other. Tam feels something hanging in the air between them. Maybe it's not just her. Then she knows she's right, because he's kissing her. He's wrapping his hand around the back of her neck, under her hair, and his tongue is sliding against hers.

She goes with it for a while. How can she not? But then, as sensation gives way to thought, she presses her hand to the centre of his chest and pushes. When he steps back, his eyes wide, she thumps him in the sternum. "Why *now?*" she hisses.

He just shakes his head slightly and stares at the ground.

She turns and leaves him there on the porch, shutting the door firmly behind her.

Upstairs in her room, she paces the wooden floorboard, flushed and angry. Why did he have to do that now? He's had all year to do that. Why did he have to wait this long to kiss her exactly the way she's wanted to him to kiss her? Ever since that night of the fishing trip and the dead wombat a year ago? Why couldn't he have done that when they first met instead of playing best mates with her and going out with skinny, cutesy Nerida Marsh? Why just as she's about to leave? When there are whole months separating the possibility of them?

And why did she have to put a stop to it? She sits on the edge of her bed and tugs at a fraying hole in her jeans and frowns. What an asshole. He probably only did it because she's leaving. Or maybe he knows about this stupid crush she's had and is trying to make her feel better? She takes in a deep breath. No, that's not his style. Not at all. The smartest thing to do would be to pretend that never happened.

But it only takes a second before Tam realises she's not feeling that smart.

She jumps off the bed and bolts down the stairs.

"Back later," she gasps at her father and Bill on her way out.

She sprints up the hill, headed straight for the one light she can see in the darkness, pulling her jacket around her against the wind. When she gets to the house, she picks up a pebble and throws it at the amber-lit window. It only takes a minute for him to appear. When he spots her on the gravel below, he gives her a slow smile. "Come up," he says quietly.

She does as she's told, slipping in the side door. She kicks off her shoes and carries them, so as not to wake Matt's uncle as she climbs the stairs.

He grins from his bed as the door opens. "How very eighties movie of you."

"Shut up," she tells him, dropping her shoes and climbing onto the bed.

CHAPTER 6

Olivia, Melbourne

Olivia lets herself in the side gate. She tiptoes through the house, scared of waking a sleeping baby. Anna is in the laundry, dragging armloads of soggy clothes from the washing machine.

"Hi."

Anna smiles wide. "Hey, little sister. You good?" she asks in that gentle way of hers. She reaches right down into the washing machine. She's so short that her head and most of her torso disappear into the tub too. Eventually she returns with a bunch of clothes clutched triumphantly in her hand. She throws them into the basket and picks it up, resting it against what her swollen belly has left of her hip.

The yard is overgrown and sunny.

Anna drops the basket on the lawn, cranks the rusted metal handle of the clothesline, and begins to peg rows of tiny singlets and bibs on the line. "You excited?"

"Sort of," Olivia mutters. She picks up a towel, shakes it out, and fixes it to the line.

"Where's your pack? I thought we were taking you to the airport?"

"You are, if that's okay?" Olivia picks up a sock and pegs it to the line. "I left it in the spare room."

"Of course." Anna grins. "Well, Steve will drive. I'm getting too huge to fit behind the steering wheel."

"How long now?"

"A week. I can't wait." She stares down at her stomach. "Your free ride is nearly up, kiddo," she tells it.

Olivia laughs and pats Anna's belly, feeling the taut skin surrounding her nephew.

When the entire line is festooned with clothes, Anna lowers herself into one of the lawn chairs nestled in the overgrown grass. Olivia watches the clothes wave in the breeze, wondering how such little people can produce so much dirty washing. She looks over at her sister, tired and pale, but happy. "You *are* huge."

"I know." Anna laughs, rolling her eyes and running her hands over her front. "My stomach is, as they say, the gift that keeps on giving."

Olivia laughs. She's missed her sister. She hasn't seen her since before exams, but she's spent more time with Anna than she's spent with anyone ever. And they've never fought. Not once. Not even a sibling spat.

They sit there in silence, sun-stunned and mellow.

"I have got to mow this lawn." Anna rubs her neck and looks around the yard. "Remember when we moved here? I never thought I'd have to worry about grass."

"Yeah, I remember." Olivia is perched on an upturned wheelbarrow and smiles sleepily, remembering how the yard had been almost entirely paved with concrete back then.

Happy to have her sister back in Melbourne after Anna's year-long stint in Sydney, Olivia came to help them unpack. The tram ride took her to unfamiliar Melbourne, blocks past the old prison. Until that moment, in her mind, the north of the city had ended at Pentridge. She had no idea that a different, sleepier Coburg lay beyond the frenzied commerce of Sydney Road. It had been the first truly warm day of the year, and instead of taking anything out of boxes, they'd sat together on the sun-warmed slabs, drinking tea among the piles of crammed cardboard cartons. Anna was pregnant with Ally then.

They laughed together at the barren backyard, its area completely paved over aside from a short stretch of grass near the back fence housing a few ailing shrubs. Within months, Steve had ripped up the concrete, letting the grass take over again.

"I'm going to lose Ally in this one of these days," Anna jokes. "I'll never be able to find her."

"It's pretty long," Olivia agrees, looking at where the weeds have reached nearly halfway up the back fence.

"Is Mum coming to the airport?"

"Nope. She's got some guest lecture thing. I had lunch with her today. We said goodbye then."

Anna's smile is weary. She, too, is used to her mother's constant unavailability. "Well, you and me and Steve can get Vietnamese tonight and celebrate."

"Okay." She looks up to see Anna staring at her. "What?"

"You okay, Livs?"

Olivia shrugs, feeling the now-familiar tide of misery wash over her. "Not really."

"I'm so sorry it went so badly. But you can still transfer into law later, right?"

Maybe. She feels like such a loser. Especially with her sister, who is raising a kid, is pregnant with another, and still manages all this incredible environmental activism work from home. Not many people know it, but Anna is a quiet storm.

A loud cry erupts from somewhere inside the house. Ally is awake. When Anna stands, Olivia does too. Before she goes inside, Anna folds her into a tight hug. "It'll be fine, Olivia. You'll be whatever you want. You will. And you're going to have an amazing trip." Anna lets her go and gives her one of her gentle smiles.

Olivia returns the smile, wanting to believe her.

* * *

It is early morning when Olivia tumbles out of those hospital doors, bone tired and wide awake at the same time. She pulls her cardigan around her, flinching at the dual assault of bright sun and the cold wind. Back in the room, Anna is passed out, the exhaustion of even such a short labour knocking her out cold. Steve is awake though, deep in a silent reverie over his baby boy.

Olivia shakes her head, unable to quite comprehend this night. That she just witnessed the birth of her nephew. That was definitely not in the plan for the evening. She got the shock of her life in the early hours of the morning when Anna came into the spare room and sat gingerly on the edge of the bed, pallid with pain. Her nephew is impatient it seems, ready to meet them a week early.

The drive to the hospital was surreal, speeding down empty Bell Street. When they got to the hospital and the midwife took them to the room where he would be born, Anna clutched her hand and whispered, "Stay." She has no idea if Anna wanted Olivia to stay for herself or for her. But obedient, she did as she was instructed.

She sinks into the curb and watches a man pace the length of the short path outside the hospital, unaware that the wind has gotten trapped under his jacket and the back of it has blown up like a balloon behind him. Dazed, she rubs her eyes and yawns. Already the whole experience has been reduced to filmic flashes for her: to small, digestible moments of drama and pain. It's those flashes she knows she will always see when she looks back on this night.

Like the way parts of her sister's body heaved and shifted as she knelt on the floor of the small shower room, deep in the last stages of labour. Olivia had stared, shocked and hypnotised by the way Anna's hips and spine, parts of the body that she had previously thought immovable, seemed to shift and buckle to accommodate Henry's movement toward the world. Her body gave in to his desire to be born in ways she never thought possible. Olivia was fascinated and horrified at the same time. Part of her wanted to run from the room at the sounds of Anna's pain.

Like the short but interminable silence that fell after the baby rushed from her sister's body, sliding into the midwife's hands in a surge of skin, fluid, and flesh. It was only for a few seconds, but it was like they all stopped breathing as the midwife stuck her finger in the baby's tiny closed mouth. The moment hung suspended in a taut silence between his entry into the world and that first cry that eventually erupted, tinny and thin, around the bathroom.

Like the sight of her sister after it all ended. Anna was crouched in the corner of the shower, the water still running over her feet. Thinning drops of blood surrounded her as they washed down the drain. She was panting quietly into her lap, her eyes closed to everything in the room. It was like she had shut down, closed off to protect herself from what had just happened. Olivia recognised, for a brief second as the midwife placed the baby on her lap, Anna's fleeting desire to push the baby away, to stay huddled in her moment of self-protection. She didn't, though. Instead, she laid a shielding hand around the tiny breadth of the baby's back and held him there while they both got used to him being in the world. Then this experience made sense for Olivia.

Her phone buzzes in her pocket. It's her mother coming to take her to the airport. Olivia swipes a hand over her face and yawns loudly. She cannot believe she now has to board a plane. She pulls herself up from the curb, her head still spinning slightly. Inside the silent room, the blinds have been closed and everyone is asleep. Anna is in the exact position she was in when Olivia left the room, and now Steve is on the other side of the double bed, his body curved around Henry. He is still wrapped tightly in the towel he was placed in after the midwife finished checking him.

She peers through the half-darkness at the baby. His face is more defined than it was when she left the room. She smiles at him. Her nephew. The child she is always going to look at, thinking how she met him the moment he came into the world.

"I'm glad I got to meet you before I go," she whispers, leaning right over the bed and smoothing a finger over his forehead. His tiny face scrunches, and he grunts and settles again. She kisses her finger and presses it to his tiny, wrinkled brow.

She takes one last peek at him and tiptoes quietly out of the room. As the sunlight hits her face outside, she hauls in a deep breath and tells herself again, *I did that.* For the first time in a long time, she feels a rush of something good.

CHAPTER 7

Kit, Melbourne

She saves Liza until last.

"Have fun, okay?" She dives at her, wrapping her arms around her neck.

Liza's curls tickle Kit's nose as they stand enmeshed in this embrace, rocking together from foot to foot as the last passengers trickle around them and that eternally polite PA voice makes final boarding announcements and missing passenger calls.

Liza squeezes her just a little harder. "You okay?"

Kit just nods. She can't speak, because now that it has come to the actual moment of watching them go, it's completely real and hurts like hell. And trust Liza to know it.

"I mean it. Have fun." She grins through tears. "See everything, do everything, be naughty. And then message me and tell all."

Liza's smile is wide, even though her eyes are terrified. "I will. I love you."

"Love you too."

Liza gives her a small, regretful smile, as if to say she *still* can't believe they aren't doing this together. Kit doesn't acknowledge it. She can't. The crying window is still wide open. She just gives her a small, dismissive wave.

Liza hikes her bag onto her shoulder and gives her a small nod, like she gets it. She shows her boarding pass and passport, waves one more time, and then disappears through the sliding doors to Departures.

Kit swallows hard and turns slowly for the exit and the bus home.

* * *

When she gets back to Collingwood, the whole suburb is steeped in a dead quiet. The rest of the world is still sleeping off Saturday night. Kit would be too, usually. Unwilling to walk the last stretch into the grim, early morning party aftermath that will be Smith Street, she jumps on a tram. On the short ride, she keeps a wary eye out for ticket inspectors. She has no idea where her travel card is, and she sure as hell can't afford to owe anyone else money.

Back at the flat, her mother and Darren are home. He's cleared the small dining table and is working on some piece of electrical something, as usual. Her mother, Annie, is dusting all the clutter and crap she calls her "treasures," her wide frame moving gingerly through the chaos. The morning sun barely penetrates the thick net curtains and the army of trinkets lined up on the windowsill. Claustrophobic, Kit props the door open to let in some air and light. This new flat feels as tiny as the all the others.

"No, hon," Annie says. "Darren gets hay fever from the jasmine next door, remember?" A cloud of dust erupts from under her duster as she speaks, sending particles dancing furiously through shafts of sunlight. Kit shakes her head. And this dustbowl's not about to kill him?

"Kitty," Darren booms by way of greeting. Then he lets off a loud sneeze that ripples through his generous frame. "Alright?"

"Hi." When her mum first started seeing him a few years ago, Kit thought he was literally asking her if she was all right. Now she knows it's just some weird British way of saying hello.

"Lizey's off then?" Annie asks.

Kit nods and leans down to pat Tinder as she rubs her grey fluffball of a body against her. Her mother still doesn't understand it's a ridiculous name for a cat, and Kit's given up trying to explain.

"You messed up there, didn't you?" Darren chides loudly for the zillionth time. He says everything loudly. "You should be on a plane instead of crowding in here with us lot."

Kit glares at him. Does he really have to rub it in? And what does he mean by "us lot"? There's two of them.

"Leave her alone, Darren. She's miserable enough."

Miserable doesn't even describe it. Kit looks at the clock on the wall above the fridge. It's only nine thirty, and it feels like a whole depressing day has passed. But that's where waking up at four will get you. "I'm going to bed," she mumbles. She trudges to her room.

"Kitty, hon. I didn't know she was coming as well," her mother calls out behind her. "You two have to sort it out."

What? Bleary, Kit pushes open the bedroom door.

"Shut it!" a voice growls.

All she can see is a mess of jet-black hair tangled over the floral pillows. But that's all she needs. This room was empty yesterday, and today, piles of clothes and handbag contents are strewn across the other bed. All the boxes Kit lugged over here have been stacked precariously next to the door, replaced by another smaller pile of bags dumped between the beds, spilling over with clothes and shoes and cosmetics.

Kit leans on the doorframe, still too stunned to move.

"Can you get in or out and shut the bloody door?" Chloe pulls the doona tighter around her. "Darren's so goddamn loud."

Shocked into obedience, Kit shuts the door, clears a space and sinks onto the other bed. "What are you doing here?" The last she knew, her sister was living down the beach at Rye, renting a place with her friends and working in a pub.

"Got kicked out of the shack. Owners wanted it for the summer," Chloe mumbles. "What are *you* doing here? I thought you'd moved out?" She asks like it's an accusation. Like Kit has no right to be here. Same way she's always treated her. Before Kit can even respond, she grumbles. "And you better sort out all that shit by the door. I'm not living in here with you and ten thousand boxes. I have stuff too, you know."

Clearly she does, because it's all over the freaking floor. Kit stares around the tiny room. How can she share this tiny, suffocating space with her sister, who dominates any space she's in, no matter how big?

Tears sting at the back of her eyes again. This summer is becoming her worst nightmare realised. She has *got* to get out of here. She finds a better top among the rubble and quickly changes into it. Chloe is already snoring under the doona. Her sister has always had the ability to go from psycho to zero in moments, like she never erupted.

She makes a quick exit. As soon as she sees Kit, her mother raises her hands and sighs. "I had no idea. I had no idea both you girls would turn up on the doorstep demanding to move back in."

That's when the guilt hits. "I'm sorry, Mum."

"Oh, don't be sorry, hon." She pulls Kit into a hug, and rocks her gently back and forth. Kit can smell a waft of sandalwood on her velvety shirt. Mum smell. It's as comforting as it is cloying. "You two are just going to have to figure out a way to share that room."

"I know," Kit mumbles. She yanks open the front door, letting in a rush of a breeze. Darren immediately sneezes again. She grins, despite her mood. "And you need to go live in one of those plastic bubbles."

He yanks a hankie out of his pocket and bellows a laugh. "Very funny, smart ass."

"Where are you off to?" Annie asks, still dusting.

"To get a job." Kit pulls the door behind her and trots down the stairs and back out onto the street. Cars roar by under the plane trees on Queen's Parade as she strides away from the noise and chaos as fast as she can. She makes her way into the heart of the suburb, where all the cafes and bars line the streets, competing for everyone's attention. She'll find another job there for sure.

And then she's going to work so that she can pay back the money she owes on rent and that stupid cherub as soon as humanly possible. And she'll be so busy, she'll never have to be at the flat. With the sudden appearance of her obnoxious sister, that can only be a good thing.

As she heads for a clump of cafés, she runs her fingers through her hair and sets her shoulders to presentable. She will have a job by the end of the day. She *will.*

CHAPTER 8

Tam, Hong Kong

Her eyes are grainy and tired, but she can't stop staring out the windows. Dawn is inching into being around them. Already, everything seems so exotic and strange, and they're not even halfway there yet. Even the air in this airport smells different.

A few hours earlier, tucked in a window seat next to Liza, she watched their approach to this city in the darkness. At first, the vast blackness of the ocean revealed nothing. Then, intermittent clumps of lights appeared, dotted close together like a constellation of stars. Islands, she guessed. As they approached, some curled like incandescent chains tossed along the surface of the water by some careless, giant hand. Finally, as the landing gear clunked from the belly of the plane, the world turned into a vivid mass of coloured lights below, some still, some moving. It took her a moment to realise they were the headlights of cars driving slowly along roads. A tiny, teeming world moving below her. She couldn't look away.

And now as a yellow smog-bound sun rises in the sky, she sees what she wasn't able to see last night, what those necklaces of lights wrapped themselves around: mountains. Everywhere. Great green masses rise out of the earth, circling the airport like an army at the ready. They're surrounded. These are nothing like those craggy, bush-bound hulks back home. These are elegant, peaked, velvety forms. So beautiful.

She shuffles down in the stiff airport seat, drags her eyes from the view and checks her phone. It's still two hours until they take off again. She shakes her head. Even though she knew how long this trip was going to take, she had no idea how it would *feel*. Those nine hours in a plane have left her feeling like something left in the sun for too long. And they have another twelve or so more in front of them.

She stretches and yawns, accidently knocking Liza's book. "Sorry."

"It's fine." She gives Tam a small smile and returns to her reading.

Tam glances at her phone again, a reflex action. But of course, there's no point. She has no service. It'll be just getting near nightfall at home. Bill will be cooking, either at his place or theirs, and her dad will be deciding whether or not to light a fire. She feels a sharp pang in her stomach and shakes her head. She's not allowed to be homesick yet.

Mai and Olivia traipse back into the Departures lounge and drop down onto the seats opposite them. Tam's barely spoken a word to them yet. Mai's talking a mile a minute, staring at her phone. She's clearly got internet.

"Jason Deith got arrested at Schoolies." She rolls her eyes and drops into her seat, eyes fixed to her phone.

Olivia just nods, an eyebrow raised.

Tam takes the chance to inspect these girls she's barely spoken to yet. They're so different. Mai is small and compact, with bobbed black hair and a round face. Olivia is average height and slim, with long light hair, somewhere between brown and blonde. Mai's snub-nosed and cute-ish, where Olivia is classically, gently pretty.

So far everything has been pleasant and polite between them all, with just a hint of uncomfortable. At least she and Liza have had a few meetings in their past. And Tam likes Liza. She's sweet. Tam stares at the other two, trying to get a read.

These two, she's not so sure about yet. Mai seems kind of loud and excitable. When she met them at the airport from her domestic connection in Melbourne, the first thing she heard as she approached them was Mai screaming "You what?" at the top of her lungs. She was clutching Olivia's arm, jumping up and down. Tam flinched.

She has no gauge on Olivia yet at all. She seems kind of quiet, too. Reserved, maybe. But she'll take that over the shrieking.

Mai shoves a shopping bag into her hand luggage. "Like I need more stuff to carry." She shakes her head. "That's the worst part of travelling, hauling your crap around with you."

"Especially the amount of crap you brought." Olivia smiles at her.

"Well, I've got to look good on this trip. I'm planning to pull. A *lot*."

Olivia rolls her eyes and smiles. "That's right, I forgot."

"And you better be my wingman."

"We'll see."

Tam can already tell Olivia has no intention at all.

"Oh no, you *have* to." Mai bounces up and down. "This holiday is my freedom march, remember?"

Olivia catches Tam watching them and smiles, her green eyes warming. "Mai's parents keep her on kind of a tight leash," she explains.

"Right."

Mai rolls her eyes. "Put it this way: they couldn't be more clichéd Asian parents if they tried."

Tam smiles, even though she isn't exactly sure what that means.

"So, if Olivia's going to let the team down, how about you, Tam?" Mai asks, pulling her neon kicks up onto the seat and hugging her knees. "You going to party? Fancy playing wingman? I'll let you have first pick."

It's like Tam has been suddenly transported into one of those gross bromance movies. "Uh, I'm kind of seeing someone," she mutters by way of excuse.

A small delicious thrill rocks through her as she thinks of Matt and of that hot, sleepless night in his attic room two nights ago. It was hard to leave that room, even to come on this trip. And although they didn't talk about it, it felt like something more powerful than a get-out-of-jail-free-because-you're-going-overseas one-night-stand. *She* definitely has no eyes for anyone else. She'd make a terrible wingman. "Sorry."

"Well that's annoying." Mai turns to Liza. "What about you, Liza? Single? Taken?"

"Um, single," Liza says quietly.

Mai is about to say something but stops and peers at Liza's book. "*What* are you reading?"

Liza holds up the paperback.

Mai laughs and nudges Olivia. "Look."

Olivia's face is unreadable as she glances at the book.

"Her mum wrote that, you know." Mai jerks a thumb at Olivia.

"Really?" Tam's eyes widen. Olivia's mother is Ruth Clayton? Tam had to read one of her books in Year 10. She's supposedly some literary genius. "One of our great women writers," her English teacher Mrs Kaur used to constantly say in this reverent tone.

"Yup." Mai moves her small backpack so an older couple can sit down near them. "She is."

"I'm going to get some tea before we go," Olivia says. Tam gets the feeling this conversation is making her uncomfortable.

"I didn't know that," Liza says, looking bewildered.

"Seriously?" Mai hooks her travel pillow around her neck and settles back. "You went to our school, didn't you? God, you must have had your head in the sand." She huddles over her phone and that is that.

Liza tucks the book away in her hand luggage, her cheeks pinking slightly. Feeling sorry for her, Tam looks out the windows again, wondering how this odd combination of girls is going to work for the next month or so. *If* it's going to work.

* * *

Liza, en route

She unfolds her legs from their tangle and stretches them out, giving her aching knees a reprieve. The athlete in her isn't designed to sit still for hours on end in small spaces. But then, no one is, really. She tucks her legs in to let a woman pass, wishing she could jog a few laps of the aisle to stretch out. It didn't help that they were strapped into their seats for the first two hours due to turbulence. For hours the plane dipped and swung from side to side in the air as they flew close to a series of storm cells over China.

Liza doesn't mind turbulence. Once, on a trip to Perth with her dad, the plane kept performing these sudden, stomach-flipping dips as they crossed the Nullarbor Desert. He told her not to worry. As long as the plane keeps moving forward, it's doing its job. Just think of it as driving on a dirt road. So when the jerking and weaving gets rough, she shuts her eyes and pretends she's in her grandad's ute out on their property, waiting for it to exhaust itself.

Mai was terrified, though. She kept clutching the armrests and letting out these little low squeals every time the plane bucked a little harder. "I freaking hate this," she muttered through gritted teeth. "We're gonna die." Liza wanted to reassure her with what her father had told her all those years ago, but she wasn't sure Mai would hear her.

Now, on the other side of sleep, the plane is moving relentlessly forward on smoother air. She unbuckles her belt and decides to go to the toilet. She doesn't really need to go, but she needs to move. She inches through the dimmed cabin, past people snoozing or watching movies, and joins the short line at the back of the plane.

When she's done, she squeezes out the tiny closet of a toilet and takes a look around. There's a small space at the end of the plane near where they serve food, and a couple of people are standing there, stretching or staring. Flight attendants chat quietly as they open and close hatches in the galley, shoving things away and pouring drinks. She notices Olivia standing by the plane doors, peering out the window.

Before she can go, Olivia spots her and beckons. "Hey, come see this." She steps back so Liza can look out the window. Far below them is a vast tract of white and black. It takes Liza a minute to work out what she's looking at. Snow. And rocks. It's mountains. Great stone hulks rising out of the earth, some so high, clouds huddle around their peaks. They seem to go on forever, sprawling beyond her range of sight.

"It's the Himalayas."

"No way." A thrill springs through her. She, Liza Hansen, is looking at the Himalayas. That's crazy.

Olivia leans her forehead on the small square of glass. "I always look out for them, every time I fly this way. It feels so weird. To think that's Nepal or India or even Tibet, just doing its thing down there while we fly over it." She shakes her head, still staring. "It's crazy." Her voice has a slight throaty husk to it, and she enunciates everything carefully. Not posh. Just measured and adult.

Liza nods. "It *is*. Ha...have you travelled much?" She bets the answer is yes.

"A bit, but mostly to the same places, to visit Dad. He lived in Shanghai a few years for work."

"Shanghai? Wow. What's it like?"

"Loud and confusing. But fun, too. He's moving there next year. I've been on a couple of book tours with mum too, to the States and Europe, but they're usually pretty rushed."

Liza just nods, feeling even more intimidated now. They stare at the view in silence. She finally builds up bravery enough to say. "I didn't know your Mum wrote that book. It's on the reading list for the course I want to get into next year."

Olivia gives her a dubious smile. "You must be the only kid in the whole school who didn't know that. You didn't have to do *The Return* in Year 11?"

"Yeah, I did, but I didn't know she was your mum. I wasn't around much. Because of running."

"Of course. You were one of those kids they always mentioned in assembly for bringing glory to the school."

Liza blushes and lets out a small laugh.

"Well, anyway, that was one less kid whinging to me about having to read that tome." Olivia shakes her head and smiles. "Like it's my fault it was on the syllabus? It was embarrassing enough having to write an essay on my *own* mother's book."

"I bet it was. What's it like? Having a writer for a mum?"

"I don't know," Olivia says blankly, like she's been asked that question a zillion times before. "She's just my mother."

Liza immediately wishes she hadn't asked and changes the subject. "So, did you really help your sister have a baby last night?"

"Yeah, well, I didn't exactly do much." She grins. "Just stood there, horrified, and rubbed her back when she asked."

"What was it like?"

Olivia wraps a strand of her hair around her finger and tips her head to one side, thinking. "Incredible, gross, terrifying, amazing. All of the above."

She laughs again. But then she can't think of a single thing to say, so she retreats to her seat.

CHAPTER 9

Tam, Algarve, Portugal

Tam tramps up the rough-hewn steps that climb from the beach up to the cliff path. Panting heavily at the top, she walks a little distance away from the path and perches on a rock. She needs a moment with this view before she can face going back.

The sun hangs low over a glittering ocean, the water a heavy blue in this early morning calm. Tam woke up early, intent on finding some silence. And she has finally found it. The beach below her is empty, abandoned by everyone here to deep, drunken sleep, or at least the privacy of rooms to finish out the party.

And if she sits in this spot and stares directly outward, or even to her right, toward the small town, a huddle of white-painted, red-roofed buildings clinging to the side of the rocky mountain, she can retain this sense of solitude. It's a beautiful place, really, craggy and sun-bleached. And even though it's headed to winter, the sun radiates just enough warmth for it to feel like a holiday.

But if she looks behind her, she knows reality will hit. This resort was Mai's pick, all part of her project to party hard and soon. One of her relatives works for a chain that has hotels and resorts all over the world, apparently, and she got them an incredible deal to spend their first five nights of their holiday somewhere warm and on the coast. A beach holiday before they head to colder places.

When Kit told Tam about their first stop, it had sounded awesome: a famous coastal area in the south of Portugal with stunning beaches and decent weather at this time of year. The pictures she'd seen looked beautiful. And it *is* a stunning place. It really is. It's the resort that sucks. Profusely.

What Tam didn't realise is that this place would just be one giant, gross party spot for backpackers, mostly British, whose only holiday intentions are to get completely and utterly wasted twenty-four seven.

Tam saw a lot of places that looked just like this on the bus ride to the town, terraced, white-painted party hubs. Their rooms are matching twins on a floor identical to all the others, with small balconies identical to all the others. The rooms are clean, but the walls and bathroom fittings bear the marks of the long line of partying holidaymakers that have come before them.

The first night, jetlagged and exhausted from the epic trip to get here, Tam barely registered anything. She landed facedown on the bed and slept for twelve hours straight. At breakfast the next morning, fuzzy and still exhausted, she immediately got a sense of the place. Girls were strolling the halls in their bikinis with just light kimono or oversized shirts barely covering them. People were slugging beer with their breakfasts, their plates heaped with hangover bacon and eggs. And by the pool, the party had already started. All day, techno beats pound from the speakers by the pool, ricocheting off the walls and making the windows tremor.

During the day, the beach is strewn with drunk or hung-over tourists, sunbaking. There's no way to get away from them, either. Tam has tried to find a way out of this Spring Break-style hell. But each end of the beach is closed off by steep reddish-brown cliffs cleaving through the white sand to the water.

The only place to go is the town. And even there, it's the same crowds, pillaging the town for souvenirs and happy hours. She wonders why everyone seems so rude and impatient even though they're on holiday. Yesterday, when she ducked into a small shop to buy a cold drink, a pair of Australian guys were demanding that the old man running it, whose English was clearly limited, find them the right kind of surf wax. She felt embarrassed. She also feels embarrassed by the girls who walk around the streets in bikini tops and shorts so short, they might as well not be wearing them. Maybe she's too prudish, but she can see the vaguely disapproving looks from the local women who run the shops and cafés.

The worst part about this resort, though, is the way it doesn't feel like it's part of the place it's in. This resort could be anywhere with a beach, really, and it wouldn't matter. It just feels like some purpose-built party palace that just happens to be in Portugal. It could be a cruise ship, for all the surrounding culture matters.

A pair of Scottish girls giggle and gossip about whatever happened to them last night on the dance floor as they begin the trek down to the beach.

She can't wait to get out of here. Mai loves it, though. She's found herself a posse, and she parties with them every single night. Olivia too. Every time they see her she has some wild story about something someone just did. And when she's not partying, she's flaked out on the beach with them or sleeping. Tam's pretty sure Liza's not having that much fun, either. She spends most of her time reading or running in the hills. They've spent the last couple of afternoons together at the beach.

Tam climbs off her perch on the rock and wonders what Lisbon will be like. That's got to be better, in a whole city of actual Portuguese people living and working. Maybe the obnoxious tourists won't be as noticeable there. She weaves around the deck chairs by the pool, dodging around a pile of vomit that hasn't been cleaned up yet. She holds her breath as she scurries past. God, she hates this place.

After a couple of wrong turns, she finds the hallway that leads to her room. They all look the same. She's so busy hating on the place, she doesn't notice it until she's nearly at her door. Sprawled on the floor like a beached whale is a guy wearing only a pair of boxers, snoring loudly. What the everlasting fuck? She nudges him with her foot. He just grunts and keeps snoring. She can smell the alcohol, reeking from his pores. She nudges harder. Nothing. Nudge evolves into kick. This time he grunts and wraps an arm around his head, the tuft of his bleached faux hawk pressed against the carpet.

A group of people saunter past and joke about his rough night. They don't offer to help, though. She swears loudly and steps over him and opens her bedroom door.

"Uh, there's a guy passed out outside room 407," she tells reception on her room phone. "I don't know where he came from, and I think there's something wrong with him." Then she hangs up and throws herself down on the bed. Closing her eyes, she listens to hotel staff try to rouse the drunken blonde whale outside her door, wishing she were somewhere else.

CHAPTER 10

Liza, Algarve, Portugal

She strides gingerly down the last steep stretch. The gravel is loose and dry, and she's already skidded a few times. A sprained ankle would not be a fun addition to this trip. When she hits asphalt, she finds her pace again, keeping well to the shoulder of the road. Cars hurtle around these narrow cliff-bound roads. They clearly have no fear of the dramatic drop from the road to the mass of rock and ocean below.

She does. So she lopes along the inside of the road, the winter sun beating down on her shoulders. Jagged red and yellow mountains stretch high above her. This has been her favourite thing so far, running through this landscape each day. It's stunning.

The hotel she's not so sure about. It's just one non-stop party. And Liza's never really known how to party. She's trying, though. Sort of. Last night she went with Mai and Olivia to the club at a resort down the road. She even put on a dress and some mascara and drank a glass of champagne with her dinner to prepare herself. The drink made her feel kind of light and brighter for about half an hour, but when she got there, she still didn't really know what to do with herself. Mai launched herself on some people she had met earlier, and a guy almost instantly bee-lined for Olivia, capturing her into a conversation. Liza stood strung between these two interactions, feeling like a loose end no one wants to tie up.

To disguise the fact she had no one to talk to, she danced. Still buzzing from her one drink (yes, sad), it was kind of fun at first. Then it got later, and the crowd got drunker, and she spent most of her time fending off guys who seemed to think sidling up really close and breathing heavily on her was the ideal come-on.

That's when she decided to admit what she already knew. This is not her. And she's pretty sure it's not just because she's gay, either. She tried to find Mai to tell her she was leaving, but she was nowhere to be found. She spotted Olivia out by the pool, deep in some conversation with a different guy on one of the deck chairs and waved a goodnight, but Olivia didn't see her.

Liza slows to a walk when she gets to the driveway of the hotel. Panting, she heads upstairs. It's only four, but everyone is already gearing up for another night. Girls pass between rooms, reeking of perfume, trading outfits. People call up and down the halls. A guy carries a tray of drinks in plastic martini glasses from one room to another. She slips into the room, escaping the toxic stink of hairspray and cologne.

Tam is already in there, leaned over her backpack.

"Hey."

"Hi," Tam grunts, clumsily folding a pair of jeans.

It takes Liza a second to realise she's packing. She frowns. They aren't due to leave for another two days. She grabs her towel from the back of her door and wipes her face. "What are you doing?"

"Leaving."

"Why?" Liza sits on the edge of her bed and watches, bewildered, as Tam marches around the room, gathering her things. "Where are you going?"

"Lisbon."

"But we're not going until Thursday."

Tam shrugs, slipping her laptop into her pack. "Well I'm going tonight." She turns around and flashes her a grin. "Want to come?"

Liza stares at her. "Um, I, uh...We can't just leave."

"Why not?"

"Because of the others."

"They'll be fine. They can just meet us in Lisbon on Thursday. We'd hardly be abandoning them. Besides, they're having fun."

"You're really not, are you?"

Tam stops what she's doing, takes a deep breath, and shakes her head. "No, I'm not." She sits down on the edge of the bed facing Liza and pulls at a strand of her long red hair. "Kit's told you I want to be a chef one day, right?"

"Uh-huh."

"Next year, I start an apprenticeship. Then I want to have my own restaurant one day."

"That's so cool."

"And you know, I came on this trip because it might be my only chance for years. And because I really wanted to see Europe and to try new things, and new foods. And I don't know," she stares down at her freckled hands and shrugs. "It's so beautiful around here. But this place, these people? It feels so soulless. And *so* high school."

Liza nods. Exactly.

"I mean, I'm in this amazing new country, and all I'm seeing is drunk people partying—which I could do at home if I wanted. And all I am eating is food I could eat at home." She folds her arms over her chest and sighs. "I want to actually *see* some of this country. I don't want this place to be my experience of Portugal."

"I wasn't expecting it to be like this, either."

Tam looks slightly relieved. Like she thought she might be the only one. "And I respect that the others wanted to start this trip off with a beach holiday, to party and celebrate finishing school, and that's cool. Mai can party her little heart out. We clearly don't all want the same things from this holiday." She shrugs. "And this afternoon, I just kind of had this epiphany that we don't *have* to do the same stuff, just because we're travelling together." Tam picks up a T-shirt and rolls it up. "I may never be here again, and I want to use all the time I have to really see it, you know?" She checks her watch. "So, there's a bus from town in a couple of hours, and I'm going to catch it. It gets into Lisbon late, but there's a cheap hostel right near the stop." She picks up a T-shirt and starts folding. "So if you want to come, you've got an hour."

Liza stares at her towel. She wants to go. She didn't know it until she heard this, but she does. Because what will she do here? The same as the last couple of days, while away the hours reading on the beach—but without Tam for company? "Do you think the others will mind? I don't want to upset them."

"I really don't think they'll care. It's only temporary. We'll just tell them that we want more time in Lisbon, and that we'll meet them in a couple of days."

"Okay then. Why not?" Liza stands. And for a moment, she feels bigger and braver and worldlier than she ever has in her life.

"Awesome. Well, get ready, then." Tam grins. "We don't want to miss the bus."

Suddenly this feels like the adventure Liza thought she was going to have.

* * *

Olivia, Algarve, Portugal

"So what do you think?" Sam asks, letting a small trickle of sand fall from his palm onto her shin.

Olivia makes a noncommittal sound and rolls over on her towel. She stares at her book and hopes he'll get the hint.

"Oh well, we don't have to decide now," he says, standing. "I'm going for a swim." He strides away to the water.

She drops her book on the sand in front of her. *We?* Where does he get the idea that they have magically overnight become a "we"? Just because they slept together *once?*

Why can she never achieve a one-night-stand? At least one that stays that way? Any time she tries it, the guy always wants something more. And she finds herself having to figure out how to extricate herself. Sam was supposed to be a thing two nights ago. And here he is. Still.

Even Will was supposed to be a one-night, friends-with-benefits thing, and he lasted six months.

And Sam's nice. Really nice. He doesn't act like a dick when he's drunk. Not like that guy Mai's been all over because she likes them all big and burly and physical comedy. And sure, it was fun to lie around with him the other night and talk and kiss, first on the beach and then in her room. But that was all she wanted out of him. But now he seems to think they're mated for the rest of this holiday. She wishes she could figure out a way to get out of it without hurting his feelings.

Something hits her in the arm. A bottle cap rolls across her towel and comes to a stop on the edge. She frowns and looks up. Mai's sitting out in the full sun, gathering a tan, perched on one of Campbell's muscled, footballer thighs. If Mai wanted a footy player, couldn't she have found one at home?

"Wake up! What are we doing tonight, Livvie?"

"I have no idea." Olivia wishes Mai would stop calling her that. It's so cutesie. It's Mai's way of making them seem closer, more intimate than they actually are. Sure, they've been friends for years, but they've never really spent that much time alone. But now that it's just the two of them, Mai keeps telling everyone they meet about their fabulous, twinned future, how they're going to the top law school in Australia next year, and how amazing everything is going to be. It's driving Olivia crazy.

"Well, what's Sam want to do?"

"How should I know?" Olivia mumbles, annoyed.

Mai doesn't notice. Or doesn't want to. "Well, we've got to make the most of our last night here." She wraps an arm around Campbell's neck and drains the last of her soft drink. "We need to party."

"You decide and let me know." Olivia pulls on a dress and stands. "I'm going for a walk."

"Want me to come with?"

Olivia shakes her head. That's the last thing she wants. "I won't be long."

Taking off quickly, before Sam spots her and tries to come along, she weaves around bodies strewn over the white sand. She frowns. Why is she being such a bitch? Even if it's just in the privacy of her own head? Mai's her friend, and she's just excited and drunk on the freedom of this holiday. She'll chill. And, Olivia has to admit, a huge part of it's the law school stuff. It's not exactly Mai's fault Olivia's completely messed up her exams. But every time Mai says anything about their uni plans, Olivia gets this sinking, gross feeling. She has to tell her before results come out.

She perches on a wide, red rock and looks out at the glittering water. This holiday is kind of strange so far. But then, she's not really sure what it's *supposed* be like. The other two took off to Lisbon two nights ago. She wasn't that surprised. Especially about Tam. She seemed to hate the place. Olivia's a little intimidated by Tam. She looks fierce, with her red hair and her broad figure and piercing blue eyes. She's nice enough, but vaguely disapproving.

She's had nothing to do with Liza yet. She joined her and Tam one night at the club. Olivia never spoke to her, but she saw her standing with some of Mai's new friends, looking completely left out. Olivia thought of going to rescue her but lost sight of her and figured she'd left.

It doesn't surprise her that they didn't like this place. Olivia's not sure she likes this place that much either. It just feels like all the parties she has even been to, only jammed into the space of one week and at the beach.

At least it's a beautiful beach. She wraps her arms around her legs and rests her chin on her knees, staring at the impossible blue of the water. There are definitely worse places she could be. She takes a deep breath and promises herself she'll try and be nicer to Mai. In her head *and* out loud. So what if she's a little too excitable? She's always been like that. And so what if she's loud? She's also sassy and confident and fun, even if she can grate a bit. Mai is just being who she's always been all through school. And maybe Olivia never totally noticed who that was until now, treated to the undiluted version.

Before this, she's always had her other friends as a buffer. And then she had Kit to escape to whenever politics got weird in her group or she got tired of all the same people and jokes and chatter. She wishes Kit were here. Sweet, fun, non-judgemental, and completely apolitical Kit. Olivia could handle all this if she were here.

"Hey, that's where you got to."

It's Sam. Of course it's Sam.

He grins, squinting down at her. "So, wanna hear the plan for tonight?"

CHAPTER 11

Liza, Lisbon, Portugal

Liza is in love. There's no other way to describe how this proud old dame of a city makes her feel. She loves its narrow winding streets and its crooked pastel buildings. She loves the endless hills and the cracked colourful tiles that decorate everything. She loves this place so much, she feels it like sunlight on her skin. Lisbon has this kind of faded grandeur, a beauty that is as decadent as it's decrepit. Everywhere she looks, there is something beautiful, or something that was once beautiful and still bears traces, even in its crumbling state.

Even now, as the tepid winter sun disappears behind the buildings and a chilly wind picks up, she feels only goodwill towards this crowded street and the polluting traffic that wends its way uphill. She waits for Tam to finish in the store, pulling her jacket around her, and stares out at the pinpricks of light that sweep down the hill to the water. Around her, the city prepares for its evening plans. And she feels like this is the kind of city that *always* has plans.

The first day they arrived, she and Tam roamed the streets, making their acquaintance. Eventually, they made their wandering way through a maze of laneways and cobbled streets up to a castle embedded in a steep hill. They sat in the gardens and ate cake and watched cats sun themselves on the castle walls. Then they wandered back, getting decadently lost, but orienting themselves with the port water below.

Last night, they saw the Fado singers in a tiny café. When the hostel manager, a young British guy, asked if they wanted to come along to see this traditional Portuguese form of singing with some other guests, they hesitated. Neither had ever heard of it.

"Put it this way," he said. "It's about the most clichéd, touristy thing you could do in Lisbon, but it's still amazing. You in?"

"We're in," Tam said, speaking for both of them.

They huddled with the others at a long table in tiny bar until late, drinking rich red wine and listening to the even richer, mournful voices of the singers. Although she didn't know what they were singing about or why, it made Liza sense some kind of longing.

Later, when a beautiful, careworn woman—the youngest of the performers—sang, it woke Liza from her wine daze. She spent a hefty part of her night watching the woman drink whiskey and chat to the owner between sets, working up a crush. A little drunk, and a lot lustful, it was kind of fun to sit there, shrouded in sound, and dream up ways they might evade the impossible and meet.

This morning, hung over but happy, they caught a train out to a nearby town and walked a wide stone path along the coast all the way back to the city. It took hours because they kept stopping to dip their feet in the water or drink coffee at small cafés along the trail. Part of Liza was itching to run, to feel her feet eat up the kilometres back to the city and the cold sea breeze rush past her.

Tam finally exits the small electronics shop, a small bag in her hand. "Want to go eat?"

They wind their way down the narrow path in silence. It's not awkward, though. Liza likes hanging out with Tam. It's easy. And she doesn't seem to need to fill up every moment of quiet like Mai.

They stop at an intersection and wait as cars roar by. Here they speed as recklessly along the narrow streets as they did along the coastal cliffs near the resort. Liza feels the urge to check repeatedly before crossing a road. That's what she's doing when Tam grabs her arm. "Hey, let's go in here."

She points at a tiny café, bright with fluorescent lights. It's plain and utilitarian, the only decorations faded posters advertising soft drinks and beer. The counter is lined with old men in overalls and work shirts, forking up food from large plates. It's nothing like the softly lit, urbane restaurants in the main square.

Liza stares, uncertain. Her first worry, of course, is whether they'll be able to order. Everywhere they've been so far has had an English-language menu. "Really? You sure?"

"Why not? Every time we walk past this place it's full. So it must be good. Besides, I want to try what people who live here actually eat."

Liza shrugs. "Okay."

* * *

"You're gay?"

"Yep." Liza blushes.

Tam just nods and stirs her spoon through her stew.

Liza looks down at her plate and does the same. It's the first time she's said it out loud to anyone but her parents. And she has no idea what Tam's non-response means. God, she hopes she's not a homophobe.

Not sure how to fill the quiet, she takes a last mouthful of her food. It wasn't too hard to order. There were the only two dishes to choose from anyway. The small, wiry old man who runs the place seemed highly amused by their presence, though. After some pointing and single words exchanged, he served them up plates of a rich, meaty stew and a heaped plate of bread. It's perfect after their epic walk today.

"Have you got a girlfriend?"

"No. I was kind of seeing someone before I left. Kind of." Liza realises she hasn't thought about Alika in days. Another reason why coming here was a good idea. "But she wasn't out."

She stares at the parade of people traipsing back and forth outside. This city is more alive at night than it is during the day. She takes another sip of her drink. "I don't even really know any gay people, except a couple of kids back at school, and I didn't really *know* them. We just went to the same school. I've never even been to a gay bar. What about you?" She rushes to add. "I mean, do you have a boyfriend?"

Tam rests her cheek on her hand. "I don't know."

"You don't *know* if you have a boyfriend?"

"Exactly." Tam gives her a small smile. "Which is why I needed this." She holds up the SIM card she bought earlier. "It's a long story. I'll tell you sometime." She stares at her phone. "And I need to call Dad too."

"How is he doing?" Liza asks. She vividly remembers when he was first diagnosed. Kit was freaked, for herself and for her cousin.

"He's better. He's over the chemo and his scans are good, apparently. Now there's just the worry about it coming back."

How terrifying. Liza doesn't know what she'd do if one of her parents got sick like that. "It must have been so scary."

"It was pretty horrible. The aunts all came flocking, though." She smiles. "That helped. Dad was a little overwhelmed by the onslaught; I don't know why. He grew up one male in a house of six women. Shouldn't he be used to it?"

"Probably. Kit used to tell me about all the crazy aunts. I could never keep them straight."

Tam laughs as she pushes her bowl aside. "*I* could barely keep them all straight and they're my family."

The owner comes over to their spot at the window and leans in. "Good?" he asks, picking up the empty bowls.

"*So* good," Tam tells him with gusto. "Obrigado."

"Yeah, amazing," Liza says. "Thank y—uh... Obrigado," she stammers. She gets shy every time she has to say please or thank you in Portuguese. She's so sure she's stuffing it up.

They exit the café quickly as more people shuffle in, looking for a seat. Pulling on their jackets, they stand on the edge of the footpath.

"So, what do you want to do now?" Tam asks.

"I have no idea," Liza confesses as her eyes follow the fairy lights strung along the street from here to the water. She doesn't really care. She just loves being here.

"There's nothing you want to do?" Tam asks, pulling her long red hair out from under the collar of her jacket and zipping it up.

"It's not that there is nothing I want to do, I just don't know what there is to do," Liza says, hoping she's not being a killjoy.

Tam just stares at her for a moment and then nods. "I have an idea, but first we need the internet." She holds up her phone.

"Why do we need internet?"

"You'll see," is all Tam says with grin.

* * *

The bar is tiny, hidden on the third floor of a crumbling, pastel-blue building. They climb the stairs and make their way into the space. The atmosphere is low-key, with just a few tables filled with groups drinking and talking. Muted music emanates from a room beyond, and Liza can see the lights of a dance floor flashing through the doorway. In the corner, two men work quickly behind the bar mixing drinks.

"So what's so great about this place?" Liza asks. Tam hasn't said a word after her mystery Googling back at the hostel. She just told Liza to get ready to go out.

"This, Liza," Tam grins and hangs her jacket on the back of a chair, "is your first gay bar."

Liza's mouth drops open. And then the penny drops as she realises the two people sitting in each other's laps in the corner are both women. Then she notices the small rainbow flag hanging on the wall behind the bar. Yep, it's her first gay bar. It looks like Tam's completely okay with the gay. She feels herself relax a little.

Tam sits. "There are rules, though."

"And they are?" Liza asks warily, joining her at the table.

Tam's grin is wide. "You have to buy me a drink because I took you to your first gay bar." Then she points at Liza. "And you are *not* allowed to desert or abandon me here if you find yourself a hottie. Dance floor, yes. Leaving the building, no."

As if that's going to happen. Liza laughs and nods, still blushing wildly. "I promise you. What do you want to drink?"

* * *

The girl is small and slender with big brown eyes. The little English she can produce is spoken in a quiet lilt. From what Liza can gather through the haze of her mild drunkenness, the gargantuan language barrier, and the deafening music, is that her name is Catarina, she studies some kind of science and lives with her parents somewhere in the suburbs of the city. In turn, she knows Liza is going to university next year, that she's from Australia, and she may or may not know that Liza is a runner. Liza gets the feeling she might think she just likes jogging. Which is pretty much true nowadays anyway.

And that is all the intel they have gathered on each other after half an hour. And Liza is quickly learning that this amount of information does *not* a scintillating conversation maketh.

Next to them, Tam chats to Catarina's friends, a sweet couple who clutch hands on the tabletop as they talk. They clearly speak better

English than Catarina, because with Tam the conversation is eager and quick.

Liza wishes for the zillionth time since she arrived here that she could speak Portuguese more than the basic hello and please and thank you. She'd like to ask this girl more about her life. What's it like to grow up in this beautiful city? What's it like to be gay here? What does she do when she's not studying? But she can't figure out ways to pose these questions without hitting a zillion vocabulary roadblocks. Only the most simple questions and answers seem to work.

She takes a sip of her Coke, tucks her curls behind one ear, and leans forward. "Do you have a job?"

Catarina nods and smiles. "Yes, in my uncle's restaurant. You?"

"In a gift shop."

Catarina frowns. "Gift?"

"Like, presents?"

Catarina shakes her head, looking apologetic.

"Doesn't matter." Liza waves a hand.

The girl nods, and they fall into another silence. Embarrassed, Liza watches Catarina stare around the bar, now full to bursting, and wonders if she wants to get away from her. From the epic stiltedness of this conversation.

It'd be awkward enough talking to a girl in a bar who speaks the same language as her. But this? She's just about to find a way to tell Catarina that it's okay to leave her, to go and find people she can actually talk to, when she turns to Liza. She smiles wide and points down the passage to the source of the music and flashing lights. "Dance?"

Dancing? That she can do. She nods and smiles. Catarina takes her hand and leads her from the table. It's a small, windowless room with low ceilings, jammed with people dancing to some Portuguese pop song. Catarina keeps a hold of her hand as she pulls Liza into the crowd, and she only lets it go when they find a space to dance. Then she smiles, runs her hands through her pixie cut and begins to move. Liza laughs, though she doesn't know why, and mirrors her.

The lights beam down and the music selection sprints through a range of light pop and dance numbers, none of which she recognises. Liza finds herself relaxing into it anyway. She always feels stupid when she dances. But Kit always says that everyone looks stupid when they dance if you really look at them, so she decides not to care.

Anyway, she's too happy to care. Now that the struggle to talk has disappeared, she's actually having fun with Catarina. Every now and then they catch each other's eye and laugh, comrades in surviving this epic communication breakdown. It's funny to think that she doesn't even know if they would like each other if they *could* talk. There's a kind of freedom in this silence. Liza smiles to herself as she realises that maybe this was the best possible scenario for her first flirtation in a gay bar. There's no way for her to screw it up by saying something dumb.

A run of songs later, Catarina pulls out her phone from her pocket. Her eyes bug wide.

"Everything okay?" Liza shouts into the music.

Catarina shakes her head. Liza follows her out of the room. Once they're in the dark passage, she turns to Liza and frowns. "Last bus in ten minutes. We must go."

"Oh." Liza nods. She's surprised by how disappointed she feels.

Catarina thrusts her hands in her pockets, sways back and forth a little and frowns at Liza, as if to say she doesn't want to leave either.

Liza smiles, not sure what to say. But she doesn't have to say anything, because the next thing she knows, Catarina rises up on her toes, hooks an arm around Liza's neck and drops not one but two soft, hasty kisses on her lips. Then, still on her toes, she meets Liza's eye with a wry smile. Emboldened, Liza giggles and kisses her again, breathing in her scent of something sweet, like burned sugar.

Catarina slowly releases her neck and says quietly, "Goodbye, Liza." She says it like "Leeza," but Liza doesn't care one bit.

"Bye," she says, although Catarina is already striding across the room. She watches her alert her two friends to the time. They hastily pull on their jackets and wave their goodbyes to Tam.

Liza doesn't join Tam immediately. Instead, she takes a second there in the passageway, the relentless music pounding behind her, and indulges in the exhilaration. She's seen the Himalayas— even if just from a plane. She's made her escape from resort hell and learned to negotiate a teeming, foreign city. And now she's kissed a girl in a Lisbon gay bar.

And now, she had better do as she's told and Skype Kit tomorrow to tell her all about it.

CHAPTER 12

Kit, Melbourne, Australia

She follows the tiny old man into the kitchen. Even when the door swings shut behind them, the urgent, vibrant strains of salsa music trickle in from the bar. The kitchen is cavernous, with wide white bench tops and a huge grill that runs across the back wall. It smells like *a lot* of meat has been cooked in this place.

He leads her past a row of fridges to the sink area and jabs his fingers in the direction of a set of shelves. "You take dirty dishes and bring here."

She nods obediently, even though this is the eighth instruction he has given her in three minutes. There's no way she's going to remember it all.

"Michail will wash." A man even tinier than this one turns from the sink and scowls at Kit. She can't tell if it's an actual dirty look or just his default expression. Either way, it doesn't bode well for a friendly working relationship.

She spotted the job notice next to the doorway as she walked slowly up the street toward the supermarket. It was posted next to a hand-painted blue sign pointing to the second floor of a building. A world music venue resided up there, according to the sign. Kit wasn't even sure what that meant. All she cared about was that the mystery venue needs a waiter. That was enough to propel her up the narrow, dark stairs.

After the spooky walk up, the place was a surprise. It's lovely, with a row of huge arched windows along the far wall, and polished floorboards stretching from a large dance space in front of the stage all the way to the edges of the vast room where long tables sit against the walls.

In the ten minutes she has been here, she has learned that the old man she is following now and his son run the place. Stav, the son, takes care of the live music and the bar, while Jim, the dad, rules the kitchen. Stav is tall, stocky, and exuberant. He talks quickly and gestures expansively during the five minutes she spends with him before delivering her into the hands of his father. Jim, on the other hand, is short, wiry, and serious. But there's a stern, paternal warmth she can feel, too. He has already assured her twice in his thick Greek accent, "I know you good girl. You be fine." She has no idea how he knows whether she is a "good girl," but she hopes he's right.

He flaps a hand at Michail and his cranky face. "Don't worry about him. He okay. You just stack dishes neatly."

Kit nods uncertainly. This has got to be the weirdest job interview ever. In fact, it doesn't even seem to be a job interview. She just seems to have the job. Why else would he be showing her where to find cutlery and serviettes?

But does Kit really want this job, working with the two smallest, oldest men she's ever seen, and an exuberant hand talker? When she went out looking for a job, she assumed she'd be working in yet another of the hipster cafés along the Fitzroy/Collingwood strip. But she's had no luck so far.

There would be upsides, though. At least here she wouldn't have to listen to co-workers whining about how they hate this job, but that they're saving to move to Brooklyn or Berlin for a year to, you know, *do art*. Here she might be the youngest person in this place by a good quarter of a century, but it might break the monotony of her other jobs. Besides, they seem to be offering employment. And no one else has done that so far.

When he finishes showing her around, Jim says, "Okay, start tonight?"

"Tonight?"

He slaps her on the arm. "Why not, huh? You come. You see if you like. We see if we like. Then we talk."

"Um, okay," she says uncertainly. Why not?

"Good girl." He slaps her arm again. This seems to be his version of affection. "You come at eight."

She walks slowly to the stairs, feeling vaguely pleased and slightly thrown by this job she suddenly seems to possess. Going up these stairs and finding this place all felt a little Alice down the rabbit hole and weird. But at least it's different.

As she wanders down the busy street back to the flat, she thinks of Liza and the others. They must be in Italy by now. She sighs. The girls have the world, and she gets world music. Whatever the hell that is.

* * *

Tam, Genova, Italy

"I thought this place was in Switzerland?" Tam dumps her pack on the ground next to the table they have chosen.

Not that it would have mattered where they chose to sit. The entire café is empty except for a couple of old men leaned up against the bar, elbows at rest on the gleaming wood. Small espresso cups and an array of newspapers litter the surface in front of them. Every now and then, one of them turns and appraises their group slowly before returning to their conversation.

Tam sinks into a seat, fighting the urge to rest her forehead on the worn tabletop. Olivia drops down next to her, rubbing her eyes. Her hair is tangled around her shoulders, and her top is wrinkled. It was a rough night on the bus. "You're thinking of Geneva," she mumbles through a yawn.

"Isn't that where we are?"

Olivia's face is scrunched as she thinks, as if messages are taking a long time to move between her neurones. Tam can't blame her. It's hard to sleep through the night when you're crushed into a tiny, barely reclinable seat while a maniac driver careens across three countries.

It got dark somewhere near the Spanish border. The bus emptied out a little, and Tam shifted away from her shared seat with Liza to one behind so they could both stretch out as much as possible. Her sleep was fitful, though.

After they passed into Italy, the driver sped up. Every hour or so, she'd wake up and stare out the window in a daze at what she could make out of the surreal view. They were on a coastal road, passing through one glittering town after another. Each seemed to cling to cliffs, their lights reflecting onto the water of the small ports and bays they huddled over. Between places, the bus shot through tunnels hewn into the rocks, climbed steep inclines, and wound quickly along the roads, stopping briefly every now and then to drop someone off. And she wished it were daylight, so she could see these magical places properly.

It was dawn when the bus came to a shuddering stop in this port town. All around them, stone buildings in a pale rainbow array of pastels and earth tones climbed up the cliffs and hills, as if stacked on top of each other. On one side, a shifting blue ocean stretched away. Tam clambered out of the bus and turned a slow, stunned circle, smelling the dirty salt air of the port.

In fact, it was so early, nothing nearby was open except this little bar café with its curious men. Desperate for coffee and sustenance, they wandered in.

"This place is called Genova," Liza says, holding up a small map she's pulled from somewhere in her bag. "One letter off. No wonder you were mixed up."

"But the Italians call it Genoa." Mai's headphones still hang around her neck, pushing her black hair forward around her face in a weird shape. It makes her look like a cartoon character. "And its nickname is *La Superba.*"

"Well, that's confusing." Tam's never been great at geography. If the girls had told her they were in Switzerland, she would have believed them. "How do you know what they call it?"

Mai shrugs. "Read it somewhere."

"Mai knows stuff." Olivia says through another yawn. "She acts like a ditz, but she's kind of brilliant."

Mai pulls an exaggeratedly modest face and grimaces.

"And she speaks nearly fluent Italian," Olivia adds. She rests her chin on Mai's shoulder. "So will she *please, please, please* order her friend who dropped Languages in Year 9 a coffee and any food you can forage from the nice man behind the counter?"

Mai laughs. "Sure. Might as well test it out. That evil witch Napolitano would be so proud."

Liza looks up from her map, eyes wide. "Ms Napolitano? I had her for Year 7 homeroom. She was *terrifying.*"

"Well she was just as terrifying in Italian," Mai assures her with a grin as she gets up. "Okay, here goes. What does everyone want?"

The rest of them wait in coffee-hungry silence, too sleep deprived to even attempt small talk.

Tam yawns heavily into her arm. She can't wait to get to their hotel in Florence this afternoon. But that's still hours away. They don't catch their train from Geneva/Genova/Genoa for three more hours.

Once they have their coffees and some bread and pastries that Mai brings back to the table, they chew and sip mechanically, not speaking. Tam stirs a sugar into her milky coffee and looks around the place with its old-fashioned paintings of ships and faded cigarette advertisements. The old men at the counter are not even pretending to be discreet now. In fact, two of them have turned right around and are staring right at them as they chat to the guy behind the counter. It reminds her of the old geezers at the local pub back home. For some of them, a hapless tourist that comes through the door looking for a beer and a counter meal is the most exciting thing that happens all week.

She watches the men a minute and then turns to Mai, curious. "Can you understand what they're talking about?"

"Us, clearly," Olivia says, breaking a roll in half and grinning. "They seem a little fascinated."

"Shh," Mai taps her on the arm. After a minute or two of concentrated listening, she shakes her head and laughs.

"What?" Olivia asks. "Tell us."

"They're arguing about her." She tips her head in Tam's direction.

Tam looks over at them. "Me? Why?"

Mai listens a little longer and pulls a face. "They're arguing about your hair and about if you could be Italian. And then they started arguing about where Italian redheads come from. One dude's saying something about the Normans, and another one's saying something about Jewish people." She tips her head to one side. "It's kind of hard to follow."

"It sounds like it'd be hard to follow in *English*," Olivia says, putting more sugar in her coffee.

Tam rolls her eyes, weary of the perennial ginger talk. It's been going on all her life. "Why is everyone so fascinated by red hair?" she asks. "I don't get it."

"I do," Mai says. "You rangas are a rare breed. In Vietnam, people would be stopping you on the street."

"Do people mention it all the time?" Olivia asks.

"They do."

Olivia gives her a sympathetic frown. "How annoying."

"It is." Tam wonders if Olivia can commiserate because people probably talk about her mother all the time. "It gets bloody boring."

"Do you ever get obnoxious dudes asking if you're a ginger down south, too?" Mai asks. "Guys at school used to ask my friend Ella that all the time."

"Yup, they do."

"Gross," Liza says.

"Assholes," Mai adds loudly. The curse sets off a small ripple among their curious observers. They clearly know *some* English.

Olivia shakes her head. "That's gross. I hope you slap them upside the head?"

"Sometimes, yeah."

Olivia grins. "Good."

This is the most relaxed they've been with each other since they started travelling together. Tam looks around at their little group, awakened now by the coffee, and feels relieved by this unexpected moment of camaraderie.

They still haven't spent much time together since the girls made it to Lisbon to meet them. Mai and Olivia wanted to see and do a lot of things Tam and Liza had already done, so they remained in these pairings, doing different stuff.

There was an undeniable air of awkwardness between them about the fact they split up too. No one really talked about it, but it was there. And Tam can feel the mutual apprehension that maybe this isn't going to work out. That they won't be able to find common travelling ground. But now, sitting here together, a thread of connection found, she thinks maybe, just maybe, they'll be okay. They just need a minute to get to know each other. If Tam and Liza can manage to make friends so quickly, surely they all can? And in this moment it feels possible. And that's a relief.

Mai turns to Liza. "They're talking about *you* now."

Liza cringes. "Oh God, what?"

"The one in the red shirt is saying you look just like his niece, and that you could easily be mistaken for someone from Calabria."

"These guys are obsessed with where everyone comes from." Olivia shakes her head. "What's that about?"

"Maybe regional differences are really noticeable or important here. Like it is with food," Tam says, thinking of all the research she did.

"Maybe," Olivia muses. "Or maybe they're just bored, and we are the only visual stimuli."

"I don't even know where Calabria is," Liza confesses.

"It's in the south." Mai looks Liza up and down. "If you don't mind my asking, what are you? I mean, you're not totally Anglo, are you?"

Liza shakes her head. "Nope."

"And I get to ask that." Mai grins. "Because people ask me *all* the time." She rolls her eyes. "Because Asian people haven't lived in Australia since, like, the Gold Rush."

"Can I ask, what's your background?" Tam asks.

"Sure. But only because you didn't ask, 'Where are you from?' all accusingly, as if I couldn't possibly have been born in Australia. Mum's Vietnamese and Dad's Chinese." She turns to Liza. "What about you?"

"Dad's half-Dutch, half-Sri Lankan."

"That explains the awesome height and colour combination. I'm totally jealous of your body, by the way."

Liza pulls a face. Mai's right, though. Tam would kill to look as lean and athletic as Liza. Everything about her screams health.

"Half-Dutch, half-Sri Lankan?" Olivia shakes her head. "I've never even heard of that combo before."

"Yeah, the Burghers," Mai says, chewing on a hunk of bread.

"You want a burger?" Olivia frowns. "It's like, eight in the morning."

Mai shakes her head. "And you call me a ditz. Burgher with an h. They're an ethnic group from Sri Lanka."

"Oh." Olivia laughs, blushing. "Oops."

Mai brushes crumbs from her hands. "So should we go and explore? Before the peanut gallery over there tries to decide if I could pass as Sicilian or something?"

CHAPTER 13

Hey Tim Tam, I just wanted to tell you that Mum spoke to your dad last night. She said he sounded really good. Like he used to, you know? I know you must be worried, even if you're pretending you're not.

How's Italy? Are you eating amazing food? Mai says the hostel is huge and loud. Don't worry, it could be worse. I met this guy at my new job who said he slept in a tent in the backyard of a hostel in Budapest for three weeks with only mice for company. So if the showers are as gross as Mai says, just be thankful you're not sleeping with rodents.

Melbourne's boring and HOT. I work ALL the time, which is probably good, because if I didn't, I might have to murder my sister. Remember what a bitch Chloe could be when we were little? Well she's gotten worse, believe it or not. She makes mum do everything for her—cooking, cleaning, washing. Such a freaking princess. And if I so much as move or speak when she's asleep, she screams at me.

Anyway, enough whinging. I hope you guys are having fun together and that everything is amazing. Give the others a squeeze for me, and one for you too. Kit xx

* * *

Liza, Florence, Italy

Showered, but not feeling so clean after those skanky dungeons the hostel calls bathrooms, Liza enters the breakfast room. It's a huge, fluorescent-lit cavern, crowded with tables and chairs. And it's currently full of backpackers stuffing their faces with the free cereal and tiny bread rolls.

She grabs some food and searches the room for the others. She can only see Olivia, sitting in the back corner, staring at her iPad. Liza hesitates. Does she want to be alone? Should she find her own table? Before she can decide, Olivia looks up, gives her a small smile, and moves her coffee cup as if to make room for Liza.

"Hey." Liza gives her an uncertain smile and sits. Olivia's wrapped in a rust-brown cardigan that sets off her eyes. Liza's never met anyone whose eyes are so absolutely green. Not just hazel and slipping there sometimes, but a mossy, olive green and lovely. "Mai still in bed?"

"She's gone to meet that guy from the resort. Campbell. He and his friends are here, at another hostel."

"Oh." Liza focuses on buttering her roll. Olivia still makes her nervous. She's nice, but there is something so quietly poised about her, restrained even, making her hard to interpret. It makes her feel more gawky and wrong than she usually does.

"Where's Tam?" Olivia asks.

"She's got that cooking class today."

"Oh yeah, that's right."

Liza sips her orange juice and pulls a face. Whatever it is, it's not juice.

"Delicious, isn't it?"

"I think I just got diabetes."

Olivia smiles.

"You know," Liza puts her glass down, "this is going to sound dumb, but I only ever heard of people having continental breakfasts in books. I never knew what they were, but I definitely thought it was going to be something more exciting than cereal and toast."

Olivia laughs. "Me too. I was kind of disappointed."

"Good. Now I don't have to feel so dumb."

They smile at each other and lapse into another silence that Liza definitely has no idea how to fill. She's used up all her breakfast chitchat. She digs her spoon into her cereal and frowns. Maybe if she hadn't spent so much time learning to run in fast circles for the last few years, she'd be better at this whole conversation thing. She wishes Mai were here. Mai can fill any silence.

Olivia scratches at a mark on her iPad screen. "Heard from Kit?"

Liza nods, relieved. Of course. Kit is their common ground. "We Skyped for a minute the other day, but she had to go to work. You?"

"I got a Facebook message. Her sister sounds painful."

"She is." Chloe's always been a bully. No wonder Kit always wanted to hang out at her house when they were younger. "Poor Kit."

"I wish she was here."

"Me too." It's so strange that they can both miss the same person so badly but barely know each other.

Olivia drops the napkin into her empty bowl. "So what are you going to do today?"

"I honestly have no idea. You?"

"I was just going to have a look around, I guess. There's a shop I want to check out later, but that's it. You feel like exploring?"

Liza considers her, feeling timorous. "Uh, sure, if that's okay?"

"Of course." Olivia gives her a quick smile, but it's hard to read. It could be a genuine smile, or it could just as easily be a polite, tolerant it-would-be-rude-not-to-invite-you smile. And now Liza wishes she could take that yes back. She doesn't want Olivia to think she *has* to spend time with her or that Liza can't look after herself. But it's too late. It's done.

* * *

"My turn for a stupid tourist confession," Olivia says as they stroll up the wide, stone pedestrian arcade. People crowd the street, the locals harried and businesslike, striding between the throngs of meandering tourists. Liza can hear the frantic jam of impatient morning traffic at the end of the block.

"What?" she asks as she loops her scarf one more time around her neck. The sun is out, but the wind is cold and wintry.

Olivia gives her a bashful smile, as if she's already regretting telling her whatever it is. "Every time I come to Europe, I get all surprised by how old everything is. And I know it's really stupid," she adds in a rush. "Because it's Europe, and stuff is *supposed* to be old. But I just get surprised by it." She shrugs. "I know it's dumb."

Liza looks up at the ornate windows and decorated walls of the buildings around them. They're so regal and elegant and unlike anything at home. "No, I totally get it. It's not just that it's old. It's, like, if we had a building like that in Melbourne," she gestures at a particularly beautiful old building on the corner, "it would be something really special, a landmark. Everyone would know it. It would be on all the tourist maps. But here it's just kind of ordinary. People just live in it like it's just normal. I mean, it has a freaking mobile phone store underneath it."

"Yeah, that's it, exactly." Olivia smiles and pushes her sunglasses up her nose. "Good, now I feel less dumb."

"Happy to be of assistance," Liza says in a mock-noble tone She looks up at the facades of the buildings along the stone street. It doesn't give her the same breathless pangs as Lisbon, but it's beautiful.

"My dad adores Italy. He took me and my sister Anna here when I was six, but I don't really remember it," Olivia says. "He's jealous I'm here."

"What does your Dad do?"

"He has an export business. Totally boring but successful."

"It's cool you got to travel so much."

Olivia just nods, her face blank, and Liza can't tell if it's a nod of agreement or a nod because she's conceding that it's *supposed* to be a good thing. Why does she feel she has to try so hard to read Olivia, even though she's being friendly and nice?

They stop at the end of the street. And there is the river, flowing muddy and restless between crumbling stone walls. The stretch of brown water is occasionally broken up by a bridge spanning the divide. On the far bank, the city escapes up the hill, looking greener and less chaotic.

"So where are we going?" Liza asks.

"I have no idea. Where do you want to go?"

"I don't know." Liza looks back and forth. She has no idea what to do, except maybe go to a museum or gallery or something. But she doesn't want to go inside, not when the sun is shining on them, however weakly.

Olivia digs her hands into her coat pockets. "Do you know what my favourite thing to do in strange cities is?"

"What?"

"Just walk around." She shrugs. "I know I'm *supposed* to go see the brochure sights and learn about history and stuff, but I really just love wandering, *and* looking at people. That's what I always do when I come places with Mum and she's got book stuff. I just put in my headphones and walk and watch."

Liza immediately conjures this image of Olivia striding through the streets by herself, encased in sound, watching the world go by. She looks happy and self-possessed, even in Liza's imagination. "You know, if you just want to hang by yourself, I can go do something else."

"Oh, no, sorry! I didn't mean it like that." Olivia grabs her arm. She looks genuinely worried she's offended Liza. "I just meant to say I like walking around outside. I didn't mean I wanted you to go away or anything. Not at all."

Liza smiles, but decides to be honest. "It's okay, really. I mean, I know we don't really know each other. That none of us really do, and that... I don't know... It's all been kind of awkward."

"It's weird without Kit, isn't it?" Olivia says quietly.

"I kind of didn't want to come when she said she wasn't."

"Me either. I bet none of us did. Well, except Mai." She rolls her eyes and smiles conspiratorially.

Liza returns the smile. It feels good to just acknowledge this mutual discomfort. She sets her shoulders. "So let's do it, then."

"Do what?"

"Walk. I hate wandering around those crowded galleries and museums, fighting everyone else to look at the same things. It's tiring. Let's just explore."

"Okay."

They wander along the river for a while until the crowds get too much and they escape across one of the bridges to where the world is instantly quieter. Higher up, the streets are lined by tall trees, and stately buildings are surrounded by manicured gardens.

They don't talk that much, except to point out something especially beautiful or strange or to decide on direction. It's not uncomfortable, though. It's easy now that they know they both want the same thing.

Later, they buy bread and cheese and fruit from a small deli and eat it on a wide stone bench with a view of the city. Olivia asks her about the running.

"So why did you get sick of it?" Olivia tears off a hunk of bread and wraps it around a piece of cheese.

Liza straddles the bench and slowly peels an orange. "I just never really got into racing. I love *running*, but racing's different."

"What do you mean?"

"I mean the competitive part, running against other girls. In training, I liked learning race tactics and—"

"Tactics? There's tactics? I thought you just had to run really fast. Like, faster than everyone else."

Liza smiles, picking at the white pith gathered under her nails. "Nope. Especially not with the 800-metre. Because you can't just like, run two laps super fast. It's too tiring. So you have to learn ways to pace yourself and how to read and beat your opponent's race too. If you've got nothing left at the end, you don't have the energy to overtake if you're behind."

"Oh, right." Olivia sits back, shading her face from the brightening afternoon sun with her arm. "So why didn't you like the racing part?"

Liza is surprised that Olivia wants to hear anything about this. When most people find out she's a runner, they just ask her if she's going to be in the Olympics one day. She tears apart a piece of orange peel, inhaling the cloying peppery citrus scent. She loves that smell. "I guess I'm not naturally competitive. At least, that's what my coach said. And you kind of *have* to be. It's not enough to train hard. One of my friends, Manda, she's the total opposite. She can get kind of lazy in training, but then she's so fierce on race days; she's like a completely different person. You can't even talk to her, she's so focused on kicking ass." She holds out a section of orange.

Olivia smiles and takes it. "Sounds scary."

It was. Liza smiles and finishes the last piece of orange, swiping at her mouth. "I think I'm just missing that competitive gene or something. When I was about thirteen and I first started running the 800, I was doing really well, winning a lot of races, even regionals. And I started hearing about this girl, Michaela Thomas. Apparently, she was getting really similar times as me, and winning all her races on the other side of town. We'd never come up against each other, but my coach started talking about how if I made state finals, she'd be my biggest opponent and all that. He even asked a coach friend of his how that girl raced, so we could prepare. I didn't really take it in, though. Why would I care about this kid I'd never met who could also run really fast?

"Of course, we both made it to state finals. And I was still kind of oblivious to it all. I just wanted to run with my friends, get taken out for pizza after, and then go back to training. That was my idea of a good time back then."

Olivia snickers into her piece of orange.

Gratified she can make her laugh, Liza goes on. "Then, when I was lined up at the blocks for my first heats, this little blonde girl marches up to me and was all like 'You're Liza Hansen, right?' She said it in this voice like I'd left rats in her lunchbox or something. But I didn't even have a clue who she was. And when I agreed, kind of nervously, that I was, she gives me this filthy look and growled, 'I'm *so* going to beat you.'" Liza shakes her head. "And I just wanted to laugh, you know? Why was she taking it all so freaking seriously?"

"She really was."

"Uh-huh. But now I kind of realise that, even though I didn't need to be a little bully about it, I was supposed to *feel* that competitive. And I never really did. And, I don't know. Maybe I've been lucky." She folds an empty paper bag, smoothing the creases neatly with her fingernail. "I've just gotten by on being naturally fast and having a great coach. But when this gets serious, like University Games or even Comm Games kind of serious, it's probably not enough. I don't know if I can care about winning enough to go through all that for another couple of years."

Olivia pulls her knees to her chest. "It would be kind of cool to win a medal though, wouldn't it?"

"I mean, yeah, of course. And I really, really love running. I do. But do I want to spend all my time doing it? For the incredibly slim chance of even qualifying to get a *chance* to go after a medal? Instead of doing other life stuff like school and actually having a social life? I don't know." She sighs. "I feel like I already kind of missed school because of it. I never went out on the weekends, I didn't really make many friends except for other girls who ran—and Kit, of course. I didn't even go on any school camps."

Olivia grins. "You missed Camp Koolamatong in Year 8? How terrible. Those wilderness walks were *wild*."

Liza smiles. Then she looks back down at the paper in her hands and frowns. "I guess I just asked myself, do I really have enough desire to win? Enough to do all the training it will take? I don't think so. I really don't. I know it sounds lazy and a waste, but I just really don't think I can be bothered. Not compared to all the other things I could be doing."

There. She's finally said out loud what she was already sure of. Because when she's presented the idea of possibly quitting to her parents and coach and teammates, she has only articulated it as vague doubts so far. But she's known. For a long time. And it feels safe to say it with certainty to someone like Olivia, because she's in no way invested in the outcome.

With everyone else, she always feels like she owes them part of her success, like all those stupid ribbons and medals in her dresser drawers are theirs too because of the time and effort they gave up to her in order for her to get them. She even feels like that with Kit. For all those times she drove in the car with them to races miles away, just to support Liza. Or when she stayed at home with her on weekend nights when Liza was too exhausted after races to celebrate even though she probably had a million invitations to go out.

And she knows that her parents, baffled as they were by having an athletic daughter, drove her to all those races, paid for all her equipment, and quietly and delightedly supported her, because she was so surprisingly good and it's what you're supposed to do when you have a "gifted" kid. And she always felt bad, luring them into this world that they had no previous connection to, only to now depart it with nothing to show for it.

And then there's her coach. She swallows. She doesn't even know how to deal with what it will be like to finally confirm Patrick's fears, after all the work he has done with her.

But right now, in this moment, Liza feels completely unshackled from expectation and the burden of her gratitude. She is free to feel these feelings.

"It doesn't sound lazy or stupid to me. It just...*is*." Olivia leans back on her hands. "If you don't want to do it, then don't do it."

Liza nods and stares up at the cloud-scattered sky. Olivia makes it sound so simple. But then, maybe it is. In fact, it's going to have to be. Because saying it out loud for the first time, Liza knows it for absolute certain. She has freed herself from racing forever. She's going to take back that time and just spend some time *being* in the world. She's going to run just for fun, in the cool solitude of the mornings. She's going to go to university and make friends with people who love books as much as she does. She's going to go out. And hell, maybe she'll even find a girlfriend.

She stretches her legs out on the grass below and wriggles her toes with the deliciousness of all this newfound possibility. She doesn't say any of this to Olivia, though. She's already talked way too much.

So they sit quietly, gathering up the sparse warmth of the sun. And Liza is a million miles away when Olivia suddenly says, “Hey, you didn’t finish the race story. Did you beat that little tyrant?”

“Nope. She beat me.”

“Damn.”

CHAPTER 14

Liza, Florence, Italy

Later, they stride back over the bridge and down one of the busy arcades. Olivia stops at a small corner newsstand.

She returns waving a newspaper. "Found an English one. I need to catch up. I've been *so* slack."

"Well, you are on holiday."

"Yeah, but me being on holiday doesn't stop the world from going to hell. And I'd like to know when it happens."

Liza raises an eyebrow. How optimistic. She's impressed someone her age actually reads the news. "What are you going to do at uni?" she asks, curious.

"Law." Olivia says, walking a little faster.

"Oh, yeah, Mai was talking about it. Cool. Where did you apply for?"

"A few places." She sounds bored. "I want to find this shop I was talking about. Do you feel like coming?"

"Uh, sure." Liza changes the subject, because clearly Olivia isn't interested in talking about uni.

The shop Olivia wanted to visit is a little vintage clothes store by the river. As she waits for Olivia to try on a dress, Liza examines a light kimono-style jacket with an embroidered floral design on the back. It's a deep royal-blue and made of some silken material. It's beautiful. She's not usually into flashy clothes, but this is one of the prettiest things she has ever seen.

"I'm getting it," Olivia announces as she emerges from the dressing room, the dress flung over her arm. She reaches past Liza for the blue jacket. She holds it up, inspecting both sides. "Oh, that's so pretty. Did you try it on?"

Liza shakes her head.

"You should." Olivia holds out her hand. "Here, pass me your stuff."

Not entirely convinced, Liza obediently does as she's told.

She pulls it on over her T-shirt. It hangs loosely on her, the sleeves draping halfway down her arms. She examines herself in a mirror.

"It looks great." Olivia traces the embroidered pattern on the back. "It's gorgeous."

"But where... I mean, how would I wear it?" Liza asks, tugging at it a little.

"What do you mean how would you wear it? Just like you are now. Over jeans and a top." She strokes Liza's arm to flatten the sleeve. "It's really pretty."

"But I feel really overdressed."

"Believe me, you're not. You just feel self-conscious because you're a really simple dresser. But this is not so over the top that everyone is going to look at you. It's just a bit more out there than you seem to wear. If people do look, they'll just be thinking you have great taste." She smiles at her. "And, you know, in the spirit of all these life changes—quitting running and everything—maybe a change is good?"

"Maybe."

"So, you know, like, wear it with confidence," Olivia adds in this totally insincere salesgirl voice.

Liza grins at her via the reflection and considers herself in the mirror.

She wishes she possessed an ounce of Olivia's style. Even though she usually wears the same basic stuff as the rest of them, jeans and boots and jackets, there's always a pretty scarf or a piece of interesting jewellery added. She has this offhand stylishness.

Liza always feels just kind of boring around her. Boring and safe. But she feels really different in this top. Sophisticated. Maybe Olivia is right. Maybe that's not such a bad thing.

"And think," Olivia adds. "Whenever you wear it, you'll be able to say you picked it up in Florence. Pretty cool, huh?"

Liza smiles. That's true. "Okay," she says, removing it carefully. "I'll get it."

* * *

They are clearly near a university now. The streets are full of students carrying books and backpacks. They stand outside a brightly lit café looking at all the student hipsters inside.

The walls are painted in bright primary colours, and origami shapes hang from the roof. "Should we go in?" Liza asks.

Olivia looks at the menu pinned crookedly to the window. "Everything is in Italian, though." She giggles. "How will we order without Mai?"

"Don't know." Liza knows about three words in Italian and one of them is "pizza."

"We could go back to where we were this morning?" Olivia suggests. "Near the hostel. There's heaps of places with English menus there?"

Those cafés that line the arcade are all basically the same restaurant, fitted out for the tourists with the same flirty waiters and chintzy menu and decor. They have eaten at places like that for the last two nights.

Maybe it's the confidence that comes with making this decision about her running. Maybe it's because she's learned a little something from Tam about taking food risks back in Portugal. Maybe she wants to feel as cool and mature as Olivia. Whatever it is, she shrugs. "We'll figure it out."

Her reward is Olivia smiling back at her. "Okay, you're right. Let's do it."

CHAPTER 15

Tam, Florence, Italy

The message comes through just as she's setting up her laptop. It's Liza.

Hey, we're at random bar with some really nice Italian students. Have you finished cooking? Want to join? I can send you the map?

Tam taps out a quick reply. It sounds fun, but she's got an even better plan.

And it comes to her like a small miracle. The connection is made, and all of a sudden, there he is, sitting on his bed in front of her. It's a little pixelated, a little fuzzy, but it's Matt.

He gives her a slow smile and she feels an instant flood of missing him. He's wearing his dark blue hoodie, headphones dangling around his neck as usual. For a second, she'd give up this trip, this place, pretty much anything, to be sitting in that room with him. Scratch that, she'd be *lying* in that room with him.

She pulls her laptop closer to her, trying to block out all the other hostel people around her. "Hey."

"Hey, yourself." He grins and tucks his hair behind both ears at once. "How was the cooking class?"

"It was interesting, I guess. The guy teaching it was kind of cheesy, and I was the youngest person there by, like, three decades. But I learned some stuff, I guess. I know more about table cheeses than I ever thought I'd know."

"Well that's good. I think."

She laughs. He knows nothing about food. Just that he likes to eat it. "What have you been doing?"

"Not much. Helping your Dad get ready for the cherries. And fishing. The squid are running."

"Really? That's early."

"I know. The wind's dropped. We caught six the other night. Big guys, too."

"I'm so jealous," she says. And she is. Because for a minute, her homesickness wants—no demands—she be down on the jetty. They'd be drinking Jack whiskey, more for the warmth it offers than the buzz, and laughing as they duck the furious sprays of ink the silvery beasts eject as they're wrestled to the surface. She can almost feel the light breeze running off the water and hear the sounds of the water slapping gently against the pylons. And she can taste the sweet, soft flesh after she fries them in spices and flour back at someone's house afterward. She takes in a deep breath, sick with longing.

"Hey, how's Dad?"

"He seems okay to me." He frowns at her. "Don't worry, Tam."

She just nods, because how does she tell him that she can never *not* worry? That worrying about her father is her job, her duty, the worst of her habits? One she can't shake even now that the doctors say there is less and less need to worry all the time? It's not that simple. Not when it's been the last thing she's done before going to sleep and the first thing she's done on waking ever since his diagnosis. And how does she tell Matt that even if she wanted to, she's not sure she'd know how to stop? She's even doing it when her mind is busy doing something else. It's always there, relentless and grim.

"It's really good to see you," he says.

"You too."

There's so much she wants to ask him, but she doesn't know how. But most of all, she just wants to know: was that last night together just that? One night together? Or if she were home, would they have become something more? Or has he already moved on in his mind? But as much as Tam wants to know, she's terrified of the answers.

So instead, she tells him about Italy, about what she's seen and done and eaten. And then he tells a story about some panicked tourists up at the blowhole who nearly lost their terrier to a ferocious wave. He was always great at telling stories; at making her laugh. But when she finally disconnects an hour later, he just says his goodbye, as if he's going to see her tomorrow, and she's left as confused as she started.

* * *

Liza, Florence, Italy

Liza surfaces from sleep and straight into a headache. What's that about? She rolls onto her back and slowly eases her eyes open until she's gazing up at a stained ceiling and a long fluorescent bulb hanging only a metre or so from her head. Thank goodness it's off. She contemplates the view for a moment and pulls a face. How does a ceiling get stained?

The room smells bad, too, like too many people cooped up, breathing in it. When they booked, they could only find space in a twelve-bed mixed dorm. It's chaotic and loud and confronting, sharing a room with a bunch of strangers doing something as intimate as sleep together. Or not sleeping. No matter what time it is, there's always someone awake, rustling or talking in hushed tones.

She rolls over onto her side again, listening to the loud snores of someone nearby, and wonders why she feels so crappy. That's when she realises. This might be a hangover. Her first.

She remembers hanging out at that café with Olivia and meeting this group of students who helped them order. Then came the cheap carafes of red wine. They were studying architecture nearby and supposedly working on a group assignment together for summer school. But really they were just drinking and telling Olivia and Liza stories about Florence and about their lives, in impressively fluent English. Then they all went to another bar. It was fun. Liza remembers feeling so sophisticated, befriending actual Italians and hanging out in secret little bars down laneways no tourist would ever usually find.

She probably only drank two glasses, but that's all it takes to make her feel rotten, apparently. She's still lying on her side, contemplating a trip downstairs to wash in the awful shower room when the sleeping lump on the bed opposite rolls over. First an arm and then a head emerges. It's Olivia. She stretches and yawns and then grins at Liza. "I feel awful."

She isn't the only one. Liza smiles, relieved. "Me too. I've been drunk exactly once in my life before," she confesses, thinking of the night she used vodka to work up some Dutch courage to tell Kit about Alika.

"Really?"

Liza blushes. "Now I know why."

They both start laughing.

"I don't—" Olivia starts to say.

"*Shut up*," someone grumbles below. "People are trying to sleep."

Olivia winces. She climbs down from her bunk bed, her bare feet hitting the ground with a gentle thunk. The next thing Liza knows, Olivia's climbing up the ladder to her bed. "Move over," she whispers, grinning.

Surprised into obedience, Liza shuffles over against the wall to make room for her. Olivia climbs right up onto the bed and lies down, resting her head on the edge of the lumpy pillow. Her green eyes, now in full stereo this close to Liza's face, are twinkling. "You were so funny at McDonald's, on the way back here, when Matteo tried to challenge you to a race up the street."

"That's right. Sorry, what an idiot."

Olivia slaps her gently on the arm. "You weren't an idiot. You were just really excited and funny. It was fun."

Well, that's okay, then.

Olivia grins. "But I did have to talk you out of racing him. Remember? You were so going to do it, and I was scared I'd lose you, or you'd fall or something. I had to work pretty hard to talk you out of it."

"You did?" Liza blushes.

"Who knew you could be so easily bribed with a McFlurry?"

They crack up.

The same voice groans underneath them. *"Shut up!"*

Liza claps her hand over her mouth to stifle her giggles. Olivia presses her face into the pillow. When she's stopped laughing, she peeks out at Liza and grins. "We better be quiet."

Olivia doesn't get up to leave, though. Instead she just rolls on to her back, flings an arm over her face and shuts her eyes. Surprised, Liza does the same, hyper aware of the press of an elbow against her shoulder.

And she has no idea how much later it is when she surfaces from sleep with Olivia still stretched out on the bed next to her. All she knows is she's still groggy and Tam is standing on the ladder of the bunk whispering to them. "Hey, are you two getting up soon?"

There's a mumble from Olivia.

"Remember, we decided we're going on that tour today?"

"Oh yeah." Olivia yawns and swipes her fingers over her eyes. "We're getting up. Promise."

Tam just looks at them for a moment, her expression unreadable, and then disappears down the ladder. "See you downstairs."

Olivia sits up slowly, rubbing her face. She turns and smiles at Liza. Even with only a few hours' sleep, she's still so pretty. She slaps Liza on the thigh and turns for the ladder. "Come on, we better move it. Don't forget, a delicious continental breakfast awaits."

Olivia clambers from the bunk, leaving just the faint nutmeg scent of her perfume behind. Liza breathes it in slowly and squeezes her eyes shut. *Don't get a crush on this girl,* she pleads with herself. *Please do not get a crush on her.*

Because that could get kind of awkward.

But she also knows it might already be too late.

* * *

Kit, Melbourne

Kit pulls off her apron, sinks down to the back steps and slides out her phone. Behind her, the sound of Colombian music reverberates through the door, a ceaseless, contagious rhythm.

She breathes in the cooling night air and checks her Facebook.

There's a message from Olivia.

Hey, how are you? I hope the new job is good, and that Chloe is not giving you too much hell. Your messages make me incredibly glad my sister is so great. But then, I never had to share a room with her, either.

We're still in Florence. It's beautiful but kind of frenetic. I hung out with Liza yesterday. She's really cool. She's different from what I expected. Then I don't really know what I was expecting. We roamed the city and then went out drinking with some Italian students. It was really fun. We took a photo for you too. Liza's sending it. Mai's busy chasing that Brisbane boy. She's convinced him and his mates to stay at the same hostel for our last two days, which means she's going to be hell-bent on partying. I know it's terrible, but sometimes I just wish she'd chill, you know? Anyway, sorry to vent. I miss you, and I hope everything is okay. Olivia xxxxxoooo

Kit smiles. Aw. Her two besties have been hanging out. That's so cool. She wishes she was with them. She's never hung out with both of them at the same time. It's weird to think they're making friends without her.

Liza's message is on her email. It's short and sweet, and she's attached a hilarious photo of a mannequin with a wardrobe malfunction posing in the window of what looks like a high-end boutique.

Hi! How's that for an epic nip slip! Florence is still super beautiful, and I still miss you like crazy. I hope the new job with the old men is working out okay. I love you to pieces. Xo

Kit looks at the photo again and laughs. She shoves her phone back in her pocket and leans back against the next step. Inside, dinner service is over, and now everyone has started on the drinking and dancing. She's been working since eight this morning, between the café and here. And she still has a couple of hours to go. After she has cleared all the tables from the dinner service, she usually helps in the bar.

The door opens behind her. Thinking it's going to be Jim telling her to hurry up, she turns quickly. It's not, though. It's Lewis, the bartender. He grins down at her and waggles his eyebrows. She grins back. She loves Lewis already. Because he's the thing that is going to keep her sane at this job. She was incredibly relieved on her first night when Jim introduced her to this short, chubby, cheerful guy behind the bar. Partly because it meant she wasn't the only person under fifty in the place, and also because he was so damn friendly. Lewis acts as if everything on earth were put there for his amusement. All night he cracked jokes, gave her advice, and made her weird, sugary soft drink combinations to keep her going through the busy shift. He even helped her deal with Michail in the kitchen, who grumbled at her every time she dropped in a plate, no matter how neatly she cleared and stacked them.

"Ah, don't worry about him," Lewis laughed. "That old bugger would only be happy if you fed everyone on paper plates and chucked them out at the end of the night. Ignore him."

And so she did. Fuelled by Lewis's give-no-shits attitude, she'd just smile her sweetest smile at him whenever Michail started up his barely comprehensible mutterings and go about her business.

And because of Lewis, when Jim handed her some notes and asked her to come back the next night, she was actually happy about it.

"Watcha doing?" Lewis asks as he drops onto a step above her.

"Reading some messages from my friends. They're in Florence." She's already told him her tale of non-travelling woe.

He nods. "Cool city." Of course he's been there. Lewis has been everywhere. While they packed up last night, stacking chairs at the sides of the room, he told her all about how he spent the last three years since he left school travelling, stopping to work for a few months in different places to fund the next part of his trip. It sounds amazing.

She sighs. If she hadn't screwed up, she could be doing that right now. Instead, she gets to go inside and duck around salsa dancers, wiping down tables and picking up beer bottles. And then she gets to go home. And if she's really, *really* lucky, her sister will be lying around stoned, watching inane crap on her laptop without headphones while Kit tries to sleep.

"Hey." Lewis taps her on the head. "No feeling sorry for yourself." It's as if he can read her thoughts. Then he squeezes both her shoulders comfortingly and tells her, "You were just meant for a different adventure, that's all."

"Okay," Kit says, choosing to believe his version of events. Because it's better than hers. She picks up her apron. "And right now, my latest waitressing adventure awaits. Who knows? Maybe I'll meet a hot Colombian millionaire who'll fly me around the world."

"That's the spirit." He takes her hand and pulls her up with him. And she laughs as he salsas his way back to the bar.

CHAPTER 16

Olivia, Trieste, Italy

Italy flies by in an indulgent whirl of scenic train trips, doughy treats, and cheap carafes of highly drinkable wine. With Florence as their base, they visit small Tuscan towns and wander around, seduced by the relentless beauty. They catch a train to Pisa, where they dutifully snap pictures of that under-performing tower. Well, actually, Olivia gets bored and instead takes pictures of tourists taking pictures of themselves pretending to hold the tower up and montages them on her Instagram. Then they elbow through crowds in Venice, taking in the copious smells and sights of that teeming souvenir shop of a city, overrun with gawking visitors and freewheeling tourist enterprise.

Then, at Mai's pleading, they backtrack to the west when Campbell and Sam and their friends decide to walk some of the Cinque de Terre, a series of worn paths traversing rustic olive groves and vineyards thriving on the terraced hills by the ocean. The path is dotted with small villages that cling like crumbling pastel limpets to the steep cliffs, suspended over rocky coves. They walk for two days, staying overnight in one of the villages. Hungry and tired from the walk, they spend the evenings eating massive plates of pasta, going to bed early and falling into deep sleep. In the weak sunshine of the morning, they brave the cold autumn water for a swim as small black crabs scuttle over rocks, before hiking into the hills again.

It surprises Olivia how much she enjoys these two days. Usually, exercise doesn't mean more than suffering through the occasional yoga class. So at first, it's hard, and she's envious of Campbell and Liza, whose fit bodies seem to eat up the steep inclines and rocky paths. But then it's fun, striding along these paths under the winter sun, cracking jokes and stopping for views or food whenever they feel like it. And even the exhaustion at the end of each day feels good. It's a kind of pleasurable, spent tiredness that plummets her to sleep at night.

At first Olivia is wary of travelling with Sam. She isn't sure what to expect after his clinginess in Portugal. And she's right to be wary.

He seems hopeful at first. Even though she hasn't engaged with him since Portugal, aside from accepting his friend request, he sticks by her side. She is careful to treat him no differently than the others, and he eventually seems to get the picture.

After Cinque de Terre, they swap the countryside for the city, catching a train to Rome. Olivia is the only one of them that really likes Rome. Sure, it isn't a particularly friendly city. But Olivia kind of admires its standoffishness. She likes the way it doesn't bend over backwards to play host to its visitors like other places they've been. Rome doesn't seem to have time to accommodate the slack-jawed slowness of tourists who gape at the ruins and traffic alike. Rome says hurry up. Rome says stay the hell out of my way. It doesn't seem to feel the need to indulge anyone. It reminds Olivia of parts of New York. Indifferent. Permanently entrenched in a game of hard-to-get. And it turns out Olivia likes her cities like that.

But now they're done with Italy. They catch a train to a port city slung between Venice and the border of a country Olivia didn't even know existed until they planned this trip. In fact, now that they're on its doorstep, she doesn't know much more about it than what a quick Google image search last night told her: it's tiny and almost insanely pretty. That and what her father said in his latest email, that it was the first new country to demand its way into being at the beginning of what would be the miserable, bloody fracturing of Yugoslavia. This is the sum of what she knows.

On the way there, she looks up from her book to see Liza staring out the train window, her mouth moving with words Olivia cannot hear. Beside her, Tam is fast asleep, head on her bag. Mai is elsewhere.

"First sign of madness, you know," Olivia tells Liza. "That's what my grandpa used to say."

Liza jumps and stares at her, looking like she's just been shaken from a dream. "What is?"

"Talking to yourself."

"I didn't know I was." Liza's cheeks turn pink. "I was just trying to remember something."

"What?" Olivia asks, curious. Liza's always elsewhere. And sometimes she's found herself wondering where it is this girl dreams.

"The words to a poem I read once. I loved it, but I can't remember it. It said something about falling in love with train rides so much that you won't be able to remember where home is any more. But I can't remember the words, exactly, though."

Olivia smiles. So she's not the only one who gets writing stuck in her head the same way you do a song or melody. "Do you remember who wrote it?"

Liza shakes her head and gives her an embarrassed chuckle. "I think I saw it on Tumblr, actually."

"Yeah, well, even Tumblr can get deep sometimes."

* * *

In the port town, they kill time waiting for the afternoon bus in a small bookshop. Olivia's found two English newspapers, so she's set. She stands in the corner and takes advantage of the free wi-fi. Will has deigned to reply to her message.

Sure, I might have some time to meet up. Message me when you hit London town.

Might have some time for her? That's it? That's all she gets? Well, at least he's responding. That's a step up from a month ago, at least. Most of the time he drops straight off Messenger the minute she logs on.

It hurts, the fact that he won't give her any time. For the last two years, he's been one of her closest friends. And even if it's her fault she let them evolve into something she was never that sure she wanted, it was only because he so clearly *did.* Now, she can't help wishing he'd just get the hell over it and be her friend again. She misses him.

Mai slaps a magazine back onto the shelf. She's been grumpy since they left Campbell in Florence. But like every bit of Mai drama, her misery is kind of comical in its overstatement. Right now, she's staring morosely at the rack of magazines, picking them up and putting them down without even looking.

"Where are the boys headed?"

Mai crosses her arms over her chest and huffs. "They're going north, to Switzerland and Germany, like any normal person would, instead of going to some place no one has ever heard of." She plucks another magazine off the shelf and actually opens it this time.

"Where's your sense of adventure, Mai? Of serendipity?" Olivia actually likes that they're going somewhere she would never have thought to go. That's one thing she loves about this trip, that everyone got to pick a destination. It's like a game of travel lotto. "It could be amazing, you never know."

"Maybe," she says doubtfully. "But can you just let me be miserable until we hit the border? Then I promise I'll cheer up, okay?"

Olivia pats her shoulder. "Okay, deal."

"Thanks." Mai flicks to the next page, and her eyes instantly bug. She holds the magazine out for Olivia to see. "Would you get a load of this?"

It is a spectacular piece of sartorial insanity based on a concoction of animal prints and leather. "Wow. Just, wow."

"Uh-huh. That beats that shop in Pisa with the furry mannequins." Mai slides her phone from her jeans pocket and takes a surreptitious snap of the spread. Then she shoves the magazine back onto the rack. "Hey, we get our results in a week. Where will we be then?"

Shit. Yes, they will be getting their results. Olivia swallows. Somehow, she'd let herself forget for a couple of days. But now D-day is only a week away, and Mai will know how badly she did. Everyone will. She clears her throat. "It's the night before we leave for London."

"Well, there better be someplace to party in this weird country, then. Because I plan to if we both score over ninety-five."

Olivia swallows again, but feigns a smile. She pats her friend's shoulder. "You always plan to party. You're going to need rehab after this trip."

"Yeah, but there's always a reason to party on this trip. And getting into Melbourne? That's a good reason."

Olivia makes a hasty retreat from the magazine rack before she can say anything else about it. There's no way she's getting that score.

Tam's perched on some steps, a large cookbook open on her lap. She looks around the small shop. Liza is combing the shelves of the English language section at the back, her bottom lip caught between her teeth. Olivia pulls out her phone again.

When she's done consulting, she heads for the back of the shop, where Liza is bent right over, her hands rested on her knees as she peers at the lower shelves.

Olivia reads the first verse of the poem she has found out loud.

"That's it! How'd you know?" Liza's eyes are wide.

"The power of Google."

"Thanks. I was going to look it up tonight."

"I was curious, too." She leans against a shelf and folds her arms. "Somehow that quote manages to be incredibly romantic and incredibly depressing at the same time."

"I think that's why I liked it. And now that we're travelling, I kind of get it." Liza tips her head to one side. "The seductiveness of always being about to get someplace, the promise of the journey, compared to the reality of the destination."

"I love travelling so far," Liza says. "But I'd never want to do it so long I'd forget what being home feels like." She turns back to the shelves.

Olivia nods, even though she doesn't really know what she feels about it. She watches Liza scrutinise the shelves, occasionally slipping a book out and scanning the back before dismissing it. Liza's always reading. She can do it any time, anywhere. Seriously. Olivia thought she was addicted to reading, but she wouldn't be surprised if Liza whipped one out at a club one night.

She smiles teasingly at her. "So I know you've read like, six zillion books since we started this trip, but there's got to be at least one in here you haven't read."

Liza laughs. "There's heaps I haven't read. But I'm terrible at choosing books. There's so much pressure, you know?"

"Ah no, not really."

"But what if I pick one, and it's bad or I don't like it?" Liza's eyes widen in imagined horror. Olivia wants to laugh. Liza's rivalling Mai for the melodrama crown right now.

"Then don't read it. Seems pretty simple." One thing Olivia's mum taught her was to never give your time to a book that doesn't grab you at the start.

"But if I hate it, I'm right back where I started, with nothing to read. And I *hate* having nothing to read. It makes me nervous." Liza shakes her head. She's got her hair tied back in a massive bundle at the top of her head and it wobbles comically.

Olivia nods. "I get that. Security blanket."

"Exactly." Liza continues to comb the shelves.

"You know, when I was in high school, I used to go back and read some of my favourite books from when I was a kid." Olivia has no idea why she's telling Liza this. "Total comfort thing."

"Me too," Liza says, without a shred of Olivia's embarrassment. "I still want to sometimes."

"Well, we can head for the kids section if you want?"

Liza grins. "No, I think I'll read with the big kids for now." She checks her watch and clicks her tongue. "I've got five minutes to find something. I should have got a Kindle."

Olivia smiles indulgently at her. "Well, you can borrow mine if it comes to that. But until then, let's find you a date." She moves in and runs her eyes over the spines, taking in titles. The books are mostly classics, but there are one or two shelves of contemporary novels. She slides out a familiar volume, surprised to see an Australian book in the collection of mostly British and American bestsellers. It's the book that beat her mother's for the Rainer Prize last year. Not that her mother cared. She's won all the prizes already. Some of them twice. In fact Ruth praised this book heavily, both in private and in the media. Olivia loved it too, with its heartrending blend of sadness and comedy. She holds it up. "Have you read this? It's amazing. And it's about travel, too, so it's kind of perfect for now."

"Thanks." Liza takes the book, looking hopeful, and scrutinises the back cover, full of gushing praise from reviewers.

"But, if by any weird chance you happen to be the only person in the world to hate it, don't hate *me*, okay?"

Liza clutches her new treasure to her chest and smiles bashfully at her. "Okay. Promise."

* * *

Kit, Melbourne

Kit tiptoes into the flat, closing the door quietly behind her. Her mum has an early shift at the hospital, and Darren didn't finish work until late.

She contemplates making a cup of tea for before bed, but decides she just needs to sleep. It's past 1am, and she has to be up in six hours to do the early shift at the café. Then she has another shift at the pub. She hates tomorrow already, and it hasn't even begun. The only good thing about it is that by the time she finishes all those shifts and gets her pays for this week, she'll have paid off the rent she owes at the old house. Now there's just the money for that stupid statue. She has already put the money she saved for the trip onto it, but there's still a few hundred dollars left to go on that embarrassment.

But once that money is paid, she might be able to find a new place to live or even start saving for another trip. She still has the plane ticket. It turned out she wasn't allowed a refund, just a date change, but she has to use it within the year. She can't imagine travelling alone, though. Maybe she just won't use it, just let the ticket run out and chalk the loss up to another misadventure, another lesson learned.

She tiptoes past her mum's bedroom, praying that her sister is out or asleep. It's doubtful she's out, though. Chloe hardly ever leaves the house, except to smoke sullenly on the front steps or to go to the DVD shop. She keeps whinging that they need to get internet so she can just download movies like everyone else. But even though she does every other bloody thing for Chloe, Kit's glad her mum refuses to shell out for something she can't afford and barely knows how to use.

There's no light coming out from under the bedroom door. Sighing gratefully, Kit turns the doorknob gently and pushes the door. Immediately, a toxic cloud of cigarette smoke threatens to engulf her. Instantly furious, Kit flicks on the light and shoves the door closed behind her.

"Turn the fucking light off!" Chloe growls, pulling a pillow over her head.

"No!" Kit marches over to the window and throws it open as wide as it will go, yanks off her top and bra, and hauls on an oversize T-shirt, glaring.

Chloe yanks the pillow off her head, rolls over, and glares at Kit. Her freshly-dyed black hair makes her face look harder. Her mum had to clean that mess off the sink with bleach and steel wool. "I said turn it off. I'm trying to sleep, for fuck's sake!"

"Have you forgotten Darren's deathly asthmatic? Do you want to kill him?"

"I didn't smoke *in* here. I leaned out the window."

"Well it smells like you've been chain-smoking. It's freaking disgusting. You can't walk ten metres to go outside? Stop being so bloody selfish."

Her sister scoffs. "Stop being such a bitch just because you're the loser who messed up her trip. It's not my fault your life sucks."

Kit fights the urge to throw something at her. "Well it is your fault this place stinks like an ashtray."

Chloe just gives her a benign smile and rolls over in bed. "Suck it up, baby sis," she mutters. "Or move out."

Steaming, Kit yanks her doona from the bed. There's no way she's sleeping in this stinking room. She storms out, pulling the door shut gently behind her, hoping none of the smoke has escaped. Darren will be wheezing all day tomorrow if he breathes that feral air.

"Turn the fucking light out!" Chloe screeches from behind the closed door.

Ignoring her, Kit stalks into the lounge room and pulls the piles of papers from the couch. She curls up on the worn cushions and squeezes her eyes shut. Being in this flat is like being in a sad prison. Her mother and Darren do nothing but work their asses off and stare at the TV, watching the world from the safety of the couch. And her sister is hell-bent on adding as little value to the planet as humanly possible. She *has* got to get out of here.

CHAPTER 17

Olivia,

Your sister asked me to send a photo of little Henry. He's long, isn't he? He's quite the miracle of cell division. And quiet, too.

You were a quiet baby. Alarmingly so. Because you weren't sleepy and quiet like this little one. You were shockingly alert. I used to find you in your crib, wide awake, and have no idea how long you'd been just hanging out, staring at the world. I always wondered what your infant brain was taking in.

I've been busy, but not writing. I'm running some summer workshops at the university. It's more enjoyable than I thought it would be, but demanding, too. The students are incredibly eager and very sensitive. I suppose that will get taken care of when they begin to publish (nothing like an editor to cure you of that). Some of them want me to comment on every single word they write. They're supposed to be workshopping each other's work, facilitated by me, but I get the feeling they're just waiting for me to bestow some essential piece of advice that will make novelists of them all. I don't know how to tell them I have no idea how to teach such a thing.

I hope your trip is wonderful. When you're in London, you should go to the Hallman Gallery. Remember Luca and Rayne? Rayne has a photography exhibit there. She'd love to see you. You spent a lot of nights sharing a cot with her daughter Sage when we were working on that little literary magazine together. She'd love to see who you've become, I think.

Mum

* * *

Tam, Trieste, Italy

The bus station is decrepit and sad. Like most bus stations, Tam is learning. So far, they all have looked and smelled the same. Used and abused. She kicks her legs up onto her backpack and bites into the sweet flesh of a pear, hoping its scent will cover the smell of sweat and stale smoke. Outside, a steady drizzle has set in. Bored, she stares idly up at the football match on the television fixed to the wall.

It's another hour until their bus will take them across the border. Then they will catch another bus from the capital, straight up to a mountainside lake where they will stay a couple of days. She's looking forward to seeing some green and to being able to breathe again. Italy has been beautiful, but the air in all the cities is choked with car exhaust, and the streets are constantly crowded. She craves air and light and room to move. This country girl can only take so much.

An old man in the corner wakes from his snoring slumber, hawks loudly, and then spits onto the floor. Tam puts the pear down. That's one way to kill an appetite.

On the television, a news bulletin flashes on, showing scenes of wet, wide-eyed people huddled on a beach, surrounded by people in uniform. As Tam tries to make sense of the silent images, the small mumsy woman who chatted loudly in her thickly-accented English as she sold them their tickets comes out from behind the counter. Pulling a chair over to the set, she clambers up and turns up the volume. The urgent, sombre voice of a newsreader fills the room. Everyone waiting looks up and watches the images of terrified women and children being lifted from a vessel by men in military uniforms.

The ticket seller pushes the chair back into the corner and stands there, hands on hips, shaking her head at the screen and ignoring a teenager standing at the ticket window. "Two hundred dead," she says to them in English over her shoulder. "Forty survive. Some of them die before boat even sinks. Imagine, children sitting among the dead for days, waiting to see if this will happen to them, too." She shakes her head again, her voice both sympathetic and disapproving, as if her ethical barometer cannot make a choice on this one. But then who could?

"They will die to come here," the woman says slowly. She shakes her head again and walks back to the counter, pulling the door shut firmly behind her.

Tams stares at the screen. This is what Olivia was talking about over breakfast the other day. All the people trying desperately to flee across the water to here, away from wars and other horrors at home. Her chest fills with quiet sorrow. So many similar images on her television screen at home too, usually bookended by admonishing speeches from suited politicians who have probably never come close to experiencing the unimaginable things that propel these people on such terrifying watery journeys. She looks at the others. They, too, are staring at the screen.

Finally, the miserable little news bulletin finishes, and the soccer match of earlier fills the screen again, the excited commentators clearly oblivious to what viewers have just witnessed in the break. Tam stares out the door into the rain, the images of the weary, resigned faces of survivors still hovering in front of her eyes. Outside somewhere, someone screams loudly. The two things probably have nothing to do with each other, but still, it feels like they do.

* * *

Lize!

Guess where I am? On the bus, of course. We're headed out to Geelong for regionals. Patrick's making us do the 400 relay on top of our own runs, and we're in crappy shape. Manda's got a cold even though it's like, a hundred degrees and has been for days. Shae's PMS-ing hard. Patrick dropped her to third leg because she hasn't been hitting her times in training, and she's pissed. And she broke up with Dave too, so she's extra pissed. I'm scared she's going to throw the baton at my head.

So, basically, my question is: where the bloody hell are you? I need you to anchor, so I don't have to do it. And I need you on the bus to keep me company and protect me from these evil, hormonal wenches.

Alika left the team. Says she's not going to run anymore, that uni and training will be too hard. Pity, she had a good shot at Uni Games. And we need her for relay. So don't you get all worldly and lazy and quit on us, too. I wish I was being all cultured and shit in Europe. Italy sounds amazing.

But crushing on the straight girl you're travelling with? Not so amazing. Bad move, Lizey-Jane. Does she know? Are you hanging around, giving her moo eyes all the time? Nah, I bet you're classier than that.

Me, I'm disgustingly single, as usual. I think the guys I hang with aren't into sweaty chicks with thighs stronger than theirs. Dumb, really. They should find out what I can do with them before they write me off.

Anyway, better go. Shae's moaning for some painkillers, and we're almost there. Got to go play nursie. Stay awesome.

Tracy.

CHAPTER 18

Tam, Bled, Slovenia

Tam dashes out onto the hostel balcony, her laptop and mug balanced precariously in one hand. While she waits for the Skype connection, she stares out into the darkness and sips her rapidly cooling tea. The only things teasing at the stillness of this wintry night are the occasional powdery spill of snow from the trees and the twinkling of lights from the town below.

She zips her jacket to her chin and grins as he appears on her screen.

"Hi." Her breath turns to steam as it makes contact with the air.

"Wow." He leans against his couch, mug in hand. "It's that cold?"

"Yep. It's freezing. Snowed all morning."

"You know, I've never seen snow. Not proper stuff. There was a bit at the top of Mount Welly when we went there. But just in the distance."

"I wish it was daytime," she tells him. "Then I could show you the view. This place is so beautiful. The Alps are just behind us. The *Alps,* Matt!"

"That's insane."

"What's it like at home?"

"Pretty hot already. Wednesday was over thirty. Northerly."

"Bushfire weather." She rubs a finger over the handle of her cup. Another thing to worry about.

"There were a couple on the weekend. Orford and somewhere out west."

"Orford?" She frowns. She always loved driving into that little town. You come down the hill and drive for a minute along the brilliant blue river before it abandons the convict road and pours out into the icy grey waters of the east coast. There, you can see all the way to where Maria Island lurks, a dark hulk on the skyline. "Was it bad?"

"Nah. They contained it pretty quick. It went over Nick's cousin's place. They only lost a shed, though."

"Good." She sighs, praying the Peninsula is spared this summer. Her dad would lose his entire livelihood if he loses the orchard.

He leans closer to the screen. "Hey, stop worrying, for Christ's sake. You worry too much."

Tam glares at him.

He just grins at her. "What are you doing today?"

"It's night, you idiot." She holds up the computer and shows him the darkness outside.

"Oh yeah. I can't keep this whole time thing sorted."

"I sent you the link to the world clock app thing."

He just grins and raises his shoulders.

"God, you're such an old man." She shakes her head. But she smiles too. She can't help it.

They stare at each other for a moment. Then she bites her lip and asks the question. "So, what have you been doing? Seeing anyone?"

"Right now, I'm seeing *you*."

"Okay then." She blushes and changes the subject. "Hey, shouldn't you be at work? I thought Dad would have you hard at it?"

"Nah, he's in town, and he doesn't trust me to do the spraying 'til he shows me the ropes. I'm going over this arvo to fix some fences. The wallabies are getting in, little buggers."

"Town? What's he doing in town?" She frowns. Her dad doesn't drive to Hobart unless he absolutely has to. Ever.

"Said he had an appointment. Bill's gone with him."

A cold sensation spreads through her chest and belly. He shouldn't have another check-up for six weeks. Just after she gets back. She timed her trip around it. Something must be wrong. "What kind of appointment?"

"No idea." He stares at her. "It's probably nothing."

She nods, but she's not sure. Not at all. Because if something *was* wrong, there's only half a chance he'd tell her. Every time she asks her dad about his health on the phone, he just brushes it off, tells her not to worry. But he'd say that no matter what. Only six months ago, he was shivering in a hospital bed, fighting a bout of pneumonia that nearly killed him, still telling her he was just fine. She chews at a fingernail.

Matt suddenly sits up and leans forward. His image wavers and pixelates as he pulls the computer closer to him. When he comes back into clarity, he's leaning his chin on his hand, staring at her. "Seriously, don't stress, Tam. He seems fine. He worked like a beast on the sleeping sheds yesterday. He couldn't do that if anything was wrong."

Tam doubts it. Her dad has a superhuman ability to ignore things like sickness and sadness and just work through it. She's seen it plenty of time before.

"He's okay, Tam. And you know, maybe the appointment's not even a doctor thing. Look, I better go," he says. "Dad needs to use my computer so he can order some stock. You be okay?"

"Yep," she lies.

"Seriously, don't stress, Tam. I'll talk to you soon." He fires one of his sleepy, charming smiles at her, and then the connection is gone.

She closes her laptop and hugs it to her chest, staring out into the darkness. Most of the lights in the town have disappeared now, and all she can see is the glistening branches of snow-laden trees catching the porch light. It must be late. She's never going to be able to sleep now, though.

CHAPTER 19

Liza, Bled, Slovenia

"Okay, this way." Dragan waves them down a steep turn toward the slate grey waters of the lake. Liza clumps down the hill, her eyes fixed on the ground as she negotiates the slippery descent. It's freezing. Her feet are ice blocks of flesh and bone, even under their layers of merino and boot. She loves it, though, the brace and sharpness of this cold, the sense of definition to everything. She's never seen the world in this glittering white.

If they were staying here in the depth of winter and she had more money, she'd love to try skiing. Apparently there are incredible slopes further up the mountains. Instead they're snowshoeing. They were talked into going by a group of young guys at the restaurant near the hostel. These guys make their money by taking tourists rafting in summer, and out on the snow in winter. That way they get to stay here, rather than leaving for the cities where all the jobs are, like so many of the other kids who grew up here.

Olivia was the only one who was not that into the idea. "I am grossly uncoordinated," she told them. "Like fundamentally, innately so. I'll hold everyone up." That didn't stop Mai from talking her into it, of course. But it took a bit of convincing before Olivia finally, grudgingly, agreed.

Liza turns to see how she's holding up. She hasn't seen her for a while. And that's strange in itself, because lately she's been hyperconscious of where Olivia is at all times, though she's doing her damn best not to show it. She spots Olivia about ten metres behind her. She's got a determined but over-it look as she gingerly tramps down the steep slope. Her cheeks are red and her nose even redder. It's cute.

It's amazing how this crush has just become a part of this holiday. Liza rolls her eyes. Sometimes she wishes she could shake it off. But Olivia doesn't make it easy for her. Now that they've made friends, sort of, she seeks out Liza's company more and more. It flatters Liza that Olivia wants to hang out with her, but she also wonders how much of that has to do with escaping or diluting Mai, versus wanting to be around her.

And Liza can't even enjoy Olivia's company, because part of her is always worried that Olivia will figure it out. That she'll know that half the time, Liza is sitting there listening to her, wishing Olivia was gay or that Liza *wasn't* gay or that Olivia just wasn't so damn attractive. It's not just about how she looks, though. She's also generous and funny in a kind of quiet, self-deprecating way. It's like the minute you get to know her a little, that initial remoteness is gone. Like it was a bad reading. Because she's not at all. And she's incredibly clever. She knows so much about the world. Yesterday, she did more to explain the conflict in Syria to Liza than any teacher ever managed at school.

Liza's yanked from these thoughts as Dragan stops at the edge of the water. He picks up an oar that is lying against a tree and yanks one end out of the snow. "We must have left this here in the summer," he says, tsk tsking as Aleks, their other guide, brings the stragglers down with him.

As everyone gathers near the water's edge, Dragan sweeps an arm out toward the lake. "The beautiful Bohinj, where I learned to swim as a boy." He points over to a rickety wooden jetty. "My father pushed me off there so I would *have* to learn."

A few people laugh. A flash of memory ripples through Liza. It was in the summer she was five. Her parents took her to Brighton Baths, a beautiful old swimming area, where an old wooden pier hems in a rectangular pocket of the ocean. Her father took her on the slide. His thick arm clutched around her waist as they plummeted down the sun-baked metal and into the glittering water. He forgot to let her go as they sliced through the surface of the water, his weight dragging her all the way to the seabed with him. Terrified, she kicked and screamed silently in the water.

He was so apologetic afterward as she cried fitful, frightened tears, but made her do it again. "I don't want you to leave here scared of this place," he coaxed her. It took some persuading, but finally she did it again. This time, he released her as they broke water, and she floated quickly to the surface, grinning and gasping, buoyant with her new little act of bravery. Since then, she's been trying to remember this moment, to repeat that bravery every time she's scared, but the older she gets, the harder she feels like it gets.

Dragan is talking again. "I wouldn't recommend anyone being pushed in today, though. I am not coming in after you. Besides, you'll probably get hypothermia before I get to you."

Liza shivers. She wishes they could come back here in summer. It must be equally beautiful then, when it's all green and lush and the water is that emerald colour she has seen in the photographs on the hostel walls.

The other guide, Aleks, is talking now, pointing toward the mountain peaks stabbing into the clouds above them. That's when a loud cracking sound rips through the valley. He holds up a hand as if to silence everyone. But nobody is speaking. He holds his finger to his lips and gazes around them. "Maybe there are some hunters out today. I hope they can see us."

The sound rings out again, and everyone starts to look concerned. One girl grabs the gloved hand of the guy next to her. A guy ducks down, holding onto a tree trunk.

Uneasy, Liza looks at the others. Olivia doesn't look scared even though Mai's got a nervous grip on her arm. She looks dubious. Liza turns to Dragan. The oar in his hand is dripping. He grins cheekily at her. "Or maybe it's just me." He lifts the oar high and slaps it down hard and flat. It hits the water with a loud crack.

Everyone giggles, but the relief is palpable. The guy under the tree stands, brushing snow from his legs. "Hey, I'm from East LA," he grumbles. "You shouldn't do that to me." He gives them all a sheepish grin.

Dragan laughs again, pleased with his joke. Liza wonders if he does it every time. "Okay," he announces. "Time to go. And the good news, my friends, is that we have walked a circle, so it's only ten minutes, and we will be back to the bus and then to the restaurant where my uncle will make us some hot lunch."

Liza can feel the mood instantly lift. He leads them off along the lake. "And even better news." He calls behind him. "It is all downhill from here."

There is a collective sigh of relief as they begin to trudge along the water's edge.

As they pull out of the parking lot, Olivia drops down into a seat next to her. She immediately pulls out her phone. "You getting any reception?" she asks.

Liza is immediately, self-consciously, alert. "I haven't tried." As Olivia taps away next to her, she shuts her book and looks around the van. Dragan's in the back, chatting up two pretty, athletic blondes from Amsterdam. Tam and Mai are up front. Mai's talking loudly to Aleks.

"I swear, this place is not for real. Tell me the truth. It's a plot!" she squawks. Aleks just laughs and kicks the small, battered van into a higher gear as they rumble out of the parking lot. Liza's already heard all this. Mai's got this idea in her head that this place doesn't really exist. It's too cute to be for real, she says. She's convinced they're in some tourist version of that old film, *The Truman Show,* and that the whole town is an elaborate film set with everyone around them actors.

Insane as it is, Liza can kind of see why she thinks this. This area is as storybook pretty as the pictures promised. It's not like Italy, where car pollution and litter accompanied the beautiful old parts of cities, and where to get to Tuscan villages, they inevitably passed through the industrial, grey outskirts of the city before hitting rolling green hills or the sea. Italy was stunning, but it was also *real.*

Of course, they haven't been to the city here yet, but the lakeside village they're staying in is ridiculously beautiful, huddled down under these imposing, snow-laden mountains. The lake is a deep green, and just a touch off centre in its still waters—as if someone planned it that way—is a tiny island with an old white church, it's belfry jutting towards the sky. And just to make things even more fairytale, a red-roofed castle imposes itself on the view of the cliffs above the hostel. And all around them are the foothills of the Alps, covered by trees gilded with snow. It's *ridiculous.*

When they arrived in the town square from the bus stop two days ago, they were dragged from their usual grumbling, tired arrival banter by an involuntary silent enchantment at their surrounds. It was only broken when Mai exclaimed loudly, "This place *cannot* be for real!"

Liza was tempted to agree.

As the bus rattles down the road, Olivia slides her phone into her pocket and sighs.

"You okay?" Liza asks.

"Yeah," she mutters, yanking off her gloves and rubbing her hands together. "I'm just trying to organise to meet someone when we get to London, and they're not making it easy for me."

"Who?" she asks even though she knows it's none of her business.

"Will." Olivia stares past her out the window. "Will Vertigan. You know him?"

Liza nods. She knows him vaguely from school. He's tall and laid-back. Friendly to everyone. "I know *of* him."

"He's in London this summer."

"You're friends?" Liza asks, instead of asking the question she wants to ask. She turns her book over and over in her hands so she won't have to meet Olivia's eye.

Olivia stares down at her hands as she continues to rub them together slowly. "We *were* friends," she says eventually. "Then we dated, which was dumb."

There is a vaguely sick feeling in her stomach. Of course Olivia has ex-boyfriends. Look at her. "Why was it dumb?"

"Because we were friends. And now we're most definitely not. I actually think he hates me now."

"Really?"

"Yeah. And I don't even really know why." She presses her lips into a thin line and plays with a scratch in the upholstery of the seat. "All I know is that he was one of my best friends, and then we went out for six months and broke up. And now he's weird and distant, and he won't let me pin him down to a time to meet in London." She plucks at the frayed leather, frowning. "I was hoping he'd be past it, you know?"

Liza nods, though she doesn't really know.

"I guess I'm just supposed to be grateful he's even talking to me again."

Liza gives her a sympathetic look. Because she has no idea what to say. The only relationship she's been in pretty much comprised of being *not* talked to. She doesn't know it any other way. And before she can summon a single sage or even vaguely useful thing to say, Olivia sits up and shakes her shoulders, as if shimmying away her mood. She points at the book in Liza's hands.

"Are you enjoying it?"

The question makes her blush. She'd forgotten about her mild freak-out in the bookshop a few days ago, forcing Olivia to help her choose a book like she's some indecisive kid who can't even manage a simple task on her own. "It's really good," she says. "Like, it's really easy to read, but it's really intelligent at the same time. She makes you really think about what it means to travel, doesn't she?"

"Yeah, and I also love how you get the other perspective too, from a person who lives in a place that people treat like a holiday destination, but it's their *home*. I never really thought about what it would be like from that side, but now I'm going to be hyperaware of it."

"So, did you enjoy today?" Liza asks with a hint of a tease.

Olivia gives her an embarrassed-looking smile. "I did in the end. I mean, I'm not much of a hiker. Or even a walker, really. But it was beautiful out there." She slides her hands in her pockets, her elbow resting against Liza's arm. "I was terrified at first, though."

"Really?"

"When we were driving up here. I think I thought we were going to be hardcore climbing or something. I don't know." She shrugs. "I think I'm just weird about trying new things. Will says it's because I'm a control freak. I think it's just because I'm terrified." She grins and pulls a packet of lollies from her pocket. She pops one in her mouth and holds the packet out to Liza.

Olivia is a surprising sugar fiend. And she's always packing some form of chocolate or lolly. Liza takes one and smiles.

"I'm such a city girl. I'm brave *there*." Olivia tucks the packet away. "I explored so much of New York on my own. And London. I caught subways everywhere and just got out and walked through neighbourhoods. But I'm not so brave when it comes to nature." She tucks a long strand of honey-coloured hair behind her ear and smiles at Liza. "You loved it, didn't you?"

Liza's mouth puckers at the sour-lime flavour of the lolly. "Yeah I did. I want to try skiing now."

"Well, you'll be doing that one on your own." Olivia smiles at her, warm and teasing at the same time. Then she pulls her beanie down low, settles against Liza's shoulder, and shuts her eyes.

The bus continues its slow rattle down the hill. Liza opens her book and tries her best to focus on anything but the warm press of this girl at her side.

CHAPTER 20

Tam, near Bled, Slovenia

When Tam's dad got sick, she didn't even know. It wasn't until he'd begun the post-operation chemo treatment that she knew anything was wrong at all. When he went for the surgery, he told her he was going to an agricultural conference in Hobart for a week. She should have known then. Her father never does stuff like that. He hates town. But at the time, Tam was just beginning to wade into the perilous waters of Year 12 and didn't have time to think too hard about it.

He never actually told her about the cancer they found growing in him. It took someone else to break that news. He even tried to do the chemo on his own. Strictly against doctor's advice, of course. It worked for a few days until the poison began to, well, poison him. On the fourth day, as he made the hour's drive back to the peninsula, he was driven off the road by it.

It was just after the turn-off out of Dunalley when an unstoppable wave of nausea left him parked clumsily on a grassy embankment, vomiting out the car window. Instead of calling for help, he just manoeuvred the ute back onto the road and kept driving until he was forced to a stop again. The town cop told her aunt Anita he found him idling on the edge of the highway outside Murdunna, waiting out another storm. The officer, who had known him all his life, breathalysed him at first, thinking he'd had a few before leaving town. Then he called her aunt, Anita. By that time, the hour's journey had taken her dad three.

She came off the school bus to find her aunt cleaning out the front of the ute. It was Anita who sat her down on the front step and told her about the diagnosis, who explained to Tam why she could hear the groaning heaves of her father's nausea all the way from the front porch.

Tam can still feel the pinch of a splinter piercing her school stockings as Anita told her what she had only just found out herself. Tam picked at the new hole and stared at her aunt as she lit one cigarette off another, a habit she'd dropped years ago.

When she heard the word *cancer*, it was like numbness and terror invaded at the same time. Common sense told her those two things couldn't cohabit. But they seemed to in that moment. The next feeling—the one that flushed out the numbness—was anger. Anger at her dad for knowing for weeks and not telling her.

And she still wonders whether, if he hadn't been defeated by the chemo, how long he would have waited to tell her? Until she noticed he'd barely eaten for days? Until his hair dropped out? Until he was cured or dead? She knows it was his stupid attempt at protecting her, the same way he protected her from her mother leaving. But it still angered her, the same way his secrecy angered her when she was eight.

After that, Tam let her father's illness take over. She wanted it to. To make up for the time when she didn't know. She worried at it like you do with guilt or anger, obsessed.

Anita moved right into the spare room and looked after her dad while Tam was at school, driving him up to town and back for his appointments. They all found a routine, one ruled by long drives, sick buckets and searching for foods her dad could stomach. Everyone helped. Friends dropped around meals and things they thought might be helpful. Rural Supplies delivered chook food and fertiliser on the regular date even though no one had remembered to order it. She even woke up one morning to the sound of Matt's silent, surly uncle puttering around the yard on his ride-on mower. And inside, Tam and her aunts tended her dad like earnest, bossy nursemaids.

Tam only *just* managed to keep her head above water at school. Mostly because Anita made her go every day. And all the teachers knew. Of course they did. Everyone on the peninsula knew. That's how things work down there. And the school gave her as much leeway as the Higher School Certificate allowed with handing work in late or half-baked. All she needed. Tam already knew she wouldn't be doing uni. She'd be doing her chef's apprenticeship. Finishing high school was an ego thing.

Each night, she scrambled through her homework. She did it in her father's room on his bad days, or on the couch on the good ones. And then they'd watch TV while Anita tapped furiously on her laptop at the dining table, catching up with her work. Matt would come over, edged out by the pervasive quiet at his house, and talk footy and weather and guy things with her dad. Or sometimes they'd just stare at the screen in that comfortable silence that guys so often seem to dwell in, but girls rarely do.

On those nights in the lounge room, life had the glittering potential of normalcy. And the way the doctors spoke, it was safe to feel like that. He'd had his surgery, and now he would finish his chemo. His hair would grow back, and things would go back to their old life

But it didn't. Not yet.

Tam was alone when it happened. She came home to a note. Anita had gone to do the shop in town. Her father wasn't in the lounge room or on the porch where he sometimes sat in good weather. She found him in his darkened room, shivering, a cold sweat filming his skin.

Panicked but on automatic, she thrust a thermometer into his mouth, fed him some water, and called the medical centre immediately. The ambulance took him straight to Hobart, to the large, concrete monolith that took up almost an entire block. It was then, on that heart-in-throat drive to hospital, as she repeatedly tried to call Anita and Matt, that Tam first considered her father might die. And looking at him then, grey-skinned and semi-conscious on that interminable ride, she became utterly convinced. And the next few days did little to persuade her otherwise. For over a week he lay, immobilised by pneumonia, pumped full of antibiotics that didn't seem to do anything in the face of his ravaged immune system.

Tam refused to leave the hospital. She sat and waited, clenched and alert, by his side. Her schoolwork remained in the cardboard folders Matt dropped in. Visitors were basically ignored. It was as if she so much as looked away for a second, she'd lose him. And the fact that his doctors, who both had kids, didn't even try and tell her to go to school, told her she was right to be scared. So she slept and ate and kept vigil in that room and waited for whatever was going to happen.

It was school holidays before the tide turned. And the same way you can't see grass growing or a flower blooming until it has happened, she didn't see him getting better. His slow inch to recovery was almost imperceptible, even though the doctors assured her it was happening. Then it finally became obvious to the untrained eye. One day, he was awake for an hour. Then another, he was alert for most of the day. Then one day, he was sitting up in bed again. Then he was reading. Then he was eating. Each step seemed like a small miracle.

He was moved into a shared room, where he befriended Bill, a dedicated roamer recovering from a second surgery for a rampant melanoma. Bill had been about to head to the timber mills for work when cancer stopped him in his tracks.

Eventually, her dad caught up on his last doses of chemo and came home. And when he left the hospital, he brought Bill, homeless and jobless, back with him. He was installed in the granny flat up the hill by the woodshed. As her dad recovered, Bill earned his keep, unbidden. He kept the woodpile constantly high, splitting logs each morning. He mended the holes in the netting around the chook shed, things her dad would never have let go in the past. And when he wasn't outside, doing her dad's work, or running errands for them, he was cooking and keeping Tam company.

Once home, at the urging of the kind but dictatorial nurses who visited every couple of days, her dad stayed in his bed for a while. But it wasn't long before he was returning to his life again. Finally, one day, Anita went home and left Tam with the recovering men and something resembling their old life. With the bonus of Bill.

But even though she could see he was better, Tam couldn't relax again. Wouldn't let herself. Not after what happened last time. She couldn't completely trust it, or even trust the reassuring words of the doctors who pronounced her father on his way to something like well. They'd said that before.

Having Bill helped, though. He brought some of the quiet humour to the house her dad had abandoned during his sickness. He was wry and enthusiastic, and he loved food nearly as much as she did. As he discovered her interest, he began to teach her everything he had learned in his years working kitchens around the country. He was no expert and was never formally trained, but he had a swag of tips and tricks to pass on. Tam loved the way he could turn *anything* into a meal.

He started bringing home different cuts of meat or seafood for them to play with. And he rejuvenated the half-hearted vegetable patch her dad had abandoned years ago. Every meal became a project, a feast, starting with an ingredient. And these kitchen sessions made her more and more certain that this was what she wanted to do with her life.

And under their care and almost constant feeding, her father has returned as close to his old self as she suspects he will ever get. So she should be relieved. But now, with this mystery appointment, she can feel that slow crawl of fear again.

She finds herself constantly staring at her phone, wishing he'd hurry the hell up and return her call. When she'd Skyped Matt again, unable to wait, he told her that her father hadn't said anything about the appointment at all.

And maybe it's because this is all she can think about that just one drink into her visit, she's telling Aleks and Yuka all of this. She hasn't said a word to the girls about it. Not even Liza. But suddenly, she is in these strangers' flat, telling them she's worried about her dad.

"I think we should hope he just had a business appointment or something." Yuka tucks her short black hair behind her ears and sighs gently. "Fathers are difficult creatures." She gives Tam a small smile as she rubs the flat piece of dough between her fingers and places it on the floured surface of the table. "Mine does not like to communicate much either." She looks over at Tam's bowl. "Now for ginger." Yuka scrapes the finely chopped ginger into the large blue bowl. Tam obediently stirs it into the mix of cabbage and sesame.

The delicious smell of frying butter takes over the room as Aleks tosses a generous spoonful into a hot pan. The onions he and Tam painstakingly cut are added, and the frying easily conquers the delicate scent smell of Yuka's gyoza mixture.

They are both showing her how to cook dumplings, Japanese and Slovenian-style. "Welcome to the post-modern kitchen," Yuka joked when Tam arrived.

A couple of nights ago, Tam asked about the potato dumplings in the restaurant. Served with a meat sauce, they were messy and rustic to look at but decadent and delicious to eat. Aleks, the owner's nephew, told her how they were made, and they ended up chatting. He introduced her to his girlfriend, Yuka, and the three of them talked food and recipes and ingredients. The next thing she knew, she was being invited to their apartment to cook a meal with them.

Tonight, he is making his dumplings with mushrooms because Yuka is a vegetarian. They live in an apartment block above a bowling alley on the outskirts of a village a short bus ride away. Aleks has lived here all his life and rarely travels, he told her. He spends a few weeks every autumn in Serbia with his cousins once the tourist season finishes. But the rest of his time is spent here running tours and helping his uncle.

Yuka, on the other hand has been travelling solidly for three years, working on organic farms in exchange for accommodation and teaching yoga for travel money. She spent her childhood in her native Japan, but went through high school in a private girls' school in Sydney. She's spending the winter here before heading to Egypt.

"I needed some snow before I go to the desert," she says with a laugh. "I'm from Hokkaido. I miss the cold in my bones."

Aleks is tall and broad-shouldered with light brown hair and brown eyes, while Yuka is short and delicately built, with a round face and wide mouth. There is a calm affection between them, an energy Tam could feel the instant she met them. She wonders what will happen when it's time for Yuka to move on in the summer.

She turns to Aleks. "And what about your father? Is your father bad at communicating?"

He beckons her over to the stove, picking up a jar of dried herb and pouring a generous amount into his hand. "Thyme." He crushes it and throws it into the second pan with the mushrooms. "My father died twelve years ago, in a car accident."

Tam's eyes widen. And here she has been complaining about her dad, who has survived so far. "I'm so sorry."

"It was a long time ago. I was very angry then, but now..." He shrugs and takes a sip of his tea. "Now I know it's just part of a larger, important cycle." He glances over at his girlfriend.

Yuka smiles and nods her agreement.

Tam wonders what he believes, exactly. He wears a small silver cross around his neck, but he seems to be talking about something else, a different kind of spirituality. There are crystals on the windowsill above the kitchen sink, gleaming among the washing up cloths, and a complicated dream catcher hangs above the bed in the corner. These things are at odds with the floral and dark wood sturdiness of the rest of the décor.

Aleks turns the heat down and leans against the counter. "But my father was the same as your father, I think. Private. He never talked to us about anything important. Just told us to be good. He did not tell us *how* to be good, though." He laughs.

"What about your mum?" Tam asks, curious.

He chuckles. Then he takes her arm and leads her to the sliding door that looks out over the snow-packed balcony. “See those flats?” He points at the windows of an apartment building across a field, standing at attention by a roundabout. Next to it is a service station, its neon lights and industrial planes so incongruent against the backdrop of the beautiful Alps.

She nods.

He grins at her. “Tomorrow my mother will ask me, 'Who was that strange red-headed girl in your apartment, and what were you cooking?'”

“Really?”

“Definitely.” He pulls the flowered curtain across the door.

“Does it bother you?”

“Of course not. Here, mothers just like to know everything their sons are doing. At *all* times!” he adds loudly, laughing. “I'm used to it.”

“It's not just here, Aleks.” Yuka rolls her eyes. “My mother calls my brother every single night. Not me. Just him. Because he's a boy and can't look after himself.”

Aleks opens the fridge and pulls out more herbs. “So it seems that everywhere in the world, fathers do not speak, and mothers make up for it.”

“It looks like it.” Tam agrees, tapping her glass against his.

Later, as Tam leaves the apartment, the container of dumplings Yuka presses upon her is warm against her chest. There has been something comforting about this visit, something that feels universal. Even though she likes the girls more and more every day, it's nice to have an experience that's not filtered through all of them. She thinks she will be okay on her own after the others leave.

Climbing onto the bus that will take her back to the hostel, Tam immediately checks her phone. Nothing. She chews on her lip and wonders if she should try calling again. But there's little point. Her dad rarely remembers he has a phone. He probably hasn't looked at it for a week.

The bus putters through the darkness, the lights of a house or a billboard occasionally breaking up the ceaseless white of the snowy landscape. She presses her face against the window, unsure if she'll recognise the stop.

Yuka told her that no matter how long she has been travelling and how long she wishes to do it, that she'll return to her cold mountain home in Japan one day. And if she doesn't, she'll feel its absence in her like a weight for the rest of her life. Aleks said he would never leave this place for long. Doesn't know how to.

Tam gets it. She craves home. Every day. It's not homesickness, exactly. She's glad she came on this trip, and she's excited for the rest of it. But she now knows she will never leave her peninsula home for a life elsewhere. She knows this as fact, the way some people know there is a God, or that they're gay, or were born to make music. It's indisputable. A truth. She feels like so many people—including the girls she's travelling with —are looking for their place in the world. Tam has always known hers. And leaving has only told her she is right about that.

CHAPTER 21

Kit, Melbourne, Australia

"Because that's what I do, kiddo." Lewis turns the key in the lock and shoves the door open with his shoulder. "I am the fixer. You have a problem, and boy, do I have a solution!"

Yawning into her hand, Kit follows him. She can still hear or feel—she's never sure which it is—the relentless beat of salsa in her system. One thing she's learned from this new job is that after a night of exposure, this rhythm gets into your system and lodges there, the same way you feel the rocking of a boat hours after you've been back on dry land. It bugged her at first, but now she's used to it, falling asleep to the hustle of those restless cadences still playing out the dance.

They are inside a Chinese restaurant. From outside, the thick red curtains covered the window. But inside, it's alive with activity as waiters clear and reset tables for the next day, chatting and laughing. The rich smell of meat and five-spice assaults her, reminding her she didn't have dinner tonight.

"Lewis!" An older man, greying at the temples, sits at a corner table among a pile of papers, smiling widely at him.

"That's the landlord," Lewis mumbles. "Be nice."

Kit frowns. As if she wouldn't be. But just to prove the point, she gives the man a shy smile.

He appraises her quickly and turns to Lewis. "New girlfriend?"

"No. This is Kit. She's looking at the empty room."

Charlie casts a slower eye over her now and nods. "You tell her about the rent, okay?" He goes back to his work.

Lewis leads her up the stairs. Even in the darkness, she can see how old and dirty they are. On the second floor, the restaurant smell takes on a different tone. It's stale and embedded. Not horrible, but not pleasant either.

At the top of the stairs, Lewis flicks on a switch, lighting up peeling, dusty walls and a high, stained roof. She looks around doubtfully.

He points at a door. "That's my room." Then he leads her along the landing. The banister feels greasy under her palms. "Now don't get me wrong, Kit Kat," he tells her over his shoulder. "I know this place looks like a shithole, but there are benefits, trust me. And one of them is what could be your room." He pushes open a door and holds out his arm as if to invite her in.

She obediently steps inside. Her mouth instantly opens. "Oh my God."

He grins. "I know, right?"

The room is huge. Like, easily bigger than her mum's apartment—than any flat she has ever lived in. And it's just one room. At the far end, two tall, dirty windows are lit up by streetlights outside, drenching the end of the space in amber light. The ceiling feels a million miles away. A regular ladder wouldn't get you there. Next to her is a loft built from thick, rough-hewn timber. And even though you have to climb a ladder to get to it, the roof is so high you could still probably stand up there without touching it.

"So, what do you think?"

She shakes her head. "I think this room is insane."

Lewis laughs and points to the loft. "The guy who lived here before slept up there."

Kit just nods.

"It could be yours for the asking, if you want me to ask Charlie?"

Kit nods. Of course she wants him to ask Charlie. She walks further into the room, still daunted by the ridiculous dimensions. And the dirt. No one has lived in here for a long time. Even through her sandals, she can feel that the floors need cleaning. But that's nothing a mop and a sweep can't fix.

He shows her through the rest of the apartment. The whole thing is just four rooms and the long landing. He opens the door to his room. It's a regular size.

"How come you don't live in the big one?" she asks.

"I think I got so used to living in tents and nooks and crannies while I was travelling that big spaces weird me out now. I tried being in there, but I couldn't sleep. I guess it's whatever's the opposite to claustrophobia?"

Kit knows she will have *no* problem with that. All she ever wanted when she was growing up in cramped flat after cramped flat was some space. Space from her family, space for her stuff, space to move.

He takes her through to the rooms at the back. "This is where the deal-breakers start coming in," he tells her. The first room is basically empty, with just an old laminex table and two chairs in the centre. And in the corner, a small shelf holding a kettle, a toaster, and some jars of condiments is nailed clumsily to the wall.

"There's no kitchen. Just this," he says.

She shrugs. She eats all her meals at work anyway.

"And then there's this beautiful place." He opens another door and grins. The bathroom is the worst room by far. The walls are a foul purple colour. Both the sink and bath taps seem to be dripping. And the window glass doesn't even entirely cover the frame. Yet, she can also see that a good scrub might drag it closer to habitable. She wrinkles her nose. God, boys are gross. Even boys as sweet and whimsical as Lewis.

"So just how cheap is this cheap rent?"

He names a price so low that she just stands there and blinks furiously at him for a moment. Finally, she says. "As in, that's the weekly price?"

"Nope, the monthly."

"Holy shit."

He grins and folds his arms. "Does that mean you want the room?"

Kit pictures living in that hangar of a room, away from her sister and that cramped flat, able to sleep when she needs to without making her mother tiptoe around her own home. "Hell yes that means I want the room."

"Awesome." He raises his hand to give her a high-five. "Oh, and another thing you should know," he suddenly says.

She drops her hand. "What?"

"Did you notice anything missing from the bathroom?"

She frowns and sticks her head back in. "Oh, where's the toilet?"

He grins. "Downstairs. In the backyard."

She shrugs. "Oh well. For that rent, I'd pee in a jar if I had to."

He grins. "You'll want to some nights, believe me."

CHAPTER 22

Olivia, Ljubljana, Slovenia

Mai's gone all out on this one. She's done her research, asked around, and found out about a club near the river that's hosting an all-night party.

Mai pulls a tight gold dress over some print leggings. "So the plan is we dance until dawn, come back to the hostel, check the internet for our scores, and then we can sleep on the plane to London."

What can Olivia say?

And that's how they all end up in this place. The club is small, but it's packed with bodies. And everyone's dressed like it's summer despite the icy temperature outside. Total denial. Everyone's sweating like it's summer, too, making the air humid and funky. The music is loud, of course, and awful. A relentless, monotonous techno beat that makes her queasy with its thumping bass.

Olivia stands by the bar, in the way but too paralysed by her complete self-disgust to move. What the hell is she doing here? She has zero desire to celebrate anything. Especially not the fact she's basically been a liar for the last few weeks. And all she can think of is the time that is ticking inexorably away. Every minute is dragging her closer to the moment where she finds out just how badly she screwed up. Where Mai finds out she's a loser masquerading as high achievement. Where everyone finds out she doesn't have any of her mother's insight or her father's brilliance.

She was supposed to *kill it* in Year 12. See, Olivia was part of the group who knew the balance. They knew how to party, but weren't too trashy either. And they worked hard too. Because her group prided themselves just as much on having brains and culture and on having some idea of what is going on in the world. For every episode of a crappy soap or reality show they watched, they took in indie films on cheap Mondays. They used chopsticks with aplomb, actually read books, and even tried to comprehend the riddle of politics. They wanted to be known in the small social ecosystem of school, but they also wanted to be worldly.

In their world, an inner-city, highly successful but state-funded high school with some of the best language and arts programs in the state, being able to hold an intelligent conversation was as valuable as being hot or knowing how to party. Of course, there were kids who sat solely in one camp or the other, but her group were the point where hedonism and high achievement met.

Olivia became part of it early and by default, she knew. It was the combination of her mother's literary fame, Olivia's good looks, and the money her parents made that allowed her to dress in the offhand, chic style she had fixed on and stuck with early. None of them were actually attributes of her own making—except maybe her fashion sense. So it always felt kind of like cheating. It also didn't hurt that she got good marks easily and could point out most major cities on a map by the time she started Year 7. All these factors combined got her there without really trying and decided who she would spend the next six years with.

She was never really close to anyone in particular. But because they matched socially, because they did the same classes and got the same results, she became one of them. It was fun, of course, having a gang to hang out with and to laugh and bitch and go to parties with. It was safe. But there were no real, tangible bonds with anyone in there. Everyone paired into best friendships or couples or sometimes both. No one seemed to notice Olivia never really did. Until Will, anyway.

But it's taken until now for any real rift to show. Anything that would demonstrate that her place among them has been purely accidental. But she knows it will become the thing that separates them as the others go to their law course and she is stuck because she couldn't keep up when things got hard. It's so humiliating, the thought of being left behind.

She clutches the corner of the bar as a couple of girls in barely-there dresses shove past her to get drinks. She can't do this tonight. She feels sick and stupid and a little like this is her last night on earth. She wonders how much trouble she would be in if she went back to the hostel.

Mai is on the dance floor already. Every now and then, Olivia catches a flash of her gold dress. She watches her friend dance, loose and happy and confident in what is coming for her. Tam is beside her, dancing her ass off in her jeans and tank, her red ponytail flying out behind her. Olivia's never seen her dance. Maybe with Tam's company, Mai won't notice? Olivia could say she got sick and had to leave.

She wishes Kit were here. Then she'd have someone to talk to. If Kit were here, she'd probably have found a way to tell everyone by now. But she's not and she hasn't. As she gazes around the room, planning her escape, she sights Liza against a wall, clearly struggling but eager to hear whatever the guy talking to her has to say. *Liza.* She doesn't seem like the type to judge. And she doesn't care about results, either. She's already told Olivia she just wants to get into an arts degree and study literature.

Before she can talk herself out of it, she weaves through the mass of bodies. Liza doesn't notice her until Olivia is standing right in front of her. She's too busy laughing at something the guy is saying. Olivia freezes, suddenly uncomfortable. What is she interrupting? What right does she have to colonise Liza's night with her own dramas? Sure, they've become friends, but they're not exactly that close.

She turns to leave, but a hand catches her arm. "Hey, how's your night?"

Olivia turns back to her and shrugs.

Liza's eyes turn instantly worried. "Hey, you okay?" She leans away from the wall, peering at Olivia.

Olivia must look as shitty as she feels. She draws a breath, braving up. "Can I talk to you about something?"

Liza nods, her expression a combination of curious and concern. "Of course."

That's all the permission Olivia needs. She wraps her fingers around Liza's wrist and draws her away from the wall, through the crowds, and out the door.

* * *

Wrapping their jackets and scarves around them, they stride away through the cluster of people outside the clubs. Their shoes clack loudly on the cobblestones as they walk along the embankment in silence.

When they get to the bridge, Olivia's favourite with the fierce fairy tale dragons adorning the end, she pulls herself up onto the wide stone barrier and stares down at the water. Liza follows suit, perching next to her. "What's up?"

Olivia chews on her lip. "We're going to get our results tomorrow, and Mai—and everyone—is about to find out that I fucked up exams." She pauses, but Liza doesn't say a word, just leans in a little closer as if to say she's listening. "And I've been too scared to tell Mai that I already know I'm not going to be getting into Law with her, because she's so excited about it. But now she's going to know, and I'm all freaked out because I really, *really* should have told her already. She's expecting me to be at uni with her and the others next year. *And* she's expecting me to have done as well as her. And I was supposed to have, but..." She pauses and takes in a huge breath. And now she's stopped talking, it's as if she's not so sure how to start again.

"What happened?" Liza pulls her legs up onto the wall and crosses them.

Olivia stares at her hands, tangling and untangling her fingers. "Will happened." She tells her about forgetting to go to his speech night. How instead of watching him as she said she would, she was at home studying for her commerce exam, oblivious to the missed calls on her silenced phone. She describes how he completely lost it when she remembered later that night and rang, contrite and apologising profusely. He called her selfish and self-centred and informed her that she was a terrible girlfriend who never put him first. It was shocking and baffling. She had no idea he felt like that.

When she tried to excuse it as a one-off mistake, it turned out she couldn't, because he had a litany of girlfriend offences to throw at her. He was so hurt. So angry. More than she—even as repentant as she was—thought he deserved to be.

They weren't exactly married. Hell, they weren't even that serious, were they? She just thought they were having fun together. These were things he apparently thought she was neglecting. Things she personally hadn't deemed necessary or even obligations in such a casual relationship. "But apparently, I was way off." She turns to Liza. "Have you ever had that? Where you suddenly realise someone sees your relationship completely differently than you, and you had no idea?"

"Sort of."

Olivia picks up a small white pebble and tosses it into the water. "I felt like such an awful fucking person. Half because of what I did, but half because I couldn't really understand why what I'd done was *so* bad, which made me think I'm probably a complete asshole. Because I was *supposed* to know."

"I guess he was more invested than you. That's not your fault. Unless you tried to make him believe it was like that when it wasn't."

"I don't think I did. But how did I not realise he felt like that?" Olivia stares at the ripples shifting outward from her pebble. Maybe she did, though. Unconsciously. Maybe that's why she always kept him at a purposeful distance.

Liza gives her a helpless smile. "I don't know. Sorry."

"So, anyway, he fired all this at me just before my last two exams. I deserved it, I guess, but I kind of lost it a little with the studying. I had a complete *I'm an asshole who doesn't deserve to exist* meltdown."

Liza frowns as she pulls her hat down around her ears. "But you didn't do anything that bad."

Olivia chews at her lip. "I think my first mistake was getting involved with him at all. I could have just stayed friends with him."

Liza laughs. "Well, you wouldn't be the first person in the world to make that mistake."

Olivia looks at her, curious, but Liza goes on. "So Will goes off at you, you melt down, then you do badly at your last two exams?"

"Yup. That's the pathetic little story in a nutshell."

"And you haven't told Mai or your friends that any of this happened?"

"No. Just Kit. Because she doesn't care. Well, she cares, but not in the way the others will." Olivia sighs. "And now I feel like such an idiot. An idiot for doing badly. But also for not telling anyone. Why did I do that? Why couldn't I have just said something from the start? Now I've basically been lying to Mai. And she's going to find out in the morning."

Liza knocks her shoulder lightly against Olivia's. "You just needed some time to get over it. It hasn't been that long."

"Maybe." Olivia watches a middle-aged couple stop on the bridge. They clasp hands and throw something over the side. It's done with such quiet ceremony that she wonders what it is they threw. They turn back, smiling. "I should have told Mai, though. We've been travelling for ages, and she talks about next year *all* the time. She's got everything mapped out."

Liza snickers. "She really does. Even *I* know all your life plans for the next three years."

Olivia smiles. "Sorry about that."

"You still can tell her. Results don't come out until morning."

"I know, but I'm scared of what she's going to say. Or what she's going to think."

"I hate that feeling. Not knowing how someone is going to react."

"But that's the thing. I probably *should* know what to expect. We've been friends since Year 7."

"Yeah, but knowing someone doesn't mean you know how they're going to react to something new. Because you've never known them in that context. That's precisely the scary part."

"True," Olivia muses. This girl is surprisingly wise.

"But you just have to do it," Liza concludes.

"Do I?" Olivia gives her a winsome smile. "Do I *really*, Lize?" she wheedles.

Liza smiles. "Yes, you do. Because you want to. You know you'll feel terrible if you don't. You *already* feel terrible."

"I know. You're right. I'm just being a baby."

Liza runs her fingers over her bottom lip, staring out at the water. "You know, if it makes you feel better, I had to announce to my parents I was thinking about quitting running *and* that I was gay in the same conversation. And I had no clue how they'd react to either of those things. It was terrifying, but I just *did* it."

Olivia looks up at her, surprised. This is new information. "You're gay?"

Liza nods, her eyes fixed to the view.

"I didn't know that." Olivia smiles. "So I guess I wasn't interrupting anything in there?"

"What?" Liza looks confused for a second. "Oh, the guy in the bar? No. *Definitely* not."

"Good. I feel less guilty about dragging you out here to hear my woes, then."

Liza finally turns and smiles at her. Then her face turns serious. "You know, even if you don't know what Mai's going to say, you just have to do it. And then it's better. It is. I think if you really need someone to know something, it always feels better to tell them, no matter how they respond."

Olivia nods slowly. She stares down at the water passing ceaselessly below them. "And were your parents okay? With the running and the gay?"

Liza tilts her head, running her finger over her lip again. "I'd say they were quietly shocked—on the running count, at least. I get the feeling my mum wasn't so surprised on the gay count. But it was okay."

"You're brave. Much braver than me."

Liza shrugs. "I don't think it was brave. It was just...necessary. How am I going to live in the world if the people around me don't know who I am?"

Olivia nods and wonders where Liza manages to gather up all this insight at their age. Especially since, according to her, she's just been running around an athletics track for the last century. Maybe it gave her plenty of time to think.

Maybe Olivia should listen to her. She pulls in a deep breath. "Okay. I'm going to go back in there, and I'm going to tell her."

"Good."

Olivia lets out the breath. "In a minute."

Liza laughs. "Take your time."

They sit there in a snug silence together, watching the stream of people crossing the bridge from one side of the river to the other, everyone rugged up against the cold. Some stop and take in the pretty scattering of reflections on the water while others trudge quickly, clearly with somewhere to be. Olivia looks up, taking in the colourful buildings and the lights strung out along the riverbank. This place is so achingly pretty despite the cold weather.

She turns to Liza. "Can I ask you something?"

Liza sets her shoulders, as if she's expecting something hard. "Okay."

"Why did you choose to come here?"

She laughs. "Believe it or not, you're sitting on it."

Olivia looks down at the wide flat stone beneath her legs. "What do you mean? The bridge?"

"Yup. I saw a picture of this bridge when I was a kid, on a postcard on my oma's fridge, with the big dragon guards and those beautiful coloured buildings in the background. They came here on holidays once, from the Netherlands. And I remember thinking I wanted to go there one day even though I had no idea where it was. So when we were planning the trip and had to pick a place, I rang up Oma and asked her where it was."

Olivia laughs. "That's random and awesome. I'm glad you did. I would *never* have come here in my life if you hadn't chosen it."

"I'm glad too. I love it." She pulls up her collar. "It's cold, though."

"It is." Olivia jumps off the wall and tugs at Liza's arm. "Come on, let's go. I've made you freeze."

"I don't mind. I hope I said *something* useful."

"You said a lot useful."

They stand there and smile at each other shyly, late night revellers streaming around them. For a fleeting moment, Olivia wonders if Liza is popular with the girls. Probably. She's cute enough. Not to mention, she's sweet as hell and oddly wise for their age.

"Thank you." Olivia reaches for her hand and squeezes it. "For listening to my sad, sorry First-World problems."

Liza lets it go and shrugs. "You're welcome." And she's about to say something else when Olivia's phone begins to ring.

CHAPTER 23

Olivia, Ljubljana, Slovenia

"Goddamn it!" Mai groans loudly. "Two weeks? Now I've got to limp through the rest of this trip?"

The nurse strapping her ankle frowns and places a finger over her lips to quiet her. Olivia smiles wearily from her spot next to the narrow hospital bed.

"I didn't even drink," Mai moans.

Olivia rubs Mai's good leg, sympathetic. Travelling and crutches are probably not going to be a great mix. By the time they rushed back to the club, Mai was outside, her foot propped on a stool, a bleeding cut on her head and a hot tea in her hand. She'd slipped outside the toilets on a spilled drink no one had bothered to clean up.

Tam was with her, surprisingly drunk, and trying to soothe Mai while they waited.

Liza and Olivia quickly divided tasks. Olivia would take Mai to the hospital, and Liza would try and get the obliterated Tam back to the hostel before she passed out.

Mai moans, quietly this time. "I just can't believe I'm such a goddamn klutz. No one else slipped in that puddle. It had to be me! All because I was chasing tail. *Beautiful* tail." She rolls her eyes and sighs loudly. "Oh God, Olivia, you should have seen him. Fucking Slovenian men." She gives the nurse a fearful glance and then grins. "I mean fucking *beautiful* Slovenian men."

The nurse chuckles dryly and pats Mai's leg. "Doctor says lie here. Two hours." She points at the small bandage on Mai's head where she cracked it on a doorframe. "Watch that. She be back to see you. Two hours." She nods curtly at them and leaves.

Mai's eyes are wide. "The doctor's coming back? Shit, she was even scarier than the nurse."

Olivia pats her leg again and grins. Mai looks bizarre in her neon outfit, sprawled against the crisp, white sternness of the hospital bed.

She tucks her arms under her head. "Okay, we have two hours to kill. You better have a good bedtime story, missy."

"You know I don't. We can fill out your insurance papers?" Olivia suggests, holding them up and smiling like a game show hostess.

"Boring." Mai points at the bandage near her temple. "And I have a head injury, remember? I can't possibly concentrate. Try again."

Olivia bites her lip and takes in a slow breath. Maybe the head injury will make it easier.

* * *

Liza, Ljubljana, Slovenia

Tam staggers along the cobblestones and lets out a little groan.

Liza grabs her arm. "You're not going to be sick, are you?"

Tam shakes her head, but Liza draws her closer to the edge of the embankment anyway. Just in case. She hooks her elbow through Tam's, partly to offer comfort and partly to keep her steady. "What's going on?" she asks gently. "You don't usually drink. Well, you don't usually get drunk, anyway."

"My dad's a liar."

"What do you mean?"

Tam just shrugs and continues to lurch along the uneven path.

"He's not sick again, is he?"

"I wouldn't know. Maybe. Maybe not. Matt told me he went to an appointment in the city the other day, but I don't know what it was for. And he never tells me anything, so he could be. Who knows?" She throws up her hands, pushing herself off balance a little.

Liza steadies her. "Can't you just ring and ask him?"

"I did. He hasn't rung back. He hates talking on the phone." Tam pulls her arm away from Liza's and crosses it over the other. She's tottering a little, but not as bad as before. "I don't fucking know, Liza. I shouldn't have come away. Not now. No matter what he said. He's so goddamn useless. He'd probably send me overseas just so he could die on his own."

Shocked, Liza turns to her. "Hey, that's not going to happen. You said he's a lot better. So did Kit. And Matt would tell you if he seemed sick, wouldn't he? And your dad wouldn't do that to you," she adds, even though she has no idea.

Tam doesn't answer. She crosses the embankment toward the hotel.

Liza wishes she knew how to comfort her. But she has no idea how to console someone as self-sufficient and as bruised as Tam. And she gets the feeling that Tam can't be comforted right now, anyway.

Tam stops halfway up the front stairs, resting against the banister. The tide of people going in and out of the hostel is forced to weave around them. She doesn't appear to notice.

"Shit, I'm sorry," she says. She tightens her ponytail and straightens her top, as if she's decided to pull it together. Or as if she's decided to *appear* as if she's pulling it together. "I'm sure he's fine. I'm being a drama queen." She smiles apologetically. It's forced, though. "Sorry you've had to put up with this. This is why I *never* get drunk."

"Don't be sorry. You're worried. And you had a few drinks."

"A few?" Tam laughs, harsh and hard. "I think I had a few just in the first hour." She stares at Liza, her head tipped to one side. "Why are you so together?"

"Me?" Liza's eyes widen. "I'm not together. I'm awkward and shy, and I have no idea how to do normal crap teenagers do. I always feel like I'm that weird home school kid in movies."

Tam cackles and punches her shoulder. "You are nothing like that. Sure, you're a bit shy, but you're awesome. Don't let anyone tell you otherwise." She does a weird inward hiccup and rolls her eyes. "And I am a gross, drunk human who needs to go to bed. No one deserves to have to put up with me. I am going to feel horrible tomorrow." She grins at Liza. "I bet you're really glad you're all buddied up with Olivia now. You won't be forced to put up with me." She checks her watch. "Seven hours until our plane. I'm going to try and catch a few." With that, she turns unsteadily on her feet and walks slowly up the stairs. "Which room are we in again?" she hollers over her shoulder.

"Eight." Liza watches her stumble inside, finishes the climb, and plonks down on one of the couches lining the wide hall. Poor Tam. Poor everyone, she thinks. They're all a bunch of hot messes tonight. Tam and her dad, Olivia and her exam results, Mai and her ankle. No wonder Liza seems together in comparison.

Tam's wrong. She isn't completely together, though. But then Tam doesn't know about this great big stupid—not to mention impossible—crush she's harbouring or how the more she tries to make it go away, the more it seems to occupy her mind. How it makes her do dumb things like sit here on the couch, yawning and waiting for the other two under the pretence of wanting to know if Mai's okay, but really so she can see if Olivia is okay.

* * *

Olivia, Ljubljana, Slovenia

She doesn't summon the bravery until they're in a taxi on their way back to the hostel, Mai's bandaged ankle propped on her lap.

The funny thing is that Mai, bless her, just goes straight into practical mode. Maybe it's the painkillers the doctor gave her, or maybe it's just not as big a deal as Olivia thought. Whatever it is, Mai just starts working the alternatives.

"Okay, so depending on how bad it is, you have two plans: Plan B, you go into Arts/Law, and you get really good results and transfer into pure law after first year. Plan C, you go into the arts degree, do law subjects for as many electives as you can, and then beg for a transfer after first year. They'll at least let you do the combined major. Then you do the law postgrad instead. It'll take a bit longer, but who cares?"

Olivia sits back against the seat and blinks. This was not the reaction she was expecting.

Mai laughs at her baffled expression. "Believe me, I've been thinking about these contingencies forever. In case it happened to me."

"This would *never* happen to you," Olivia scoffs. "You've never got less than a B in your life."

"Neither have you. And look what happened? You just never know. And anyway, it doesn't mean I stopped being terrified it was going to happen. Not with my parents breathing down my back."

Olivia nods. She can imagine. Mai's parents are nice, but they're also kind of scary.

"Okay, confession time."

Olivia smiles. "Isn't it already?"

"True. So here's mine. *I* was so freaked out about exams I kept having these, like... I guess they were panic attacks, where I thought I couldn't breathe and I was going to die. I'd have them all the time. I'd sit down to study, I'd have one. I'd go to the library or the gym, I'd have one. I'd try to sleep at night and I'd have one. And when I wasn't having them, I was terrified I was about to have one. I didn't know what was happening. It was scary."

"Oh Mai." Olivia grabs her friend's hand.

Mai laughs and stares out the window. "They started happening so much during the study break that I stole mum's Medicare card and went to a doctor. I thought maybe I could talk them into giving me some pills or something to chill me out. But instead I got this righteous hippie guy who told me I was too young to depend on pills and that I should take up yoga or meditation."

"What did you do?"

"Nothing. Just sucked it up and did my exams. Haven't had one since."

"Good." Olivia shakes her head, feeling even worse. Mai is so much tougher than her. A guy calls Olivia a selfish asshole and she completely crumbles. Meanwhile Mai's having constant paralysing anxiety and probably still killed it.

Mai squeezes her hand. "So you fucked up. Don't worry. You're *so* smart. One fuck-up won't stop you. If you want to be a lawyer, you'll be a lawyer, Ols, trust me. If not, you'll end up doing something amazing, so who cares?"

Olivia smiles. In all her fear about telling Mai, how did she forget the bit where she's always been steadfast, loyal, and Oprah-level *you go girl.* Of course she's going to be supportive.

"It'd be cool to do Arts/Law, anyway. I wish I could do a combined major," Mai admits. "So I could try some other stuff, but my parents would crack it. I mean what if there's something else out there I want to do? Something that I don't even know about?"

Olivia blinks again. She had no idea Mai even entertained feelings like that. She always thought she was focused on this one thing and that she was going for it come hell or high water.

"Oh well." Mai scoops up the pile of insurance papers in her hand as they draw closer to the hostel. "Too late. I'll take some cool electives."

Too late? Olivia shakes her head. How can they be eighteen and *anything* already be too late? What is wrong with their dumb school system that you are supposed to have what you want to do with your life set in stone before you even begin to have any kind of life? It's so stupid.

She pats Mai's good leg. "I'm so sorry I didn't say anything earlier. Especially when things weren't okay for you. I was just totally humiliated, and I couldn't talk about it with anyone."

"Well, at least you had a reason to freak out. I'm embarrassed I couldn't hold my shit together during my bloody *high school* exams. How am I going to be at uni?" She jabs Olivia's arm. "Please don't tell anyone."

"I won't. But promise you'll tell me if you're freaking out again ever?" She points at her, stern. "Don't do that alone."

"Okay. I promise."

"And promise you won't tell anyone why I failed. I can't believe I let him get to me like that."

"I can't believe you're going to see that loser in London." Mai shakes her head. "I'm officially pissed at Will." She plays with her chunky silver bracelet, looking thoughtful. "I think he must have been completely in love with you, you know. That's the only explanation for the maximum losing of shit."

"Maybe." Olivia doesn't want to think about him any more tonight. She checks her watch. "Results should be up in half an hour. God I feel like such a loser. What will the others say?"

"Who gives a shit? If those bitches back home care, they're not your friends." Mai tugs on her sleeve. "But they won't care, Livs. They all love you."

Olivia smiles and stares out the window. A light fog drifts up from the river. The streets are quieter now as the sky lightens from black to the indigo promise of morning.

Mai digs a finger into her leg. "You know I don't care if you don't get in, right? As long as we're still friends. We don't have to do the same course. We'll still meet for coffee and movies and bitch about our lives and stuff. I just don't want to lose you guys." She laughs. "Maybe you and I can meet up and go to yoga or meditation together. Doctor's orders."

Olivia grins. "Good idea."

And right then, she realises she's never given much thought about the reason for Mai's hyper excitement about them all going to university together. She'd just been putting it down to Mai's usual extreme exuberance over everything. But now she realises it's something more. It's different for Mai, an only child whose parents, from all she's heard and seen, spend their time running their successful business and only come home to hammer home that she needs to become as successful as they are. Coming to school was probably a reprieve for Mai. So were her friends. Mai doesn't have a sister like Anna, or even a friend outside her social group like Kit. All her other family lives in China or Vietnam except an aunt and uncle in Adelaide. She has her school friends and her parents, when they deign to come home. How lonely it must be. No wonder she's clinging to them all so hard. And Olivia decides to let her from now on.

The cab pulls up outside the hostel, which even at this hour is lit up like a beacon. "Come on," Olivia sighs. "Let's go get some internet and face the music."

"Yup. Let's do this thing." Mai picks up her crutches and drops them instantly. She laughs. "As soon as I figure out how to get out of this car."

Olivia giggles. "Hang on a tick, invalid." She quickly pays the cab driver and clambers out the back.

By the time she has come around the car to help Mai and her crutches out, Liza is trotting down the steps towards them. "Thought you guys might need some help. The building has no lift, remember?"

Olivia tips her head back and sighs. "Oh God, that's right." She's already unbelievably tired, and now there are three flights of stairs and a one-legged Mai standing in the way of the few hours of sleep she might be able to snatch before their flight. She shuts her eyes for a moment, gathering the last shreds of her energy.

When she opens them, Liza's already helping Mai hop from the car. She smiles. Thank God for Liza.

CHAPTER 24

Tam, London, England

She misses the call. It takes her too long to recognise the source of the sound disturbing her shaky drift into unconsciousness. Groggy, she lies there and blinks at the now-silent phone, waiting until she is awake enough for the world to make sense.

The trip to London was horrifying. Tam was shaken from her sleep in the dorm by Liza and hustled through check-out, the airport shuttle, and airport security. She's still not sure she woke up or even fully sobered up until they were waiting in the departure lounge for their flight to be called. And with sobriety came the hangover, chased by a tidal wave of nausea. She bolted to the toilets, making it just in time.

On board, she dozed fitfully through the bumpy flight, her head on Liza's shoulder. She wanted to sleep, but she kept waking. It was partly from Liza leaning forward every now and then, excited about the view of the Alps, and partly due to her own invasive self-disgust. It frightened her that she couldn't really remember Mai's accident last night or much about getting back to the hostel. She's never been that drunk in her life. Not even close. And now, with this hangover, she knows why she never will be again.

She pulls the soft sheets up around her neck. The one upside to this day is that Mai's cousin, the one who got them the resort deal in Portugal, came through again, getting them a deal on a hotel in London. Tam cannot believe how grateful she was to be finding her way to sleep in this clean, quiet room high above the clamour of Russell Square. It beats the hell out of riding out a hangover jammed into a bunk bed in another hostel, trying to ignore the sounds and smells of a crowd of people.

All she can see of Mai in the other bed is her bandaged foot raised up on a pillow above the covers, and her crutches abandoned on the floor next to her. A small snore erupts from somewhere under the covers. Total shutdown. Tam is envious.

They were ordered into bed the moment they arrived by a tired, fed-up Olivia. "You two go to sleep." Olivia told them the moment they checked in. She parked Mai's suitcase in the corner of the room. "We non-trashy folk will be in the other room. Text if you need anything."

Tam's never seen her so over it. But then, they are all on minimal sleep, and Olivia had to carry Mai's stuff as well as her own.

"Hey, I held your hair for you on muck-up day, remember?" Mai yelled after her. "So don't you get all righteous!"

Olivia just laughed and closed the door.

And that's the last she saw of them. Now they're probably checking out London while Tam and Mai lie here, good for little more than the tenuous work of cellular repair.

Her vision returned, she stares at the screen of her phone. It doesn't supply the number. But now she's seen this missed call, there is no way she can get back to sleep. She dials voicemail. It's her dad. "Tamo, it's me. Call me back when you can." The sound of his voice wakes her completely. She immediately dials the number, but it rings and rings. She imagines it on the car dash while he works at the orchard, or left by his bed while he watches the news.

She tucks her phone under the edge of her pillow and slides down the bed. What she would give to hang out at home for a night. She wouldn't give up this trip, but she'd love just one night—half an hour even—of sitting on the front porch with her dad and Bill, eating dinner and talking about mundane stuff like the weather forecast and why the salvia should have been pruned shorter last year, or what to do with all the broad beans Bill grew when none of them even like them.

* * *

Olivia, London, England

Olivia and Liza can't be bothered being tourists. They eat a late lunch at a café down the street and then, daunted by their own tiredness and the chaos that is central London, they traipse back to their own room and sleep away the afternoon.

Olivia wakes, confused, to darkness and the sound of peak hour humming somewhere below. Liza surfaces minutes later. They stay put for the night, camping on one of the double beds and eating a picnic dinner patched together from groceries gathered at the small supermarket next door. They drink a glass each of cheap red wine with their food, a late celebration. Olivia did better than she thought. She won't make Law, but she should make Arts/Law.

The combination of wine, exhaustion and good news has given her a buttery, soft feeling. Like things are going to be okay.

The TV is on, but they don't watch it. Instead, they talk. Liza tells her about her ex, a deeply closeted girl from her running team. "It was so clandestine. We barely even spoke. She wouldn't even acknowledge me unless we were alone."

"Sounds like an awesome relationship." Olivia laughs sympathetically. "Though I'm not sure how you actually knew it was a relationship."

"I guess it wasn't, really," Liza says. "It was just sex." She blushes. "She just kind of jumped me one day, on camp. I don't even know how she figured out I'd be into it. Maybe she didn't. She never told me. She's pretty shy." She sips her drink. "I guess I thought she'd start talking to me eventually." She shakes her head. "But no."

"So how long did it last?"

"Five months." Liza blushes again and tightens her ponytail. She's scraped her curly hair right back. She looks older like that. Her eyes seem bigger and her cheekbones more defined. "But the time we spent together would add up to maybe a week?"

"Wow." Olivia shakes her head. And Will thought she was bad at communicating. "That's a long time *not* to talk to each other."

"I know, right? I shouldn't have let it go that long. I shouldn't have let it go a week." She flops back on the pillows, frowning.

"But that stuff is always easier to see later." She should know.

Liza just nods, her eyes fixed to the ceiling.

Olivia changes the subject. The conversation spins to books eventually. She tells her about being constantly asked by teachers about her mother's novels.

"I hate it most when they ask about *Lowlands,* because that's the one that's supposed to be about her actual life. They always ask me how much of the stuff in the book is true. I don't know. I was, like, four when she published that thing. Then Mum and Dad married and they bought a house and Dad started his business. They "grew up", my dad says. Of course, they divorced not long after. Still, my life wasn't like that book at all. Not the parts I remember." She sips her wine. "And it's annoying enough being asked about her all the time without people thinking they know *my* life, too."

"I bet." Liza puts a grape in her mouth and chews it, thoughtful. "I've never read it."

"Me either," Olivia confesses. She's read other books of her mother's, though. There was *The Return* in school, of course. The state curriculum meant she had to, much to her English teacher's discomfort. And she read another once, curious. She thought the books would be somehow familiar, given they're a product of her own mother. But nothing about the worlds she created was recognisable. She didn't expect her mother's writing to move her either. But it did. *Lowlands* probably would though, with its autobiographical bent.

Liza plucks another grape from the bunch. "There was a movie too, wasn't there?"

"Yep. I went from kindergarten to film set for months."

"You were there?"

"Yep. It was filmed where we used to live before Mum and Dad married. Mum's best friend directed it, and Mum consulted on it. We were there every day."

"Was it fun?"

"My memories are good. Lots of Mum's friends were in it. It was loud and like this constant party. Then Dad would come and get us after work and take us to Grandma's house. I always wanted to stay, though."

"Did you understand what was happening?"

"Not that much, I guess." Olivia is actually enjoying telling Liza this stuff. Maybe it's because Liza's interested in *Olivia's* experience of all this, not in her mother's, which is all her teachers and friends' parents have ever cared about. And most of her friends avoid talking about it because they're trying to show they're too cool to care that Olivia's mum is kind of famous.

Liza plays with the edge of a plastic bag, wrapping it around her finger. "You know, I was so embarrassed that time at the airport."

"When?"

"When Mai noticed I was reading your mum's book. I really had no idea."

Olivia laughs. "Don't worry, I know you didn't. You turned bright purple."

"I was so scared you'd think I was trying to show off."

"No." Olivia smiles indulgently at her. Liza's cheeks are pink. She's so cute and awkward when she blushes. "Do you know I've never watched the film? I have it on my computer, but I've never been able to bring myself to watch it."

"Why not?"

"I don't really know. Maybe because then I don't have to answer people's dumb questions about it."

Liza looks incredulous. "You're not curious?"

"Maybe. But I'm also completely weirded out by the idea. I mean, I know it's mostly about Mum, but still. It's some version of *my* life, before I was even aware of it. And it's this story that everyone knows."

"I can't even imagine that."

Olivia rests against the pillows and slowly sips her wine. The urgent voice of a newsreader talks about something to do with North Korea, but she ignores it. She can catch up later. She's enjoying hanging out with Liza.

Finally, Olivia gives her a bashful smile. "Okay, so I *am* kind of curious about the film, though."

"Of course you are." Liza sounds as if she was just waiting for her to admit it. "You have it on your laptop?"

Olivia nods.

Liza leans forward. "Let's watch it. Sate your curiosity. And if you hate it or it's too weird, we'll just stop and watch something else."

Olivia takes in a deep breath and shrugs. "Okay, why not?" she says, letting out the breath slowly.

CHAPTER 25

Tam, London, England

She slides out of bed, tiptoes into the bathroom and shuts the door behind her. She perches on the closed toilet seat and dials home.

This time, he answers after a few rings.

"Dad, it's me."

There's a silence, and Tam isn't sure if it's a delay or just her dad registering her presence on the phone. After a small forever, she hears him again. "Tam, how are you?"

"I'm okay." He doesn't need to hear about the diabolical hangover. Wouldn't *want* to hear about it. "More importantly, how are you?"

"I'm alright. Getting ready for the pick." He goes on, as if everything's normal. "Bill's got this idea we should start a shop and do the whole self-serving picking bit on the orchard for the tourists. Said a mate of his has done it at his place up the east coast. And the folks from big cities in China and Japan love getting the fruit themselves. He says if you get yourselves onto being some part of a day tour from town, you're set. What do you reckon?"

"Sounds good," Tam says hurriedly. She shivers. It's cold in the bathroom. "Matt said you went to town the other day?"

There's another brief silence. "Yep. Had to take Bill down. He's been feeling a bit crook. The doc down here wanted him to see the big doc, just in case."

"And what happened?" Tam grabs a piece of her hair and begins to twirl it nervously around her finger.

"Not much. They're bit worried about his liver. He's going back in for some tests and stuff next week. They'll know more then."

Tam presses her knuckles against the corner of the sink. Why is she always feeling two conflicting feelings at once? Right now it's relief it's not her dad and dread over Bill battling for supremacy.

"You there, kiddo?"

"Yeah, I'm here. I was just thinking. When does he have the tests?"

"Monday. Doc wants to get onto it as soon as possible."

"That doesn't sound good."

"He's probably just being careful. Let's not worry until there's something to worry about."

She pushes her knuckles harder into the cold porcelain. It already sounds like there's something to worry about. She, of all people, knows how good her dad is at playing things down. Tam frowns. "If he's sick, you *better* tell me."

"We'll tell you. Don't worry, Tam."

"I *do* worry, Dad." And before she can stem it, her fears transmute into anger. Because anger's easier than fear. "Because you went and had a whole goddamn operation without telling me. Remember?"

The silence is long. "Love, I was just trying to let you get on with things. You were trying to get your HSC done, you were working. I didn't want you to worry unless we had to."

"Yeah, well, unlike you, I think a cancer diagnosis is kind of a *had-to* point," she says loudly. Too loudly. She hopes she hasn't woken Mai.

"Yeah, maybe you're right. I sh—"

"Maybe?" Tam repeats loudly. "No maybe. I'm right. And if something's wrong with Bill and you don't tell me, Dad, I'll never forgive you. Don't you dare leave me hundreds of fucking miles away not knowing anything, okay?" Hot, bitter tears press at the back of her eyes. "Promise?"

"Alright," he says reluctantly.

"Good. I have to go." She hangs up on him.

Because she has no idea how to go back to normal conversation. She shuts her eyes, the phone still held tight in her hand. Instant contrition sets in. She *never* fights with her dad. It feels awful. And she already feels awful enough today. She unlocks her phone and types a quick apology. She has no idea when he'll see it, but at least she's done it. Now she can sleep. Maybe. She pulls herself from the toilet seat, washes her face, and pads back out into the hotel room.

"Everything okay?" Mai asks from somewhere under her covers.

"Yeah," Tam mutters. "Sorry about that. Go back to sleep." She crawls into her own bed, shuts her eyes and tries not to think about anything.

* * *

Olivia, London, England

The glass of wine helps. Definitely. Because instead of feeling cringe-y and awkward, Olivia's feeling loose and warm as they watch this story of her mother's early adulthood unfold. It's a good film. Great, actually. She can see why it's become cultish. So perfectly does it capture the fine line everyone seemed to walk in that crazy, creative scene she was a part of—the line between love and fear, addiction and dependence, opportunity and crisis. If the book is anything like this, she can understand why people of her mother's generation speak about it with such reverence. Even if you never lived in a world like this one, in this wild, bohemian household, dancing on the fringes of society, there's something so familiar about the way the characters are living out their youth.

Maybe Olivia's not quite there yet, but she knows it's telling some kind of universal truth about early adulthood. And watching it, she feels one of those rare bursts of pride in her mother, in her ability to articulate these nameless things. Usually she's too busy being purposefully blasé and occasionally annoyed about her mother's fame to recall the simple fact of how talented she is. To be able to admire her.

Just over halfway through the film, there is a tense scene in the kitchen. It's the start of the household falling apart. A child sits in the corner on a man's lap, playing with a painted paper butterfly, oblivious to the ruptures about to impact her life in the film. Olivia is shot to awareness by a complete recall of this moment. The sounds of the argument being played out around her as she played with the hand-painted cardboard figure. The smell of Ed's leather jacket, laced with tobacco and aftershave and a thousand venues played. The tingling numbness in her feet as they hung, marooned above the sun-cracked linoleum.

She remembers all of this. Apart from knowing she was in a scene. She must have known at the time. She must have been told she was pretending to be someone else's child being told to be quiet during the dialogue. She must have realised they were playing out the same scene over and over for retakes, surely. But somehow it's lost its spot in the crowded memories of her childhood. She holds her breath and watches a six-year-old version of herself play someone else's silent child.

Before she summons the bravery to admit what she's just realised and say quietly "That's me," the scene changes to a shot of a woman singing on a beach.

Liza sits up, eyes wide. "What? Where? You didn't say you were *in* it."

"In the last scene, in the kitchen. I forgot. Or I never knew. I don't know." She shrugs helplessly, still stunned by her forgetting.

Liza immediately presses her finger on the trackpad and rewinds. "I want to see."

Olivia shrugs as she drains the last of her glass of wine and pours another. She's going to need it. Liza leans forward, grinning, as the scene starts. Eyes wide, she points at the short-haired, scruffy little girl. Her grin is teasing.

"Yep, that's me." She says it drily, playing casual to hide her embarrassment.

Liza presses pause, staring at the still, blurred image of Olivia, and laughs. "You were so little and cute! But you don't remember?"

"I do remember sitting there for hours, on Ed's lap. He told me this long, convoluted story about the butterfly I'm holding. But I don't remember knowing I was in the film. I'm sure I did. I just don't have the memory." She leans forward and giggles, pointing. "Oh God. Look at my big buck teeth!"

Liza wraps her slim, brown fingers around Olivia's arm and shakes it gently, giggling. "They're so cute. What happened to them?"

Olivia runs her finger over her straight front teeth. "Peter McFarlane came up in Grade 5 and asked me if I could spare two bucks." She flushes. "And when I realised where that joke was going, I went home and begged for braces. That's what happened to them."

They laugh. Loud and long, in that way you do when it's not because something's that funny, but because you've found someone who laughs at the same dumb things as you.

Olivia's finally laughter slows to a smile. "I'm not sure what was worse, though. The buck teeth or the three years of having food and crap stuck in my braces. That was *not* pretty."

"Well, you're incredibly pretty now," Liza says. Then she turns bright red, and her teeth come down hard on her bottom lip.

Olivia stares at her, charmed *and* thrown.

Still blushing wildly, Liza gives her a flicker of a glance and then stares at her drink. "Sorry, I didn't mean... I mean, I might be a little bit tipsy." She holds up her glass and then deposits it on the bedside stand as if to be rid of it. "And that sounded like I was—" she fades out and purses her lips, looking flustered.

But the funny thing is, Liza's mortification just makes Olivia smile. It brings on a sweet rush of a feeling— one she couldn't describe if she had to. And before Olivia is even aware she's going to do it—before she even registers she *wants* to do it—she leans forward and pushes a kiss onto Liza's frowning mouth. And just as quickly, she draws back a little, hearing the sharp intake of Liza's breath.

The air stills around them. Olivia tenses for a reaction, but Liza says nothing. Doesn't even move. Her stomach starts to churn. Was she reading this all wrong? Was she reading anything at all? Still, the wine keeps her on the right side of brave. She takes a hold of Liza's wrist and asks a question that comes out in a tentative whisper. "Was that okay?"

The question hangs there for a moment, and then Liza tips her head to the side, looking deliberately thoughtful, as if considering whether it was okay or not. And Olivia can't tell if she's being serious or teasing.

"I don't know," Liza tells her, completely straight-faced. "You better do it again."

And even though she still has no idea if Liza is teasing her, Olivia does as she's told. Because having done it once, she seems to want to do it again, to fulfil the curiosity that one impulsive kiss has presented. She moves in slowly this time, wrapping her fingers gently around Liza's other wrist as she leans closer, hearing the automatic slowing of breath between them. She takes her time now, testing it out, indulging in the renewed press of their lips. She inhales Liza's light, vanilla-sweet fragrance. That scent is already insinuating itself into her memories of this kiss.

When she draws back, her pulse is working so hard, she can feel her blood moving through her whole body. She didn't see this one coming. And she has no idea what she's doing, but she knows that right now, she wants to be doing it. She looks nervously at Liza.

Liza's expression makes sense this time. First it's surprise, and then half a breath later, it's a playful smile accompanied by a slow, teasing shrug. "Yeah, it was *okay*, I guess."

And Olivia's laughing when Liza leans in to kiss *her* this time, curling an arm around her neck and drawing her back against the pillows.

CHAPTER 26

Kit, Melbourne, Australia

Kit lies spread-eagled on her mattress, staring up at the city haze sky through the dusty windows. Her windows look like bifocals, half-clean and half-dirty. She's managed to clean the bottom panes by climbing out onto the wide windowsill with a wet sponge, but the top section is too high to reach.

It doesn't matter. She's in heaven anyway, lying here in this peaceful cathedral of a room while the world barrels along the street below. The cars and trams are noisy as hell. So are the drunk people screeching all the feelings into the night until late. But there's something about hearing the noise while being totally separated from it that makes her feel even more tranquil.

She's making the leisurely drift back to sleep when there's a tap on the door.

"Come in." It can only be Lewis. The landlord never comes up here.

She hears his footsteps behind her but doesn't move. He guffaws loudly. "I love what you've done with the place!"

She giggles and looks around. What she's done with the place is precisely nothing. Well, aside from a fiendish clean. Then she dragged up her futon, a small set of drawers, a lamp, and a rug her mother gave her, a pretty, green, Persian-style thing.

She didn't put the mattress up to the loft like Lewis said the last tenant did. Instead, she's placed it in the dead centre of the room. Then she laid the rug and the lamp next to it. She loves having the bed like this, unmoored and tiny in this vast space. At night when the lamp is on, and she's lying within the radius of its beam, watching something on her laptop or just dreaming, she feels like she's on her own personal island.

Lewis is clutching his laptop in one hand and a coffee in the other. "Hey, do you mind if I sit on your windowsill and Skype my mate? Internet's being wiggy."

"Of course." She waves a hand lazily at the window and yawns. She half-listens to him chatting and laughing to someone on his computer and stretches her legs out. She likes living with him so far. He treats everything like an adventure, even the mundane stuff like shopping and cleaning. It's a radical shift from sharing with her insane sister.

She wriggles her toes under the sheet, feeling decadent and rested. She doesn't start at the café until midday, so she's got a little bedtime in her yet. Especially given she's working double shifts all weekend. She's worked so much that she'll have the Statuegate repair paid off by the end of next week. Then she's going to start saving.

"Hey Kit," Lewis calls. "Come here for a sec. Meet my friend, Daniel."

She sighs. Does she have to? She's about to pose that question when he starts beckoning enthusiastically from the windowsill.

"Alright." She inches out of bed and wanders over, stretching. The sun is hot and bright over by the window. She leans out the window and squints at the screen. A floppy-haired blonde boy with a baby face and blue eyes smiles at her. "Hey, Kit. So how're you putting up with Lewis, then?" He has an English accent, the clipped, friendly kind that makes her instantly attracted to a guy, no matter what he's actually like.

She smirks. "Just."

"Hey," Lewis protests.

"Just kidding." She pats his arm affectionately. "I love him to pieces. So, where are you?"

"Ukraine."

"No way. I thought you were going to say Canberra or Sydney or something. What are you doing there?"

"Working in an orphanage. In the west."

Kit nods. Not that it makes much difference to her that he's in the west. She couldn't point Ukraine out on a map if she had to. But she doesn't tell him that.

"Away from the fighting," he adds.

Again, she's forced to simply nod. She's going to have to pick up a newspaper someday soon. And to think just yesterday she was showing off about knowing where Slovenia is. No one at the café had even heard of it. Now she feels clueless all over again, her usual state when it comes to geography.

"I was going to go with him," Lewis tells her. "But I couldn't organise my visa from Spain because my passport was due to expire. So I came home. I might try again in a few months when I've saved."

Daniel flicks on a light. There is a shelf of books behind him and thick, green curtains covering the windows. "You'd love it here, man," he tells Lewis. "The people are pretty nice, once you get used to the whole no-smiling thing. The kids are nuts. Mostly good nuts," he adds with a grin.

"What's the orphanage like?" Lewis asks.

"It's better than most, apparently. The director does a lot of international fundraising stuff. They get a lot of donations from religious groups in the States. I think I'm the only non-Christian to ever darken their doors. I mean, the place is really run-down, and they can't afford to do everything they need to fix it. And the place stinks like bedwetting and rising damp, but the kids are looked after, and the teachers here are pretty good."

"What do you do?" Kit leans her elbow on the windowsill, intrigued.

"Assisting in English classes, mostly, and wherever else I can help. The director really wants the kids to get the language down so they have a chance at getting a job later. Here, when these kids turn sixteen, the government turfs them out onto the street and they have to figure it out for themselves. A few are supported for longer if they go to a vocational college or something, but not many. Then you just have to hope they stay safe and away from drugs and trafficking and all kinds of dangerous crap." He shrugs, looking weary.

Kit nods. They're so lucky in Australia.

He goes on. "Andrei tries to find them places to live and work, but he can only do so much." There's a banging noise behind him. "Hang on a sec." He calls out something in what Kit assumes is Ukrainian. A door behind him opens and two boys stick their heads in, grinning.

They say something to him. It's in English, she thinks, but the computer's microphone doesn't pick it up.

Dan laughs and waves them away. "No way!" he shouts. "Nyet!"

The kids just laugh and slam the door behind them.

Daniel turns back to them and grins. "Two of the nuttiest."

"They look cute. Do you get paid much for this?"

He laughs and shakes his head. “God, no. I don’t get paid a cent. It’s all voluntary. I stay with one of the staff member’s families in town, and I pay for all my own food and stuff.”

“How long will you work there?”

He shrugs. “I don’t know. Six months at least. Maybe a year? As long as I can take it. It can be a little bit depressing sometimes. Some kids have been through some seriously horrible shit.”

Kit nods, though she doesn’t know.

“We’re hopefully taking them down to a camp in the summer, if we can get enough volunteers. I want to stay for that. It looks beautiful, and I kind of want to see them have some fun.”

“That’s really, really cool.” She is completely impressed by this guy. She checks her watch. “Crap, I have to get ready for work.” She smiles and waves at Daniel. “It was really nice to meet you.”

He smiles. “You too, Kit. See you.”

She gives him one more wave, and makes a run for the shower.

CHAPTER 27

Olivia, London, England

Sunlight knifes under her eyelids, bringing her to waking. As consciousness kicks in, she feels the shifting of a body next to her, and the covers lifting. She opens her eyes enough to see Liza stand and pull on a T-shirt. Olivia rolls over, her bare skin sliding over the sheets, and watches Liza escape the bed. She makes it a couple of steps before she trips on the corner of the other bed, stubbing her toe.

"Shit." She sits down and rubs her foot.

Olivia can't help herself. "That was pure elegance."

Liza looks up and smiles wearily. "Yep, I'm like a gazelle, they say." She yawns into her hand. "Need the bathroom?"

She shakes her head. Liza limps into the bathroom and shuts the door.

Olivia rolls onto her back. Well, Liza seems to be pretty normal about this. That's good, she guesses. She hadn't really thought about what to expect from this morning. But then, Olivia hadn't really expected to *have* to think about what to expect this morning. So you know, it looks like she still has a lot to learn.

She definitely learned plenty of new information about Liza last night. Not that she's ever given it a second's thought, but she wouldn't have expected Liza to be so confident and alive in bed. But now maybe she's realising that you shouldn't assume shyness automatically goes hand-in-hand with a lack of confidence.

She didn't expect it would be so easy either—in a good way. Sometimes when she's sleeping with someone for the first time, it just kind of feels like two people having sex in the same place. Less like having sex *with* each other and more like sex *at* each other. It's like a physical version of an awkward first-date conversation. But last night wasn't like that. It was like they were both present and were acknowledging they were present, laughing and checking in with each other, like they'd been doing this much longer. And somehow, that made it hot and weirdly fun.

She didn't expect to laugh either. But that's how quickly they relaxed into it. The first time was when things began to turn into something heated, serious. As they lay across the bed and kissed, Liza's hand began to smooth its way up and down Olivia's belly and ribs, but never seemed to stray any higher. Then it stopped altogether, with her fingers splayed over the base of Olivia's ribs. As she slid her leg over Liza's in the urgency of the moment, all Olivia could think was how desperately she wanted to animate that hand, to coax it out of its reticence. But it didn't move. Unsure if Liza was simply too shy, she put up with it for a while. But then it became too much. Or really, too little.

Frustrated, she decided to lead by example and boldly slid her hand straight up Liza's singlet, moving her hand over the cup of her bra. Liza gasped slightly, broke from their kiss, and sat up over her, grinning. "And here I was being all polite." Her voice was husky and teasing. She leaned over Olivia, kissed her, and laughed again. "My mistake. Sorry." And with that she grabbed the bottom of Olivia's T-shirt and began to slide it upward, dropping the kind of decadent kisses over her stomach and ribs that made Olivia's responding giggles quiet instantly. There wasn't a trace of reticence after that.

It was surprising and a little confronting. Surprising because Olivia wasn't expecting anything like that to happen...well...*ever*, and confronting because Olivia never expected she would be the one to instigate it.

But will it stay fun? This is what she wonders as she listens to the shower sounds in the next room. Because this has the potential to become super awkward. She shuts her eyes and runs a hand over her forehead. Will this be another one of her disaster one-night-stands? Where she can't shake it—or them—off? It certainly has all the makings of one: sleeping with a girl who is travelling in a small group with her, with nearly two weeks to go. What could go wrong?

She lies there dwelling in her own dumbassery. What made her do this? And with Liza? But before she can question herself any further, the bathroom door opens. Olivia flicks a switch to normal, and tries to exude an air of casual, like last night wasn't a big deal. Which, of course, it wasn't. Liza doesn't have to know that Olivia is not usually in the habit of sleeping with girls or even of making the first move. That can be her little secret.

Liza pulls a tangle of clothes from her case. Her bare brown shoulders are wet, and her hair hangs in a dripping mess down her back. It's the closest Olivia's ever seen to it hanging straight. Liza throws some clothes onto the end of her bed and turns, running a brush through her hair. She gives Olivia an amused look. "Well, last night escalated quickly."

Olivia lets out a small shotgun of a laugh. But she blushes too. Then her gaze flicks back to Liza, not really sure where to go from here.

Liza studies her for a moment. Olivia can feel her face turn redder. She breathes slowly, trying to stem it.

"You okay?"

"Yeah, of course," Olivia mutters, immediately defensive. Why wouldn't she be? She attempts an offhand smile. "Of course," she says, softer this time.

"I'm assuming we'll be keeping this one quiet?"

"Probably best, yeah?"

Liza nods. "So, do you think the others could figure it out if they walked in right now?" Liza asks, tying her hair back into a tight ponytail.

"Mai would wonder what was up."

"Why?"

"Well I don't usually sleep naked. Not when I'm sharing a hotel room with someone I don't know that well, anyway."

"Right, of course." Liza steps over to Olivia's case and pulls out the oversized singlet she often sleeps in. She holds it up, smiling. "Want?"

"Thanks," Olivia mumbles. She catches it and sits up. While she pulls on the singlet under the sheets, Liza drops her towel and begins to get dressed. Olivia can't help blushing at her fleeting nudity. Which she knows is dumb, because she spent plenty of time up close and personal with that very nudity last night.

Why does Liza seem so much more relaxed than her? When she was the one who admitted last night she's only ever slept with one other person in her life? But here she is swanning around half-naked, casually wondering out loud if anyone will catch on to their drunken hook-up.

Olivia contemplates what would happen if Mai did guess what went down last night. "I think I'd be in big trouble."

"Why?"

"Oh, you know. What's that stupid saying—don't shit where you eat?"

Liza frowns. "I think that's what you say when someone sleeps with their boss."

"Oh." Olivia makes a face. "And now I think you think I have done us both a disservice by using not only the wrong analogy but a gross one."

Liza chuckles and zips up her jeans. "Yeah, well, I'm mortally offended."

"I apologise." Olivia smiles and tries to comb the worst of the tangles from her hair with her fingers. "But you see where I was going, right? The whole 'don't screw the crew' thing."

"Yeah, I see where you were going." Liza pulls her tank top down and smiles at her. "Well, now we're both kind of dressed. Are we Mai-safe?"

Olivia waves a hand between the two beds and raises an eyebrow. "Notice any difference?" Hers is a whorl of sheets and bedspread, while Liza's is an impeccable specimen of four-star hospitality.

"Oh. Yeah. That *might* give it away." She picks up the covers and ruffles them a little.

Olivia laughs. "Now that looks *exactly* like someone picked up the sheets and made a half-assed attempt to ruffle them to pretend they slept in them. Bet you never pulled this trick on your parents to convince them you were home all night."

"Nope, I definitely didn't." This time, Liza rips the covers back and climbs bodily into the bed. She wriggles around, kicking the sheets up. Olivia laughs at her extreme thoroughness.

"Better?"

"Better." Olivia hauls herself out of bed, grinning.

"Okay, anything else? You seem to be the expert in covering of tracks." Liza puts her hands on hips. Her smile is wry and teasing.

They stand there, locked in what she is certain is mutual amusement and relief at finding this morning so un-awkward so far. And suddenly Olivia finds herself debating just how stupid it would be to kiss her again right now in this new light of day. Right when they're working so hard to make sure last night is safely sealed into yesterday.

That's the duel she's fighting when, luckily, there's a loud rapping on the door.

Liza eyes widen, and she grins. Olivia quickly scans the room, spots the two wine glasses on her bedside table. "I'll just be taking these with me." She grabs them and slides past Liza. She hears a quiet chuckle as she shuts the bathroom door behind her.

As she rinses the glasses, she hears Mai. "Thank God you're awake," she whines. "Tam's gone somewhere, and I can't get my bloody sock on over this dumb bandage. Help!"

Olivia smiles. It looks like they're going to get away with it. She turns on the hot water and slides under its bracing jets.

CHAPTER 28

Liza, London, England

Liza doesn't quite get London. Sure it's fine, and she likes the accents and the free galleries and that statue with the horses leaping out of the water she saw from the cab the other night. But other than that, she's just not sure what the fuss is about. Of course, it's only their first proper day. She can't really count yesterday, when they barely left their hotel room. But already she can see that it doesn't have the same erratic charm as so many of the other cities they've visited so far. Maybe if it had been the first European stop these stately old buildings and the palace might seem interesting to her. Beautiful even. But she's popped her ye olde architecture cherry. And now they just seem kind of bland and reserved after the extravagance of Italy and Portugal.

And everyone seems so fierce here, so intent on getting places. It feels like negotiating the city streets is a cutthroat battle everyone is waging but no one can actually win. It's cold too. Nowhere near as cold as Slovenia, but she hadn't factored in the rain. All morning it has fallen in a slow, steady drizzle, forcing them to huddle under umbrellas. Well, to wield umbrellas would be more accurate. The battle for overhead space is even fiercer than the one for footpath.

They eat a late breakfast and then decide to head to a gallery. Olivia doesn't come. She's gone to see one of her mother's old friends for lunch.

Mai's a total trouper at the Tate, which is full-to-bursting with every other tourist trying to avoid the weather. She limps around, negotiating the crowds and cramming herself into the packed lifts between the floors.

"Aren't you exhausted?" Liza asks as Mai pauses for a moment, breathless, in the middle of a passageway between rooms.

"Yep. My ankle hurts, my arms hurt, even my hands hurt from these things." She slaps the padded handgrips. "But I don't care. I'm going to see a Warhol. A goddamn real Warhol, Liza!"

Liza tips her head to the side. "But isn't the whole Warhol thing that he kind of got everyone to do his work for him? So is it really a *real* Warhol?"

"Don't know." Mai starts swinging down the hall. "And I do not care. Let's go."

There's one thing you can never fault Mai on, and that's her enthusiasm. She looks for Tam. She's dragging her feet behind them, frowning. "You okay?" Liza's starting to feel like camp counsellor with all this checking in on everyone.

Tam gives her a small smile. "Yeah. I'm okay." She bumps shoulders with Liza. "What about you?"

For a fleeting second, Liza wonders if she knows about last night. But there's no way she could. "Me? I'm fine." They follow Mai into a room dominated by a giant wire and blue glass installation.

Liza stares at it. She doesn't really understand sculpture. Especially the abstract stuff. They don't make her think or feel anything, even though they're probably supposed to, so she just feels dumb and unsophisticated. There have been other things here that have moved her. Earlier, on the first floor, she'd been completely transfixed by a short video about a mayor who transformed his poverty-stricken city just through painting all the buildings vivid colours. People started taking pride in their city, and visitors came from everywhere to see the buildings. A "utopia of colour", he called it. *That* made her feel something. This lumpy pile of glass and wire just makes her think, *Wow, that's big. And blue.* And she's pretty sure that's not what she's supposed to be thinking.

Feeling like a totally failed gallery-goer, she leans against the wall and yawns into her hand. Olivia would have liked that video too, she thinks. And just like that, her mind's on last night.

Last night was amazing. All kinds of amazing. But she still has no idea how or why it happened. She follows the others through the crowds into another sculpture-packed room. She wanders between the artefacts, pretending to examine them, but her mind is completely elsewhere. Because she slept with Olivia last night. *She slept with Olivia.* Shocked doesn't even begin to describe how she feels about that, though she thinks she did a reasonable job of hiding it this morning.

Even when she began to feel those awkward, crushy feelings for Olivia back in Italy, she knew straight away that it was one of *those* crushes. Those futile, distracting ones you have on No Chance Girls. The kinds of girls everyone notices: hot and *taken* because they're never available to people like Liza, even when they are. They're the stylish, attractive ones from school or the street who are just biding time between hipster boys with perfect facial hair. Or they're the pretty, geeky girl in the bookshop who likes the same books as you. Or the cute girl behind the coffee machine with the twinkle in her eye, and it takes you a while to realise it's a twinkle she has for *everyone*. The ones who only ever seem to like boys. Or even if they don't, Liza's too damn shy and awkward to find out otherwise, because they seem too far out of her league in the first place.

Liza wishes she wasn't such a clichéd sucker for *that* girl. But she is. She's always harbouring a crush on at least one of them at any given time. Maybe if she knew any actual lesbians, she might be crushing on them too. But the only one she knows is so deeply closeted she couldn't find her way out with a torch and a map.

But Liza has always known the conditions of her infatuations too. It's never been about *getting* those girls. Because she never for a second thought she would. They are what they are, and she is who she is: a quiet, geeky lesbian-in-training with crazy hair and no social credentials. And besides, she knows these straight-girl crushes are probably just something that happens when you're gay and the majority of the people around you aren't. They are and have always been frustrating yet delicious distractions for her to ponder while she goes about her day, hoping one day she'll meet someone who she can actually have valid—and reciprocated—feelings for.

And she knows that this is not Olivia. Olivia, with her prettiness and her cool chick résumé, was slotted immediately into *that* category of girl. No chance at all. But now, in some crazed topsy-turvy London land, they've gone and slept together. And now it's going to be even harder to tuck this crush tidily back into the No Chance category, because Liza is stuck feeling a whole big bunch of feelings. Because she learned all kinds of things you can't unlearn last night about Olivia. Like how the curve of her lower back feels under her palm. Or how pale the skin of her belly is in comparison to the rest of her body. Or the way her breath catches slightly when you kiss her throat.

And it wasn't just the sex part that's thrown her either. The sex she can, at a push, slot into the too-much-to-drink and vulnerable category of one-night-stands. The most confusing part is the rest. The way they talked to each other, both before and after. The way it was all so *easy*. Everything about last night was fun and funny and strangely sweet. And it's that intimacy they found so easily that's going to make it hard to shake off.

And there's the bit where Olivia instigated it. Sure, Liza made that dumb comment about her being pretty. Still, Olivia's reaction is nothing less than perplexing.

It's too much like it was with Alika. She still remembers her shock that night it first happened. It was one of the first hot, muggy nights of the year, and they'd been training all day. It was after dark, and they were supposed to be in their rooms at the training camp, but it was too stuffy in the bunkrooms. Instead, tired but restless, they were walking around the grounds. Liza remembers being surprised that Alika was even talking to her, telling her about her large, very religious family at home in Melbourne, and about migrating here. Before this, Liza had known nothing about her.

When they'd done a full circuit of the grounds, they sat down on a rock under a tree and talked. That's when it happened. Liza was telling her about something to do with training or school when Alika just leaned in and kissed her. It was fierce and feverish and, as stunned as she was, Liza went with it. Because even though she'd pretty much figured out she was into girls by then, they weren't exactly lined up at the door to do *this*. And *this* was kind of irresistible, in a way it had never been with the few guys she'd kissed.

They never spoke about it, but whenever they were alone, it only took minutes until Alika would be pressed up against her, urgent. She always thought that Alika would talk to her eventually, would acknowledge the *them* that had been created, however superficially. But she didn't.

And even with no thread of a relationship between them, it wasn't hard to be physically attracted to this striking, big-eyed girl with her ropes of black hair and long, toned limbs. And over time, there were feelings. Because Liza has discovered she's not the kind of person who's able to do these kinds of things without developing at least some kind of sentiment. And she assumed that the same was happening for Alika. Now, with the benefit of hindsight, Liza realises that Alika was simply testing something out about herself. Liza was just the control group.

And now here is Olivia grabbing and kissing her out of the blue. It feels uncomfortably familiar. Only with Olivia, Liza has no clue about her motivations. She seems pretty damn straight. And there's that Will guy to back that theory.

Liza knows last night probably means nothing to Olivia. Still, she'd love to know what made her do it. Maybe it was some tipsy, straight girl experimentation. And Liza *did* leave the door wide open for that with her dumb comment about Olivia's looks. Maybe she was just flattered into kissing her? Or maybe she's kind of open-minded and was just scratching an itch?

Whatever it was, Liza's not an idiot. The one thing she knows is that there is no way it was the same thing for Olivia as it was for her. That's why, from the moment she woke with Olivia's arm pressed against her back, she knew exactly what they would be doing this morning. Sealing over last night into the drunk, slightly regrettable past so they could move on from this aberration in the social order. And she dutifully played her part to help put things back to the normal she was positive Olivia would want.

Still, even as she prepares to act like everything is fine, she keeps being overwhelmed by a small flood of sensation when she thinks of last night. It's not just that sensory memory of sex, an echo of that physical pleasure. It's everything else, too. She and Alika never had one single conversation or even exchanged a smile that was as close to being that deep or affectionate. And it's those parts that make Liza feel as bereft as the sex. But Olivia doesn't need to know any of this.

She's yanked back to the gallery by Tam's hand on her arm. Mai has parked herself down on a bench seat, leaning against a window overlooking the brown Thames as it glides between rows of self-important buildings. She looks exhausted and grumpy, bereft of her gung-ho attitude of half an hour ago.

"Sorry," she mutters. "I'm getting really tired. I think I'm going to find me a Warhol and then go. This bloody ankle."

"Of course," Liza says, sympathetic.

"I can't believe you made it this far," Tam adds admiringly.

"You guys can stay, though." Mai hauls herself to her feet. "I'll go back to the hotel."

"No way." Tam shakes her head. "It's raining, and the Tube will be impossible on your own. We're coming, aren't we, Lize?"

"Of course." She's missed half the gallery already, what with her brain being on high Olivia rotation. What does it matter if she misses the rest?

Mai smiles wearily, running her hand through her black hair. "Thanks, guys. I'm so sorry."

"The perils of chasing tail on slippery floors, hey?" Tam says.

"Don't remind me. I would have landed him, too." Mai limps off.

They find her a Warhol and head back to the hotel in a taxi. Liza stares at the rain-slick street, full of hurrying pedestrians, and the shops decorated with lights and trees. Christmas is only two weeks away. People juggle shopping bags and wrapped packages under large umbrellas, looks of grim determination on their faces.

As they near the hotel, she's struck by a thought. It's probably going to be incredibly awkward to share a room with Olivia tonight. She knows she can play normal. Hell, she pulled it off this morning. But that's not going to stop it from feeling weird.

Her problem is solved by Mai, anyway. When they get back, Mai hops straight into Liza and Olivia's room to see if Olivia is back from lunch. She is. Mai immediately drops her crutches, throws herself down onto Liza's bed, and lies down with a huge sigh. "Thank God!"

Liza follows, bringing in Mai's daypack.

It's immediately obvious that Olivia's in a weird mood. She doesn't look at anyone as she folds her clothes and listens to Mai's chatter about their day.

Mai interrupts her own rant. "Hey, how was Will?"

Olivia just shrugs and balls up a pair of socks.

Tam clears her throat. "Um, I'm going to go and get a coffee. You want to come, Lize?"

"Sure."

As they walk down the passage, Tam turns to her. "Seemed kind of tense. I thought maybe Olivia could use some space."

Liza nods.

Tam grins. “Can’t do anything about Mai, though.”

The drizzle has stopped, so they wander around with takeaway coffees warming their palms, checking out the small parks and the shops. Here in Bloomsbury, Liza lets herself love London a little bit. Only because they’ve entered Virginia Woolf territory.

They don’t hear from the others until dinnertime. They’re curled up in Tam’s room when Olivia knocks on the door.

“Hey.” She’s smiling now, which brings Liza more relief than it probably should. “We’re thinking of getting some pizza and eating it here. Mai’s still pretty sore and tired. I’m tired too.” She doesn’t look at Liza.

“Me three.” Tam jumps off the bed. “I’ll go with you to get it. I need to grab some phone credit.”

“Sure,” Olivia says through a yawn. She runs her fingers through her hair and gives Liza a small smile as she waits for Tam to pull on her boots. “What do you like on pizza, Lize?”

Liza can’t help blushing slightly. “I don’t mind. I like most things.”

Olivia nods, her gaze lingering on her thoughtfully for a moment before she turns for the door, Tam at her heels.

Liza goes in to check on Mai. She’s got her foot up on a pillow and her iPad in her lap. “I just talked to my parents.” She rolls her eyes. “That was fun.”

“Now I know you’re lying.”

Mai cackles and tosses her iPad onto the mattress next to her. “Hey, do you mind if I stay in here with Olivia tonight? She’s kind of wigged after today.”

Liza nods, ignoring the small trickle of disappointment. “Of course.”

CHAPTER 29

Hey Anna,

So guess what? I finally pin Will down to a time and place to meet. I figure out the Tube and the map and get to this café he picked, but then he doesn't even show. And when he finally answered my messages on FB an hour later, he was all like, "Oh sorry, had to work through lunch." That's it. Not even a sorry. Like it was no big deal. Like I haven't come from a zillion miles away.

Of course, I wanted to say "Well couldn't you have let me know that a bit earlier?" but I didn't. He's being such an asshole. Instead I just said fine and organised another time. Because if I get all pissy, he might never meet me, and then we'll never sort this out.

God, Anna, why do I need things to be okay with him so bad? I mean, I don't want to be with him. I just don't want things to be so shitty between us. Or am I just being some selfish ass who can't bear someone thinking badly of them? Sometimes I think maybe I am. But I don't know how to do it any other way.

So I'm going to not be angry, and I am going to reschedule to have a civilised beer with him in a couple of days and hopefully convince him he doesn't have to hate me and that we can still be friends.

Sigh. Sorry for unloading. I hope you're all good. Give Ally and Henry kisses for me, and tell Steve to do the dishes.

Love you.

Olivia

* * *

Kit, Melbourne, Australia

All Kit can see ahead is a packed work roster, short sleeps, and impossibly early mornings. And even though she has a new, amazing place, is now almost debt-free, and will be able to cut her shifts back soon, it's all kind of bringing her down *right now.*

She clutches her cup and watches her mum scratch a twenty-cent piece across the small scratchie card. Annie's motions are slow and deliberate, as if her meticulousness might increase her chances of winning a prize.

They're sitting out on the teeny balcony of the flat, avoiding Chloe, who will be up any minute. Apparently Chloe is finally starting to house and job hunt today. Of course, her mum doesn't outright say they're avoiding her. But just after Kit arrived, they heard Chloe's alarm go off in her room. Annie flicked the kettle off before it had quite reached full boil and poured boiling water quickly into their cups. "Best clear the decks, hon," she said with a grin.

It's nice out here. There's still a slight hint of morning cool in the air. Kit tries to enjoy it as much as possible, because she knows it's bound to be roasting later. She sips her tea and watches Annie move to the next row of letters, scratching at the silver sections, a cigarette lodged between two fingers. "Why do you even do those, Mum? You never win a cent."

Annie smiles benignly at the card. "You bought them for me, so don't you complain."

It's true. She did. Her mum is always buying scratchies when she's got a little extra cash. Kit knows money's pretty short for her mum and Darren at the moment with Chloe leeching off them. Annie probably can't afford any treats like this at the moment, so Kit bought them with her meagre tips from last night.

"You're quiet." Annie gives her a shrewd look. "What's bugging you, Kitty?"

"Nothing. Just tired."

"How's the new place?"

"It's really good."

"Good." She pushes the failed scratchie away and sits back, her plump frame overwhelming the small metal chair. "You know, I'm proud of you, love."

Kit pulls a face. "Proud of me? What the hell for?"

"For getting yourself out of trouble. For working really hard to pay off your debts. For taking responsibility for your actions. These are all admirable things."

Kit can't help feeling just a bit pleased. She really *has* hauled her ass out of trouble for once. And it's nice someone actually noticed.

Annie suddenly leans forward and puts a hand on her arm. Her nails are bright blue and orange this week. That's one thing she's always got the cash for, her fortnightly manicure. "And you're doing it all even though you missed out on your big trip with the girls." She shakes her head. "If I could have given you the money, I would have, you know."

"I know. But it was my mess. I had to fix it."

"It's still getting you down, though?"

"A bit, I guess," Kit admits. "But it's not just that. I just wish I knew what I wanted to do *now*. Soon everyone will be at uni and I'll just be schlepping away at my jobs, doing nothing. I kind of wish I had applied for something now."

"What would you have studied?"

"I don't know."

"Then it would've been silly to go, wouldn't it? University's far too expensive these days to go in without a goal. *Life's* too expensive. Set your goals first."

Kit grins at this little foray into self-help speak. "What's *your* goal, mum?"

She lifts her chin and cackles. "Not me, kid. I'm old. I don't have to have goals. Not anymore."

"That's depressing."

"No, it's not. It's a relief."

Kit gives her a dubious look and sips her tea.

They sit in silence as the street busies itself under them. A bunch of kids from the commission flats dance past in a gaggle of jokes and loud laughter. Kit rests her foot on the edge of a bright blue planter box and sighs. "I guess I just feel like now that I'm nearly done with paying everything off, I wish I knew what I was going to do next, you know?"

"I know hon. But it doesn't have to be uni. Just because everyone else is going. You need something to look forward to, that's all. You'll go off to uni when you know what you want."

"Yeah, but *when* will I know what I want?" Kit frowns. It never used to bother her that she wasn't as driven as her friends. But now she's being left behind—on this holiday and in life—she just feels like a loser.

"You'll think of something, kiddo. You're bright and you're sweet and you've always been able to talk to anyone." Annie jabs a finger in her direction, smiling. "You've always been a charmer. I used to find you chatting to strangers in the supermarket. And your teachers always adored you."

Kit giggles. Both, she'll admit, are true.

"That's a skill. And not everyone has it, believe me. Look at your sister."

Kit's eyes widen, shocked. Her mum is usually so careful about being democratic about them both. Annie winks at her, and they dissolve into laughter.

When they've stopped laughing, she says. "And you'll find the right way to use that talent in your life. Don't worry. I've got to believe that."

Kit smiles, feeling the vaguest threat of tears behind her eyes.

Later, as she walks to work, she thinks about how her mother said it was a relief not to be expected to have dreams or ambition. Annie is only forty-two. Kit wishes she had a better life, not just this small one made up of the flat and Darren and her shifts at the hospital. But at the same time, that's all she seems to want. And Kit knows she probably can't change that.

Annie has so much blind faith in her, though. It makes everything feel...possible. So right there, under the leafy sprawl of the plane trees on Moore Street, she decides to find something, *anything* to aim for this year. She may not be going to uni, but she can't let this year slide by in a non-event of work and parties and sleep either. She won't let it. It has to count for something. And for a moment, she finds some faith that she'll figure out what that will be.

CHAPTER 30

Olivia, London, England

"I don't get what you want, Olivia."

Olivia presses her lips into a thin line and stares at her coffee. This meet-up has already turned. Jackknifed, actually.

The first ten minutes were okay as they ignored that giant tusked creature in the corner and caught up the past month. At first, it was easy to play the catch-up game, to assume the role of old friends who haven't seen each other for a while, rather than exes who left things pretty badly last time they saw each other. He told her about the flat where he's living, in the once-dodgy now dodgy-slash-hipster pocket of Islington. Then he told her about his internship at a firm near Barbican. And she did all the right things: smiling, asking questions, reacting.

But then it was her turn. As Olivia told him about her trip so far, the places they'd been, the things they had done, she could see the mild flickers in his expression. Then, when she finished filling him in on the last few weeks, he didn't say anything at all. Just nodded and stared at some people at the next table, like their post-work drinks were far more interesting that anything she had to tell him. She couldn't fight the feeling that it was like he just didn't want to hear about her having a good time. But it seemed like his mood turned at that point.

It was fine until she, a little miffed by the childishness of this reaction, asked, "What's wrong?"

"What do you mean?" It sounded accusatory.

She instantly backed down. "Nothing," She eyed him, wary, and decided to try and move on by acknowledging the elephant. "Look, it's good to see you. And I'm really sorry. For everything that happened back home."

"I know you are." His voice was airy as he turned to watch the next table again, acting slightly bored, as if they've already been through this.

Olivia quietly bristled. Well, if he knows, why does he act like she needs to say it again and again? She didn't respond. Instead, she sipped her coffee. She noticed a couple of girls surreptitiously checking him out. She wasn't surprised either. He will never lack for female attention.

And London looks good on him. He's wearing black pants and a neat blue shirt, a concession to the internship. His hair has been cut a little shorter too. She would never have thought it would suit him, but it opens up his pale blue eyes. He looks grown-up, like a smoother version of himself. At school, he was always a little scruffy with his old T-shirts, faded jeans, unbrushed hair. That was Will's look. A non-look. This is different. But good different.

And that's when he says it, as if he's been stewing on it while she's been thinking these things about him. "I don't get what you want, Olivia."

She stares at him, surprised. He keeps shifting his gaze between her and the next table, giving her brief, suspicious glances. At least they seem suspicious. Like he thinks she's some devious game player who's only here to make his life a misery for her own fun, but he hasn't figured out exactly *how* yet. It makes her want to cry. Why does he think this?

"What do you want me to do?" His voice is even colder now.

"I don't want you to do anything." She shrugs helplessly. "I just wanted things to be okay again."

He puts his drink down and frowns. "Oh, you're ready to be friends, so I have to be? Is that it?"

"I hoped you were. Look, I—"

"Well I'm not. You know, you kinda broke my heart a little."

Shit. She knew he was upset, but she didn't realise he was *that* upset.

He folds his arms over his chest. "And now you're demanding *I* be okay about it."

That isn't fair. A flicker of anger draws her back from the misery brink. But she pushes it away, determined to stay calm. "I'm not demanding anything from you." She gives him a tight smile. "I just miss you. I miss being friends with you."

He unfolds his arms and lets them hang by his sides, staring at her, as if rendered speechless. By the level of her crappiness, apparently. He shakes his head super-slowly. "All you think about is your own feelings, Olivia. It's so fucking selfish."

That's when the tears start stinging. She leans forward. "I didn't me—"

He leans forward, matching her intent. It's all she can do not to move away. "Look, Olivia, I am nowhere near ready to be friends with you, okay? I actually thought you were here to..." He trails off, his face flushing.

Her eyes widen. Oh God. Did he think she wanted to try and get back together? An acid wash of nausea flushes through her. Her throat goes dry. Woah. How badly has she fucked up? Again?

He pushes his glass away and goes to say something, but stops himself. Then he runs a hand through his hair, still looking anywhere but her, and pushes his chair back. "I have to go."

A second later, he's gone, and she's just sitting there, reminding herself to breathe. She registers the stares of those girls who were admiring him earlier in her periphery, clearly titillated by this tense little scene. As she stands, she turns to them, her face stonily impassive. Their eyes flick nervously away.

She doesn't take the train. She's too harassed and hurting for the battlegrounds of the Tube. Instead she strides blindly along the street with the rest of the early evening crowds, trying not cry. To think she chose to come to London largely because she'd get to see him, maybe make amends. What a fucking waste. She swipes angrily at her eyes as she walks, the world reduced to a teary blur. She wishes she were back home. That she could jump on a tram to her sister's and sit in Anna's backyard playing with Ally, drinking tea, and talking out her misery with the wisest person she knows. But instead, she's on her own, wrestling for space on the streets of London.

And did he really think she wanted to be with him again? After what happened? When his whole issue seemed to be that she was never into him *enough?* Why would that suddenly change?

Never *ever* has she been so unaligned in her feelings with someone. Sure, she's often found herself the less interested party, but not like this. No one's ever claimed love and definitely not while she was feeling little more than the tender feelings of an easy, uncomplicated relationship. She doesn't even know yet what love is supposed to feel like.

She clenches her jaw as she weaves her way through crowds of shoppers. It hurts, knowing there is nothing she can do about Will now. They are too separate in their stances. He has none of her good friendship intentions, and she has none of his bitterness. Okay, well, maybe after that meeting, she has a little of his bitterness.

How did she get this so, so wrong? She hates hurting him—she hates the thought of hurting anyone—but there is no way around this. Feeling yet another assault of tears, she ducks down a quieter street. Here she can walk without the world witnessing her mini-meltdown. Here the houses are huge and sumptuous, wrapped around a fenced garden in the centre of the block. She begins to breathe again.

For the zillionth time, she wishes she'd never started anything with him. When he first came to their school, he was absorbed quickly into her social circle. They became instant comrades. They liked the same music, the same TV shows, and they shared the same tongue-in-cheek humour. At lunchtimes or at parties, they inevitably found themselves in corners together, trading silly observations about their social world. They studied English and Politics together and did their homework in the state library after school together and then went out for noodles after, talking into the night. Olivia finally found the person in their group who felt like *her* person.

Olivia was seeing James back then. She'd met him at an eighteenth at the local lawn bowls club, the new cool, ironic place to hold parties. He sauntered up to her, all confidence and charm, and struck up a conversation. He showed more social skill in five minutes than some guys at her school had shown in the five or six years she'd known them.

By the time the five minutes were up, he'd already asked her out. A private school type, James was all flowing cash, after-school sports teams, and private tutors. Of course, a lot of kids at her school had the same upper-middle-class benefits, herself included. But their parents were more likely to be successful creative types, politically aware and socially conscious. And they were more likely to buy and renovate houses in the inner north with solar panels and raised vegetable gardens planted in the front yard. Meanwhile James' parents were both executives and owned a suburban palace in Kew. Same but different.

She liked James, though. He was a good conversationalist, he laughed easily, and he liked good movies. It was easy to spend time with him. And it was also easy to break up with him when she got bored, too, using the time and distance it took to get between their houses and the increasing pressures of VCE as excuses. And he slipped out of her life as easily as he'd ingratiated himself into it.

Will happened at another eighteenth, about a month later. Later she realised Will had probably been waiting what he had decided was the sensitive amount of time post-break-up. They'd all eaten dumplings and danced in the city. And it was one of those rare, perfect nights when everything came together just right: the right group, the right venue, and the right collective mood. You can never know where or when they're going to happen. They just do.

She was vaguely aware of his extra attentiveness that night, but she was having too much fun to question it. Yet, when she looked back at it the next day, it was obvious. She remembered how he was always at her side, handing her drinks, ready to dance. And as she drank those drinks and danced it out, she remembers feeling vague flickers of concern about what this might mean. She thought they were so firmly, so happily in the friend zone.

Her suspicions were confirmed on the last tram home. They huddled near the door, joking and laughing and taking pleasure in the simple joy of being in a pack. She was listening to someone's old story about the Year 9 camp she didn't go to when she felt fingers curl possessively around her own.

And she let it happen. Because why not? She was more than halfway to drunk and feeling that electric radiant feeling you get when everything is in its place and the night's been exactly what you wanted it to be. Ending it with a hand holding hers seemed kind of *right* in the moment. And besides, hadn't she kind of been letting this thing become possible all night, however semiconsciously?

And that tipsy reasoning is how she ended up kissing him against the wall of the old shoe factory as he walked her home. And then, because she didn't have a reason not to let him, she allowed him to take her hand the following Monday as they walked from school to the café across the road. And then they just seemed to slide from friendship to couple without her ever quite deciding if she wanted it. It was simply some chain reaction that everyone around her seemed to think of as inevitable.

And it was good for a while. He was the same great company he'd always been. He was affectionate and kind of ironically chivalrous with her. And he was both talented *and* generous in bed. And she loved it when he read her stories in bed afterward, in the soft light of her lamp, acting out all the voices, making her laugh.

So while maybe he didn't one hundred per cent light her fire in the way she expected the *right* guy should, it wasn't hard to let the relationship happen either. It was like the classic best friendship with benefits. And she figured he felt the same.

It was always Will that called or messaged first, though. And it was always Will that came up with ideas for dates, for things they could do without the others. And it was nearly always him that leaned in for the kiss or grabbed her hand on the street. Not that she wasn't into any of those things when they happened, but it just didn't occur to her to instigate them. She told herself—and him—that she was just distracted by other things. Like study.

At first, he was okay with it. Then he began to show moments of frustration with her distance. It always blew over quickly, though. She'd apologise and be extra attentive for a while, and he'd be happy again. But after a handful of these tense moments, she started to feel the relationship more like an added pressure than a pleasure. She'd get irritated and impatient with him. She told herself that it was because of everything else. They were getting to the pointy end of the school year, her dad was working from Sydney, meaning she had to travel and visit him every few weeks, wasting valuable study time on travel. She had this constant feeling she was falling behind. There was only so much attention she felt like she could pay him, that she wanted to pay him.

And she forgot to go to his speech. That really hammered it home. For both of them. Sure, she might forget to call him back sometimes, but to miss something *this important?* She couldn't blame him for being so hurt. It became the final straw neither of them had seen coming. But she also couldn't help admitting to herself that when it did come, it was almost a relief.

The whole thing with Will had felt so out of her control. Like she just responded to little moments, to his little demands, without ever knowing what she wanted. Maybe this is her problem. She just lets things happen, and then regrets it when they backfire.

She chews on her lip as she considers this version of herself. She didn't just let things happen the other night with Liza, did she? And she still has no idea why she did it. And with Liza. But there's no way in hell she can deny the fact that she made the first move. And the second.

She kissed a girl once before. But it was a random thing, and she was definitely *not* the instigator that time. She was at a party, a housewarming for one of the guys who graduated last year. She was lined up for the toilets and found herself in a conversation with the girl next to her, a serious-eyed Arts student with a twenties bob and a dry sense of humour. She doesn't remember exactly what they talked about—something fluffy and dumb and party-appropriate. Then this guy staggered down the hall and started talking at them. Well, slurring at them, to be exact. It didn't take long for his "just being friendly" chatter to turn leery and gross either. And despite their overt disdain, he was drunk and relentless.

Just when Olivia had decided they were probably going to have to put up with him until it was her turn to use the toilet and someone else would become his victim, the girl suddenly turned and wrapped her arms around Olivia. She pressed her body close and then kissed her, soft and slow, putting on a show. Olivia still remembers the feel of the girl's fingers running lightly over her shoulder blades, and the way her tongue teased. Then the girl pulled away and turned to the guy, her eyes narrowed. "Fuck off." Calm but icy.

People in the queue behind her laughed, and a couple of them chimed in, telling the guy it was time to disappear. He flapped about with an apology and then stumbled drunkenly down the hall to harass someone else. Then the girl turned to her, laughing. Olivia was still reeling slightly, but she laughed, playing cool.

The girl leaned in and kissed her again, a quicker, cursory peck. "Thanks!" she said brightly. Then she shoved Olivia gently in the direction of the now-empty bathroom. By the time Olivia came out, still a little shell-shocked, the girl had disappeared. A few people in the queue eyed her and grinned. Red-cheeked, she ignored them and hurried past.

Dazed, she wandered back into the party to find Will and the rest of her group. When she told the others what happened, they laughed and teased and demanded Olivia point her out. But she didn't see the girl again.

Will was intrigued by the whole thing, asking her about it later as they walked home through the damp, leaf-littered autumn streets.

"Shut up!" She punched him gently in the arm. "You just want to get off on the idea of me and a girl."

"Maybe." He grinned and hooked an arm around her neck, pulling her in for a kiss of his own. "Was it hot?" he asked, waggling his eyebrows.

She just giggled and kissed him back. She didn't tell him that the electric little rush was still with her. Like it had just happened. Why bother? She put it down to the thrill of the unexpected and forgot about it.

Now, after Liza, maybe she's not so sure.

She returns to the busy high street near the hotel, rejoining the crowds. That's two girls now. But does it have to mean anything? She folds her arms over her chest and sucks in an impatient breath. Hasn't she had enough revelations about herself lately? Isn't it bad enough she's discovered she's a shitty girlfriend and a failed-before-she-even-began law student? Without having to consider the fact she might be a little bit gay too? *And* that maybe she's been too stupid to figure it out before this?

She shakes her head as she strides the last block to the hotel. She can't even contemplate this right now. Not after today. She will not be giving airtime to a scattering of clues in the shape of party kisses and an impromptu one-night-hotel stand. There's no room in her head for that right now.

* * *

Upstairs, the room is Mai-less, thank God. She throws her bag on the bed and stands there, relishing the quiet. She doesn't know what she'd do if she had to field an interrogation about what just happened at the pub. She needs some time to just stare into the void for a bit. But as she sinks onto the edge of her bed, she's overwhelmed by a wave of self-pity, and it all starts up again like a relentlessly bad song.

Why does she feel *so* stupid? And so conflicted? She has absolutely no idea what to do with the incompatibility of her heartbreak over losing Will's friendship and her anger at him. *Or* what to do with this newfound confusion about this thing with Liza. A thing that was merely pushing at the periphery but is now maybe surfacing to be something more important.

A quiet knock shoots down these thoughts. She contemplates not answering it but decides against it. She breathes in deep, trying to relax the tearful tightness in her throat and swipes under her eyes to clear any smeared make-up.

It's Liza, of all people, standing in the hallway, her hands jammed in her pockets. When she registers Olivia's expression, her shy smile turns into a hesitant frown. "Hey, you okay?"

Olivia shrugs, mostly because she doesn't know what to do now she's faced with yet another source of her confusions.

"Did you see Will?"

"Yeah." And that's all she has to say on that one. But that's all she needs to say, because Liza just nods slowly and gives her a sympathetic frown. Olivia shrugs, as if to say *so be it*. "Where are the others?"

"Mai's meeting up with Campbell. Turns out he's in London and neglected to tell her. She found out via Instagram." Liza gives her an *eek* look and smiles.

Olivia rolls her eyes. The saga of Campbell continues.

"And Tam's Skyping Matt downstairs."

"Right." She wonders if Liza's looking for someone to hang out with. Olivia's not sure if she can do company right now. Especially Liza. Not with all this weirdness. She decides to move things along. "So, what's up?"

Liza purses her lips and drops her gaze to the ground. Olivia grits her teeth. Clearly this is not going to be some breezy "hey, how are you?" conversation.

Finally, Liza speaks, digging her hands even deeper into her pocket as she does. "I... I'm not sure if you're avoiding me or..."

She falters, and Olivia doesn't fill the silence. Because how can she, really? It's true. She *has* been kind of avoiding Liza. Not avoiding, exactly, but just not engaging in the way she did before this. They'd been firmly on their way to becoming friends. Close, even. Now, for the last few days, they've reverted to being casual acquaintances travelling in the same group. And they both know it's been Olivia's doing.

Liza takes another breath. "I guess I just wanted to say that I really don't want things to be awkward with us. Maybe I'm paranoid. Maybe I'm imagining it, but I feel like you've been a little bit weird the last couple of days, and I don't know if it's got anything to do with me. But if it does, I just want you to know it doesn't have to be—"

A shock of exasperation hits her. Here's yet another she's doing wrong today. Olivia holds both hands up. "Do we have to do *this?*" It comes out brittle and distant, as though she's questioning Liza's right to be entering into this conversational territory.

Liza flinches a little, but she's dauntless. "But that's what I'm saying. We don't *have* to do this. We can be fine."

But Olivia can't do any part of this conversation right now. She can't see anything beyond the confusing shitstorm of feelings today has pelted on her. Even when Liza is just trying to make nice. The last thing she needs right now is for anyone to be nice to her. She doesn't deserve it. This is all too much. Too much at once. Here's Liza asking her for something, something her reeling brain doesn't know how to give in this moment.

She turns and sighs loudly. "Everything's fine. I just need a minute, *okay?*" She glares at Liza, still thick inside her self-hatred. "Just a freaking minute."

Although Liza's eyebrows lift in mild alarm at her outburst, she nods calmly. "Okay, I'm sorry." She jerks her thumb behind her. "I'm going to go."

And she's gone.

Olivia pushes the door closed and leans against it. But there's no sense of relief. Just instant remorse. She just took out her mood on Liza. And all Liza did in return was to calmly give her the time and space she asked for.

Goddamn Liza.

She yanks the door open. Liza's walking slowly down the hall, those hands still jammed into her pockets.

"Hey Lize!"

Liza stops and turns, but doesn't come any closer. "Yeah?"

"I'm *so* sorry. For snapping at you. That was obnoxious. I'm just..." She trails off, giving Liza a helpless look.

Liza holds up her hand, as if to say Olivia doesn't need to finish whatever she's trying to say. "It's really okay. It is. I just wanted to say *we're* okay, you know?" She smiles and then continues her journey down the hall.

Olivia nudges the door closed and drops onto the bed, relieved that at least she hasn't hurt someone else today.

She flops back against the mattress and stares at the stark white ceiling. What is it with Liza? There's this...*simplicity* to the way she deals with things. It's not simple like it's naivety or emotional immaturity, either. She's quiet, but she's so *certain*, too. It's clear-eyed, like she dwells so entirely and comfortably within herself. Maybe it's because she's clear-hearted.

Something that Olivia has learned today she apparently is *not*.

CHAPTER 31

Tam, London, England

Tam plucks a piece of raspberry from her overly-floury muffin and pops it in her mouth. There is no taste, just a vague, sour hint of frozen-then-defrosted nothing. The raspberry canes at home will be fruiting any day now. While she has been gone they'll have done their hardest work, slinking around the sheds, shooting up tall, thorny spears and making a roof of wide, flat leaves for the chooks to hide under on the hottest days.

They always seem to just *appear*. One minute they're these short, blackened sticks hacked down after the last crop, and the next, they're towering over her head. Every year, she promises she'll catch them in the act of growing, but she always misses it. They're sly like that. But later you can't help but notice them, listing under the weight of their plump, pink treasures. She and Bill will have to do a lot of cooking to get through the crop this year.

She rests her chin on her hand and frowns. *Bill.* She still hasn't heard anything yet. Just an email from her dad saying they're waiting for results and that they'll let her know soon. She wishes those doctors would hurry up, and they could just know. She hates this strangled, tense feeling and the way that every time she starts to have a good time, it will suddenly invade the moment.

And she's sure the girls are tired of her moping too. She's trying her best. She is. But it's hard to hide. She doesn't really want to tell them, though. Because then it's *really a thing.* Liza sort of knows something might be wrong, after whatever she told her on that drunken night in Ljubljana. But the other two are oblivious. They probably just think she's constantly in a crappy mood or something.

Mai, on the other side of the table, couldn't care less right now, though. She's too busy with her morning social media rounds. So far, she's taken a picture of her bandaged foot, and one of her breakfast, a huge greasy bacon roll coupled with an equally huge cappuccino in an odious lime green cup. Tam's sure that by now, half of Melbourne has seen those images. Sometimes it seems like Mai spends more time orchestrating her digital presence than she does being actually present.

She sips her coffee and watches Mai work furiously at her phone. This girl can produce more information with two thumbs on a tiny screen than Tam can do on a keyboard, even after an interminable semester of Year 9 touch-typing class. Tam doesn't get it, this need to keep everyone constantly updated on what she's doing. Doesn't she want to save something to tell people when she gets back? And who really needs to see a greasy bacon roll in a bad London chain café, anyway?

Hanging out with these girls makes her feel so dated and stupid. Sometimes, when they're talking about things like Instagram and Snapchat, she feels like an old aunt watching the young folk in wry, estranged amusement.

She watches Mai's face as she types. Tam can count on one hand the times she and Mai have spent alone. Yet, here they are having breakfast together. Well, can you really call it "together" if Mai has only dragged her eyes from her phone maybe three times since she sat down? Probably not.

She stares out the window, watching the world go past. Even the schoolkids seem to have the London pace down, hauling heavy-looking bags higher onto their shoulders as they march. The thought of making her way to school in these crowds every day gives her instant claustrophobia. She thinks of her own walk to school, down the dirt track, past the cow fields and the old junk house where they always forget to lock up their goats, to the bus stop on the edge of the highway. She and Matt and Tracy from the goat house were the only ones out there on those cold, clean mornings.

The table shifts under her elbows. She drags her gaze back to the café. Mai is struggling to get up in the narrow space between chair and table.

"What are you doing?"

"I just need some sugar." Mai picks up her crutches. "Ours is empty."

Tam jumps up. "Hey, stay there. I'll get it." She ducks over to a nearby table, grabs the sugar, and brings it back.

Mai's already sunk back down into her seat, crutches still in hand. "Thanks," she says, gratefully opening the pot.

"That's okay. Let me know if you need anything else. I'll help."

Mai smiles, but she looks kind of uncertain. "Thanks." She gives her a polite smile and picks up her phone.

Tam frowns. Is Mai afraid to ask her for help? What kind of impression is she giving her?

She sighs, blowing out the breath between pursed lips. Matt used to always joke that she was kind of intimidating. She's never understood it. She doesn't *feel* like that. And the thought that Mai might not feel like she can ask her a small favour makes her feel like crap. Because what does that say about what they think of *her?* She wishes she could explain what's going on, but the thought of saying it out loud makes her feel sick.

She's going to have to make more of an effort, though. At least be a bit more cheerful or something. And to kick it off, she leans forward. "Hey, I'm going to get another coffee. Want something?"

Mai tears her eyes from her phone. "Uh, sure. I'll have another coffee."

"Great." Tam gives her best effort at a companionable smile and gets up from the table. But she feels like a fake.

* * *

Kit, Melbourne

"Shit!" Kit hisses, shaking her hand. "Ouch!"

Lewis grins. "I told you, grip the handle lower and it'll be easier. And you won't hammer your hand, either."

Kit does as she's told. This time, with a few hard taps, the nail is driven cleanly into the plaster. A scattering of brick dust showers the floor, tickling her bare feet. She'll have to sweep again later.

"There." Lewis picks up the frame. "Easy, right?"

"Yeah," Kit mutters, pretending she doesn't care. But she can't help feeling a little proud of herself.

He grins. "Next I'll teach you how to use the power drill. It's only fair, after everything you taught me about the finer details of the Laundromat yesterday."

"Yeah, well that's because I can't deal with the thought of someone washing their clothes in shower *while they're wearing them.* Not at twenty-one."

He just chuckles, completely unembarrassed. Then he hangs the framed photo on the wall and straightens it. He handles it delicately, reverently even, which makes her smile. "Can't have Beryl hanging crooked, can we?"

They've named their new kitchen matriarch Beryl, after Lewis's grandmother. They found the picture in a pile of framed pictures at the op shop across the road. As they searched through shelves of kitsch junk, they fell in a kind of hysterical love with this studio portrait of a middle-aged woman. Posed formally against a pastel background, she stared up at them with a patient, benevolent smile. They stood there, making up stories about Beryl and her life until they were too attached to leave her. So they didn't. And now here she is, in all her glory, beaming down at them from the kitchen wall.

Lewis flicks on the kettle and appraises their work. "I think it's perfect the way the sunlight from the window catches her face, and how she can see everything that happens in the kitchen. The heart of this home," he says dreamily.

Kit giggles. "You're an idiot."

"But a loveable one, right?" He makes them both a cup of tea without asking.

"True." She sifts through a small pile of dropped petals in the middle of the scratched table. They picked the flowers on the way home from work last night. They don't have a vase, so they begged an empty jar from the staff at the restaurant. So here they are, a bunch of pretty little purple things displayed in an old shrimp paste jar. Kit smiles. Classy as the rest of this place.

But at least they're making an effort. The apartment looks much better than when she first came and looked at it. As soon as Kit moved in and started cleaning up, Lewis stepped up too. It was like he just needed some encouragement or company, and now he's more than willing to make this place more liveable, borrowing the tools from Charlie to hang pictures and paint their new sideboard. The place is still old and rundown as hell. Nothing will ever fix that—especially not Charlie. Kit doesn't care, though. That's what keeps the rent so mind-bogglingly cheap.

Now she actually likes sitting in their little kitchen/dining/living room, eating at the table and staring through the window at the mundane, curious, and downright creepy things that go on in the laneway backing the restaurant.

Lewis puts a steaming cup in front of her and reclines in his chair, kicking his feet up onto the windowsill. He sighs decadently like they've been working all morning instead of just putting a hole in the wall for Beryl.

She smiles and slowly scoops three spoonfuls of sugar into her tea.

He grimaces. "That is *gross*. You know, when I was in Mostar, I ordered this tea at a café, and I didn't realise their style came with sugar in it. It was so sweet, my teeth hurt. I bet yours is like that." He shudders.

Kit shrugs. She likes it like that. "I have no idea where Mostar is."

"Bosnia-Herzegovina? The Balkans? Former Yugoslavia?"

She shrugs each time he names a place. "Nope. Never heard of any of them. I'm terrible at geography."

"I was too before I went anywhere. Hated it at school. It's hard to get excited about something you haven't experienced. Travelling made me actually want to look at maps."

She gives him a cringe-y look. "You know, the other day when we were talking to your friend Dan on Skype, I had *no* idea where Ukraine was or what he was talking about with the fighting and stuff. I just nodded and acted like I did." She gives him an embarrassed smile. "Then I had to go look it up."

He chuckles and stares into the sunlight pouring in the window and rubs his round, stubbly face. "I'm thinking of going there. I'll go work in London for a few months, help at that summer camp. Then I'll do some travel."

"You're going away *again?*"

He grins. "I call it the seven-month itch."

"Why do you travel so much?"

Lewis frowns. "Why wouldn't I?" He spins his cup around on the table. "Because it opens up your world. And because every time I come back here, I feel happy to be home. But then after a few months, I get bored and restless and ready to go again. I don't know." He shrugs.

"Just have to, I guess. And I love doing the volunteer work, because it feels like you're giving something back at the same time, you know?"

"Do you think *I'd* like it?"

"Kitty, you'd love it. Trust me."

"What about working in the orphanage?"

"You want to?"

"I mean, it sounds really amazing. Scary, but amazing."

"You should totally come." He gives her a high-five. "Travel buddies!"

She slaps his hand and laughs. Idiot. "Do you think I could do it?" She blinks at how fast this suggestion has solidified into something. She was just putting a barely-formed idea out there. But now that it's hit the air and Lewis's brain, it's become a real, tangible thing.

"Why not? I bet you'd be great. And we'd have all kinds of adventures."

"Would you want me tagging along?"

"Why wouldn't I?" He gives her that exuberant smile of his. "And you know, I reckon if you can live together, you can travel together. And we're doing that just fine."

"True."

"So why not?" He shrugs and drains his tea.

She laughs. That's his response to everything. *Why not?* And maybe he's right. Why not? She's still got a plane ticket. She's cleared her debt now. And if she helps out at the orphanage, she'll be actually *doing* something, too. Maybe this is the way she is going to make this year count.

"We can work in London for a bit afterwards, save some money. Or go to Ireland, even. And we can easily get around on the cheap from there. It'll be fun." He grabs her wrist and squeezes it. "You wanna?"

"I think I wanna," she says slowly, her eyes widening as she says the words.

"Awesome." He claps his hands together. "It does mean we'll have to leave this palace." He looks around the room, frowning. "But Beryl will take care of it. And whoever rents our rooms will have to promise to honour her as sovereign head of this household."

Kit laughs, but she's only half listening. She's too busy being stunned. What has she just committed to?

It's another one of those moments when she feels like life is skidding out of her control. But unlike those other disaster times, like moving in with her boyfriend when she's about to take the most important exams of her life or agreeing to a massive, ultimately house-wrecking party, this seems like it's actually a good thing. She's just about to ask Lewis how much money he thinks she'll need to save when her phone starts ringing. She glances at the screen. It's her mother. That's weird. She should be at work now.

She picks up the phone. "Hey, Mum. What's up?"

CHAPTER 32

Liza, London, England

The stone bench under Liza is cold and hard, but she doesn't feel like moving. Neither, apparently, does Tam. Instead, they stare at the ornate shapes of the palace in silence. Liza gets the feeling they're both too deep in their own miserable thoughts to do more than this. She presses her palms against her coffee cup and glances at Tam. Yep, she looks as glum as Liza feels. And as if she heard what Liza is thinking, Tam turns to her, her frown giving way to a slight smile. "You want to talk about it?"

Liza returns the smile but shakes her head. "Not really. Do *you* want to talk about it?"

"Nope," Tam says, definite.

They grudge a laugh and then drop back into the safety of silence. Crowds of people wander back and forth along the damp paths, peering at the palace and the dignified stone buildings that surround the park. It's stopped raining, finally, but the trees are still dripping from last night's downpour. Last night, as she lay sleepless, Liza listened to the consistent, spiritless patter of the rain hitting the window until it exhausted itself somewhere near morning. They woke to a sodden, stilled world.

Not far from their bench, squirrels scramble busily up and down the trunks of trees and across the grass. Liza watches as one sits up on its haunches, vigilantly alert, as Tam crunches on an apple. He's rewarded for his patience. When it's down to the core, she tosses it onto the grass near him. He bounds over, beating out a couple more squirrels who fling themselves from the trees in pursuit of the morsel. As he nabs it, the others flock over and begin to squabble for it.

Tam chuckles. "Oops. Maybe I shouldn't have done that."

"Maybe."

They watch the hairy little fiends fight it out, as the original one defends its treasure.

“Wow.” Tam folds her arms and stares at them. “They’re kind of like fluffy seagulls.”

Liza laughs and nods. No meal on the beach back home ever fails to attract a frenzy of overly assertive gulls. “*So* true,” She digs her chin into her scarf. “Only these little guys are much cuter.”

“It’s amazing what a fluffy tail can do for your cute cred. Because that’s the only thing separating them from rats too.” Tam checks her watch. “Hey, that guard-changing thing is happening in five minutes.”

Liza nods but doesn’t move.

Tam shrugs, letting out a heavy sigh. “Meh, I think I’ve seen it in a movie anyway.”

“Me too.” They grin sheepishly at each other and settle in, snug in their mutual apathy.

The crowds have mostly cleared now. A small child runs along the tree-lined path ahead of his mother and her pram. He stops to stare at a squirrel a few metres along the path. He points at it and looks back at his mother, wide-eyed. She smiles and says something encouraging. The squirrel begins to move closer, and the child freezes, looking both delighted and terrified. It picks up speed, coming straight at him, and the kid inches back, but the squirrel is relentless. Liza notices the sandwich in his hand.

Tam chuckles. “Uh-oh, that kid’s a goner.”

The squirrel runs straight up onto his sneakered foot. The boy shrieks and kicks it off, then turns and runs, screeching for his mother. The squirrel scampers after him. Liza can’t help giggling even though the kid is crying now. He drops his sandwich and throws himself into his pusher. The mother moves out from behind it as if to defend the kid, but the squirrel just snatches up the sandwich and bolts back to a tree. By now, Liza and Tam are both laughing quietly.

“Still think they’re cute?” Tam asks between giggles.

“I’m just glad it wasn’t me,” Liza admits.

“When cute animals go bad,” Tam says, in a deep TV documentary voice.

Their laughter fades back to silence as the boy and his mother disappear across the park. Tam turns to Liza. Her cheeks are flushed from the cold, and her freckles have subsided under the pink. She always looks as if she belongs outdoors, Liza thinks. The quintessential country girl.

"You've been kind of quiet lately. Quieter than usual. You really okay?"

"I don't know. Yeah, maybe. You?"

"Maybe."

They laugh again.

"We are doing *awesome*," Tam says.

"Yup. Awesome."

"Anyway, I just wanted to check," Tam says. "I feel like we're the closest each other's got to a friend on this trip. Maybe it's the Kit connection, or maybe we're just more alike. I don't know. I just feel more comfortable with you, I guess. I mean, the other two are nice, but it's not like we're all the best of friends." Tam's lips thin out. "That's not mean, is it?"

"Not at all. I know what you're saying. We're all still figuring each other out. It's only been a few weeks."

"It feels like we've been away for longer, though, doesn't it?"

"It really does."

Liza wonders if Mai and Olivia are being as apathetic today as Tam and Liza. Because London sure seems to have brought out the *meh* on this trip. Neither of them wanted to come when Tam and Liza said they were going to the palace and to Westminster, prime tourism spots they hadn't even sighted yet. Mai wasn't sure she could manage the walking, and Olivia seemed pretty happy to stick with her.

Liza can't help thinking Olivia's avoiding hanging out with her. She wishes she hadn't tried to talk to her last night. She really wasn't expecting that kind of reaction from her. Olivia's never snappish or angry. Liza's timing probably wasn't great, though. She knows that outburst wasn't all about her but whatever happened during her drink with this Will guy. She feels guilty now, throwing the minor issue of their friendship at Olivia when she was probably right in the middle of dealing with her issues with him.

But she couldn't help it. Olivia has been kind of distant, and she just wanted the weirdness to stop. Because then she could stop thinking of them sleeping together as a mistake. And she just wanted to smooth their way back to friendship, to let Olivia know that the distance isn't necessary, because Liza doesn't expect or want anything from her.

She'd be lying, of course. What she actually wants is an entirely different thing. But it's out of the question. She draws in a breath slowly. How did she jump from Alika to this? What's wrong with her? She thought she'd done her worst by dating someone who couldn't be and never wanted to be out. Who knew Liza could aim for something even *more* complicated? But now she's got herself into a mess of feels with a straight girl. That's a whole new world of unexplored bad idea. And an even more futile one.

Tam nudges her, dragging her back to the park. "Hey, I'm starving. Wanna find out if English fish and chips really are superior to ours?"

Liza swallows, swatting away all these pesky, miserable thoughts. "Why not?" She stands. "But I already know they're not."

* * *

Dear Olivia,

Hey, favourite sister. How is the trip? Sorry I haven't written more. I can't even use Henry as an excuse, because he is such a ridiculously good baby. Steve keeps asking what's wrong. Why isn't he constantly squalling like Ally did? The worst we've had from him is one epic code brown. From the top of the nappy all the way up to the neck of his Gro-suit. It was spectacular. Especially because it was Steve's turn.

Anyway, I just wanted to ask, are you okay? I wish the reception hadn't been so awful and we could have had a proper conversation. Let's try again soon, okay?

I miss you. So does Ally. She asked out of the blue the other morning while she was watching TV if you were coming over tonight. She was quite outraged that you were not. Oh God, Livs, how the hell do you explain the concept of geography to a three-year-old? She just kept asking questions and asking questions, and I just kept giving her less and less satisfactory answers. I even pulled out Dad's old atlas and showed her where London was on the world map. But of course, she didn't get the scale thing at all and kept insisting you could just swim or get a boat across those 'bits of water' (you know, those pesky little Atlantic and Pacific Oceans). Steve and I both laughed when she said that, which mortally offended her, of course. Cue hissy fit. So, long story short, Ally says COME HOME NOW! And if I was as selfish as I feel, I'd say come home too. I miss you.

It was fun looking at the old atlas. Do you remember how you used to use it to follow your book characters around the world? I was looking at the map of the States, and you've painstakingly mapped out this trip across the eastern half of America. I wonder whose it was?

Anyway, if you want to talk, Skype me soon.

I love you,

Anna

* * *

Tam, London, England

Tam picks at the fish with her fork, flaking at the white flesh under its thick prison of batter. Then she drops her fork.

Liza grins at her. "Verdict, Ms Foodie?"

Tam laughs. "I don't think any serious food critic would be eating fish and chips in this place." The chipper they have found is a tiny little joint with only three tables and a steady stream of people lining up and leaving with packages of hot food under their arms. There is a light coating of grease over everything, from the walls to the ceiling fans to the tabletops.

"Nah," Liza shakes her head. "I've seen the cooking channels. Isn't it totally hip right now to be into basic stuff like burgers and greasy food?"

"True." Tam grins and stabs at her food. "Okay, well, the fish is dry as hell."

"Agreed." Liza has barely touched hers either.

"But the chips are kind of great."

"Agreed again." Liza picks one up, inspecting it. "But I've got to say, fish and chips is just kind of weird without the beach. And I miss potato cakes."

Tam nods, thinking of the potato cakes at the fish and chip van back home. They'd always go on Saturday afternoons in summer and check out the surf, eating crisp golden disc after crisp golden disc as they looked out over Pirates Bay and the distant, coasting specks of wet-suited surfers.

“Did you always want to be a chef?”

“I always liked cooking classes,” Tam says. “But I never really thought about it as a proper job until last year.” She tells Liza about her weekend job at the café, working in the kitchen. How she learned to love the hustle and stress of getting meals out fast and well. And then about Bill and his impromptu cooking lessons, lessons that broadened her horizons in both ingredients and method. Before that, she didn’t realise food was something you could play with, experiment with. That if you knew some basic rules, you didn’t always have to have a recipe. Cooking, she learned, could be this serendipitous, spontaneous thing.

“So what’s your *favourite* food?”

“Thai. Definitely.” Tam grins and rubs her hands together. She still remembers the first time she tasted Thai flavours. It was a soup she had in a café with Kit in Melbourne. It was a fragrant combination of pumpkin, coconut milk, lemongrass, and lime leaf. But she didn’t know that at the time. Tam had no idea what she had tasted, aside from the familiar, mellow sunshine flavour of coconut, but knew she had to figure out how to recreate it. For months, Tam tried to hunt down that taste in her own kitchen, but never got it. It wasn’t until later, when she went to a Thai restaurant with her Aunt in Hobart, that she recognised those flavours. Finally, she had the key. She went home and pored over recipes online, learning about Thai ingredients.

“That’s what you’re doing in Thailand, right?” Liza asks. “Cooking classes?”

“Yup, I have a week-long class in Chiang Mai after you guys leave. And then one in Vietnam.”

Liza sighs. “I wish I was going to Vietnam.”

“Are you looking forward to going home, though?” Tam realises she’s never heard Liza say a word about homesickness.

“I am and I’m not, I guess.” Liza picks up a chip and contemplates it. “Part of me would love to keep travelling, but the other part of me is kind of excited about getting back. I don’t know. Now that I’ve decided to stop training, I’m kind of excited. I just want to, I don’t know...” She tips her head to the side. “I know it sounds dumb, but...*feel* real life; do regular stuff. I feel like I missed everything.” She puts the chip down and sits back, chewing her lip. “You know, I went to the same school as Olivia and Mai for six years, and Olivia and Kit are really close. I barely knew them when we left for this trip. Because the whole time, I was always at training or in the library doing my homework, making up for being at training. I never met anyone or did anything. I always had to leave things early or not go at all. You know, I didn't even go to a slumber party when I was younger. Not if you don't count sleeping at someone from the team's house before we drove to a meet in the morning."

Tam wants to tell her she's not missing much, but she just nods.

"And I'm excited about starting uni, too," Liza adds.

"What do you want to do after?"

"I want to teach English and Lit."

"Really?" Tam can't imagine Liza commanding a classroom. "From athlete to English teacher. That's quite a leap."

"I know, right?" Liza laughs. "Most of the girls on my team were going into sports medicine or physio. I was *definitely* the odd one out. And, let me guess, you think I'm too quiet to teach?"

Tam grins and shrugs. "It is kind of surprising."

"I know. But I had this Lit teacher in Year 11. He was really soft-spoken and serious, but he was also really great. He liked us, and he loved books. He kind of made us want to listen to him anyway. He didn't have to yell or threaten like some of the other teachers." She pushes her plate away and swipes her curls back from her face. "I figure if he can do it, so can I."

"Of course," Tam tells her. And she believes it, too. She holds up her glass of Coke. "To knowing exactly what you want in life."

"Well I wouldn't go that far." Liza laughs and touches her glass to Tam's.

"Okay, then to *feeling* life."

CHAPTER 33

Olivia, London, England

"I'm a bit scared of uni," Olivia admits to the guy.

They're in a bar close to the hotel. They decided to find somewhere to go out for their last night in London. Well, they had to, because Mai threw down her iPad this afternoon, diagnosed herself with a diabolical case of cabin fever, and demanded they go out. And even though Olivia could tell no one was really feeling it, they agreed. Because it's hard to say no to Mai.

And they haven't really done much going out since arriving in London. It's partly because of Mai's ankle, of course, but Olivia thinks it's because they're tired. She had no idea travelling would be this exhausting, but it is. You can't just take a night off travelling. You can't just get away from everyone and everything. But tonight, they are making an effort to say goodbye to London properly, in the form of outfits and eye make-up and a bar Mai could limp to.

The guy Olivia is talking to is Australian, a friend of Campbell's. His name is Nick. He struck up a conversation at the bar, and she could immediately tell from his manner that he'd worked up to doing it. The spontaneity of his greeting was so patently *un*spontaneous. Guys are so obvious sometimes. It makes Olivia wonder if they really believe they're being stealth and suave. Still, he's sweet. And it turns out he went to her school but finished a few years ago. Of course she's all the way in London and meets a guy from her own school. He's doing a university semester on exchange in London.

"Don't be scared. Uni's fine," he assures her. "It's fun, too."

"I'm just nervous of the workload. VCE was bad enough."

"VCE is bullshit." He leans against the wall next to him and crosses his arms over his chest. "Trust me."

"But it's the only way to get into uni. So you kind of have no choice."

"I know, but that's the thing. When you're doing it, they put you into this constant state of panic about it all. Like university is going to be the hardest thing you've ever done in your life." He rolls his eyes.

Olivia smiles hopefully at him. "So it's not?"

He shakes his head. "No. VCE was way worse. Because they make such a big deal of it. And they justify it by telling you uni is just as hard and they're just preparing you for it. But it's not that hard. Sure, there's times when it's stressful, when you have a million things due or exams. But there are times when it's easier too, and you're just going to classes and doing your thing. I mean, think about it: how many uni kids do you see partying?"

"A lot." Olivia lives a couple of blocks from one of the most prestigious universities in Melbourne. She's seen that partying up close.

"Yeah, and most of those kids still get degrees." He grins, swirling the last of the beer in his pint glass. "So stop worrying."

She laughs, dubious. "Okay."

"Seriously, you're going to be fine. Sure, you have to motivate yourself, because the lecturers and tutors don't give a crap whether you hand in your work or come to class. And it takes a little while to get the hang of how it all works, but it's fine." He finishes his beer. "Can I get you another drink?"

Olivia has a quick mental debate with herself, in that way you always have to when guys want to buy you drinks. Because you have to wonder, what are they really buying? But he seems harmless, and it couldn't hurt to hear more about uni. She smiles. "Sure. Just a beer, thanks. A small one, if they have them in this country," she adds, eyeing his pint glass dubiously. She's trying to make it a rule not to drink from glasses as big as her head. She has a feeling it will work out better in the morning.

He takes her empty glass, flashing what he probably thinks is a winning smile, and then turns slowly toward the bar, his eyes only leaving hers at the last second. Olivia sighs. Yep, he's flirting. *Damn.*

She leans against the wall and looks around the pub. And the first thing her eye catches is Liza sitting at a table with Mai and Tam and Campbell and a bunch of his friends, Mai holding court. But before she can meet her eye, Liza quickly looks away. Olivia can't read her expression, but something about it makes her want to figure it out. And she gets the feeling it's not one hundred per cent happy. A feeling she doesn't recognise bubbles through her. Thrown, she glances in her direction again, but there are people obscuring her view now.

She gnaws at a snag on her fingernail and sighs, tired of going over and over all these confusions in her head. She's done way too much thinking the last few days about everything, about uni, about Will, about Liza. Well, not about Liza, exactly but about what happened.

And Olivia has pretty much decided that she was just reacting to a mood and a moment. That somehow the combination of finding out Liza is gay with starting to feel so close to her meant she maybe subconsciously—and stupidly—thought that the only way she could show these newfound feelings of intimacy was by kissing her. Dumb. As if her being gay ruled out Liza's availability for friendship. And, of course, she was a little drunk. Olivia shakes her head. Not her best work. Especially now, after seeing Liza's face. Of course, maybe it has nothing to do with Olivia, and she should probably just check her ego.

Everything that happened after the kiss was probably just the product of too much red wine and getting carried away with a new and surprisingly hot little experience. And now she's being awkward because she wasn't expecting to do or enjoy any of that. She's decided not to make it such a big deal in her head. So what if she's enjoyed some hook-ups with girls? Fluid sexuality is a thing, right? But it doesn't mean anything about her and Liza particularly. It just means maybe she likes being with girls sometimes too.

"Here—that small enough for you?" A beer is thrust in front of her face, contained in a small glass with a handle. She takes it with a polite smile. "Thanks."

"So, where are you going to be studying?" he asks, leaning against the wall, entrenching himself firmly into the rest of her night.

She takes a slow sip of her beer, buying a second to drag herself back into this moment. She can't help feeling like she's strung between two small but vital things, but she has no idea what they are, exactly.

* * *

Tam, London, England

Mai gives the grey industrial landscape outside a royal wave. "Bye, London. You were…limpy."

Liza laughs. "And rainy, too."

"And incredibly crowded." Tam kicks her legs over her backpack, using it as a footrest.

"And, I hate to say it," Olivia adds, "but kinda *cranky*."

They laugh as the train rumbles toward Heathrow.

"Whose pick was it, anyway?" Tam clutching her coffee, and looks around at them.

Olivia raises her hands slowly and cringes. "Me. Sorry, guys."

Mai grins and pats her leg. "Don't be sorry. I still kind of liked it. I like a city with a bit of attitude." She rests her head against the window and sighs. "And I loved staying in a fancy hotel. Thanks, Cousin Le."

"Yeah, thanks, Cousin Le. And I still liked seeing London. But I could just never *live* anywhere that crowded." Tam shudders.

Mai grins at her. "That's because you're a bumpkin."

"True," Tam muses. She can't really argue with that.

"It's going to be even more crowded in Thailand, you know," Olivia warns her.

Tam shrugs. "I know. But there'll also be sunshine and Thai food, so I'm okay with it."

"Mmm, chilli in everything." Olivia wriggles happily.

"Hang on, whose pick was Thailand?" Mai asks. "You chose Italy, didn't you, Tam?"

"Yup."

"It was Kit's," Liza says, staring out the window.

"Oh, of course."

"I wish she were here." Tam plucks at the lid of her coffee and frowns. It's so unfair they'll be there without her.

Olivia frowns. "Me too."

Liza nods, clutching her book to her stomach. "Me three."

Mai holds up her coffee cup as the train enters a tunnel. "To our absent friend."

They all solemnly tap their coffee cups together. "To Kit."

Mai suddenly leans over her seat and nudges a couple sitting in front of her. The woman turns around, surprised, and clutches her suitcase handle closer, as if nervous.

"Sorry to bother you," Mai says super-politely. She holds her phone out to the woman and then gestures at the four of them. "I was wondering if you could please take a photo of us?" The woman looks confused at first, like maybe she doesn't understand English. But then she seems to understand what Mai wants. She takes the phone and holds it up, smiling.

They lean in together, Liza and Tam hanging over the back of the seats, and grin at the camera. The woman takes a couple of pictures and hands the phone back.

Mai checks the photos, grins, and types something. Finally, she looks up. "'Kit, we miss you, we love you, and we wish you were here.'" She presses the screen and nods. "Sent!"

* * *

Olivia, en route to Thailand

Olivia loves planes. Loves being strung in little limbos of coming and going. And she always thinks it's funny how planes never really feel like they're moving unless you're taking off or landing. Sure, you can hear the engines at work, and feel the shifts and bumps of fluctuations in air pressure outside, but you can never really feel the sensation of moving forward.

It's not until you look down, like she is now, that you can sense forward momentum. Way below her moves an undulating landscape of brown and green, obscured every now and then by the occasional scatter of white cloud. She wonders who's down there and what they're doing. Are they enmeshed in the same humdrum mundanities of the everyday that she would be in if she were at home?

She registers the sound of the toilet door opening and closing behind her but still jumps at the sound of the voice over her shoulder. "Hey."

She ignores the immediate apprehension that steals in and turns and smiles. An eye mask sits askew on top of Liza's head, tangled into some curls and making her hair appear even wilder than usual. Olivia plucks at it and chuckles.

Liza grins and yanks it from her head, combing her hair back with her fingers. "Yeah, I don't know how you guys travel with someone so glamorous either." Her smile disappears into a yawn. She waves the mask. "I don't know why I bother. I can never sleep on these things anyway." She peers out the window. "So, what country are you gazing at this time?"

Olivia smiles, remembering their first real conversation. It's strange how quickly things change. How at that time, Liza was just this friend of Kit's that Olivia was suddenly lumped with. And Liza probably felt the same. And now she's beginning to know this girl. She knows that she likes to hear about countries and cities Olivia has visited. She knows now how she was scared of the dark until she was twelve. She knows about the one time she came last in a race because her bra strap broke while she was running and she became completely distracted. She knows how those dark curls bunched at the top of her head are so much softer than they look. "Kazakhstan, I think."

Liza turns to her, eyes wide. "Kazakhstan? This is what I know about Kazakhstan..."

Olivia waits, but not a word comes out of Liza's mouth. She laughs and nudges her shoulder against Liza's. "*Fabulous* dad joke."

Liza gives her a self-satisfied smile. "I thought so. So, my oracle on all things current affairs, what do *you* know about Kazakhstan?"

Olivia shrugs. "Not much, really. Except they moved the capital city twenty years ago."

"What do you mean? They just moved a city somewhere else?"

"Well, no. I think the old capital is still there, but they didn't like it. So they built a new shiny one on the other side of the country and shifted everything important up there."

Liza shakes her head slowly, still peering down. "Wow, you'd be so annoyed if you had some low-level government job and were suddenly told, 'Okay, time to move across the country', wouldn't you?"

"Yeah, that would really suck."

Liza stares out the window, her fingers drumming on the emergency exit. "Do you like to write?" she suddenly asks.

"Me?"

"No, the flight attendants. Yes you."

"I guess, why?"

"No reason, really. I could imagine you as a journalist."

Olivia raises an eyebrow. "Really?"

"Yeah. I don't know. It makes sense. You know a ton more about what's going on in the world than most people our age. And you really care about it too. And if you can write..." She shrugs. "I don't know. Just a thought."

A thought indeed. Olivia's always semiconsciously ruled out the idea of any kind of writing because of her mother. Who would want to live out a career full of endless comparisons? But maybe journalism would be different enough. "Maybe."

"But you want to do Law, right?"

"Yeah," she says, even though that is becoming less and less of a sure thing all the time. Olivia wonders if maybe she's just been caught up in the idea of law. That it was just something to be seen to be striving for at school. But now she's going to enrol in a combined course, she could try some other things out too. She tucks that morsel of a thought away for later and returns to the view.

They lean shoulder to shoulder, looking down at the world moving below them. And the silence that falls between them is easy and intimate. And even though things have been so weird, Olivia is deeply glad she's come to know this girl standing beside her. They've only known each other for a few weeks, but she instinctively seems to understand more about what drives Olivia than anyone else does, except maybe Anna. She's trying to think of some non-intense way to tell her how much she likes that when a hand presses gently on her arm. She turns.

The flight attendant smiles politely. "Girls, the seatbelt sign is on. Back to your seats, please."

CHAPTER 34

Tam,

It's a stunner of a night here. There's one of those red sunsets dropping over the hill, and the air is as still as anything. It'll probably mean bad weather tomorrow, but for now, I'm on the veranda making the most of it.

Your dad wanted to call you, but I wanted to tell you myself. Sorry it isn't a phone call, but it just seemed easier in a letter. I got back from the docs this afternoon. It's not good, kiddo. They found it in my liver, which I guess you know is pretty bad. The doc's talking about all the possibilities for treatment. Operations and transplants and all that kind of thing. But it looks like they have to do a whole lot of figuring out if me and my liver are right for it or worthy of it or some rubbish. What the doc never asked is whether I want it. He just assumes. But you have to weigh these things up, don't you, kiddo? Chance and probability against how you want to spend what might be your last days on this earth. I don't know. We'll see.

Anyway, I hate telling you this while you're on your big adventure. You've had enough bad news and tough times for one year. But I know you'd want to know too. And I know you're mad at your dad for not telling you when he was sick. But forgive him for it. Because right now, writing this letter to you, I know exactly why he found it too hard.

The other thing I need to tell you is that I'm going back up north. To my sister's in Bundaberg. Whatever happens to me from here on is something only family should have to deal with.

And the weird thing is, a part of me is looking forward to going back, now that I know it's happening. It's an odd kind of homesickness. Who knew that after all these years of avoiding it, this soul would suddenly be shocked back into craving that hot sun and that burning sugar cane air?

Anyway, it's getting dark here on the veranda, and I bet Matt wants his computer back. Stay safe and learn some incredible recipes. Then come up there and cook for me one day, will you? I'll show you what miracles can be woven from the stickiest, darkest sugar we can find from the cane fields

Keep being the incredible kid you are.

Bill.

* * *

Liza, Kata, Thailand

The last few hundred metres are hard. Harder than they've been in a long time. It's the humidity. The air feels thick and soupy, like she has to push through it. It's hard to feel like she's pulling enough air into her lungs. Most days, unless she's really dragging, she'll speed up for the last stretch, just to prove to herself she still can. But not today. Today it's all she's got in her just to finish the run.

It's incredible how quickly she's shed the skin of being an athlete. In the training sense, anyway. She misses the girls. She even misses Patrick. But she doesn't miss the rest. The only part that is left is the part that craves the act of surging forward, numbing her mind to the simple, cleansing power of movement. Running without a goal. Just moving.

Here, she's taken to running on the road. It was a matter of the better of two evils in the end. One of the first things Liza learned in this beachside town is that you can't rely on a footpath staying a footpath for long. You can't go more than twenty metres without it being used as a place for groups to congregate or hawk goods. As a temporary resting place for large objects. Or even as a car park. And sometimes it will just disappear altogether. It's just too crowded and unpredictable.

And that's not even counting the constant stream of people. Tourists, schoolkids, traders, and pets all crowd the narrow strips of uneven concrete, making it impossible to move quickly. The road, of course, can get just as crowded, but Liza's already figured out which are the quieter streets to take as she runs away from the beach and up into the peaceful neighbourhoods in the hills.

But even with all this figured out, there's less pleasure to be found in running here. It's just too hot. And sticky. And she always feels like she's sweated out every ounce of fluid in her before she's been on the road five minutes.

She likes Thailand, though. It definitely feels the most exotic of all the places they've been, even with the crowds of Australians they've seen here. She likes its buzzing, frenetic energy, because it comes with smiles and colour and beautiful beaches. *And* with smells and tastes and sights she's never experienced before.

Exhausted and coated in a thick slick of sweat, she takes the last stretch slowly, pacing through the corner as if she were on the final bend of the race, and strides across the sticky tarmac to their bungalow, which lounges, low slung and heavily windowed, opposite a long stretch of coast. Here, by the water, a light breeze lifts the hairs, sweat-clung to her face, bringing a hint of relief.

She stops outside the bungalow, leans over her knees, and pants it out. As soon as she's capable, she kicks off her runners, tears off her socks, and heads inside. Olivia and Mai are both there, relaxing under the air conditioner. Liza shivers as the cold air hits her damp singlet.

Olivia's sprawled on the bed, reading. Mai's on the couch, her feet kicked over the back of it, tapping away on her iPad. Liza gives them a wave and heads straight for the bathroom, panting. She flicks on the shower, waits for the water to run as cool as it's going to get, and sticks her head under it. She'll have a proper shower after she's drunk some water. But right now, she needs instant relief. The coolish water streams through her hair, over her neck, and down her face. When her hair is drenched, she wraps a towel around her head. Cooler already, she makes straight for the small refrigerator in the kitchenette and hunts out the big bottle of water she purposely left chilling before her run.

But it's not there. Clicking her tongue, she checks again and then glances around the room. There it is, next to Mai on the floor, half-empty and probably room temperature again by now. *Crap.* She frowns but doesn't say anything. She should have told them it was hers. This is one of those things about sharing a space, she's learned. Nothing's sacred. Or private.

One of the teeny bottles of water the staff leaves each day inside the fridge door will have to tide her over until she gets up the energy to go buy more.

"How was your run?" Olivia asks without lowering her book.

"Okay," Liza gasps between gulps of the water. She finishes off the bottle and tosses it into the recycling, then grabs another and drinks it down. Sated finally, she stands there, hands on hips, staring into the middle distance, feeling her body and breath begin to calm. Drops of water fall from her hair onto her face and shoulders.

"You didn't see Tam, did you?" Mai asks, her eyes fixed to her screen.

Liza shakes her head and swipes at her forehead with her arm. "No. Why?"

"I don't know. She was being weird."

Liza frowns. "What do you mean, weird?"

Mai points at her iPad. "She asked to borrow this before, to read her email. Her laptop wouldn't connect to the internet or something. And she was sitting here, checking, and then she suddenly just dumped it on the couch and left."

"She looked really upset," Olivia adds.

"Did you ask what was wrong?"

Olivia shakes her head. "No. She left kind of quickly. Bolted, actually."

"You didn't go after her?"

Mai shakes her head. "No," she says slowly. Guiltily even.

Liza looks at Olivia and then back at Mai again. "Why not?"

Mai shrugs. "I don't know. Tam's kind of...intimidating."

Liza's eyes widen in disbelief. "So? You just said she was really upset."

"Yeah, but she makes me nervous," Mai counters.

"Me too, a little bit," Olivia adds quietly in a voice that tells Liza she already knows it's not a good enough reason.

Liza shakes her head, flooded with irritation. "So what? We all helped Mai when she hurt her ankle. And Tam's been carrying your stuff, and helping you get around, just like the rest of us. And you don't help her because you're *slightly intimidated?*" She points at both of them one by one. "You know, you two can be pretty damn intimidating, too. I was nervous of both of you when we left on this trip. Hell, maybe I still am a little bit now. But you know what? If either of you seemed really upset, I would still come after you." She feels bad as soon as she says it, but at the same time, she doesn't have time to worry about their feelings.

"Sorry, but that's a pathetic excuse. You know, Tam's been waiting for some news about her dad. He's been really sick this year." She flings off her towel, pulls on her sandals, and lets out an impatient breath.

"We didn't know that." Olivia is sitting up on the bed now, looking incredibly guilty.

"Well, you do now." Liza turns on her heel. "I'm going to find her."

She heads straight for the beach, mostly because that's where she would go if she were upset. Everywhere else is too crowded and loud, and there's nowhere else to go, really. She ducks across the road in a brief break in the traffic and jogs across the grass to where the sand starts.

And she was right. Because by sheer luck, or maybe because of Tam's flaming hair, she spots her immediately, sitting cross-legged on one of those ubiquitous beach lounges for hire right near the path. It isn't until she gets up close that she realises Olivia is right behind her, barefoot and panting.

Nervous now, Liza rounds the seat and stands in front of her. "Hey."

And even though she says it quietly, Tam jumps. Her face is a blotchy red, and her eyes are pink from crying. She gives Liza a tiny smile and drops her head again.

Liza drops down next to her. "Is it your dad?"

Tam shakes her head but doesn't say anything.

Olivia perches on the lounge opposite. "Are you okay?" She leans forward and presses her hand on Tam's wrist. "You seem really upset."

Tam shakes her head and sniffs loudly. Before she can say anything, Mai arrives, hobbling, red-faced, across the sand to them. She drops down next to Olivia, panting, and looks between them, silently asking what she's missed.

Liza tries again. "What's happened?"

Tam takes in a deep breath, swipes her eyes clear of tears, and tells them about her Dad's friend, Bill, whom Liza has heard her talk about so many times. Her cooking mentor. As she fills them in on some miserable, frightening news she's just got, Liza lets out a slow breath, horrified. How scary.

As Tam talks, a young boy comes over, standing at a discreet but intent distance, waiting for payment for the lounges. Liza cringes. She hasn't got a cent on her. But Mai saves the day, pulling a couple of notes from the pocket of her cut-offs. She thrusts them at him with a small smile. He goes to make the change, but she waves him away.

They listen to the rest of Tam's story while waves pound the beach and tourists and hawkers stream around them. It's so strange, Liza thinks, to be caught in this little pocket of grief while people drink and eat and swim around them, safely ensconced in their vacation happiness.

When Tam finishes, they are silent for a minute. Liza doesn't say anything, because she has absolutely no idea what to say. What could possibly make Tam feel any better? She's too scared to touch her either, to offer comfort with an arm around her or a hand on her back. Tam doesn't seem like the type of person to want that kind of comfort.

It's Mai, of all people, who speaks first. "That sucks. Big time," she says, with her usual bluntness.

"Yeah, I'm so sorry," Olivia says.

"Me too," Liza adds. "You love Bill."

"I do," Tam says. She begins to cry again, with quietly awful, choking little sobs. And now Liza can't help herself. She puts a hand on Tam's back, pressing lightly. When the sobs finally subside, Tam speaks, her voice still grizzled by tears. "I can't believe he's not going to be there when I get home." She shakes her head. "I might not ever see him again."

"You could go see him when you get back. With your Dad maybe?" Liza suggests.

"I guess. I might never see him *well* again, though." She takes a deep breath and sighs loudly. "Like he was. Oh God, what if he decides not to get treatment?"

No one answers at first, letting Tam slide back into her misery. Then Mai stretches her bad foot out on the sand and speaks into the silence. "You know, my grandmother died of cancer when I was eleven."

Liza frowns. Does Tam really need to hear that right now?

"Stomach cancer. She was seventy." Mai tucks her hair behind her ear and bites her lip. Liza's never seen her look so vulnerable. "The worst part was that she refused to be treated. No one told me, but I found out anyway. And I was *so* mad at her. But I couldn't tell her I knew either, because I wasn't supposed to. I'd just overheard my parents talking about it. But when she died, I was *so* angry. In fact, I was so pissed at her that I couldn't even be sad for ages." She blinks slowly, staring down at her hands. "I mean, now I'm older, and I kind of get it. She was old, and the treatment for that cancer was really harsh. She probably didn't think she'd survive it. But still."

"I think it's the same for Bill," Tam says. "Not the age part. But the treatment sounds so intense. I think he'll only do it if he thinks it would give him a good chance. Only if it's worth going through."

Mai nods. "Still, that's shit and terrifying and totally un-fucking-fair. I'm so sorry, Tam."

"I'm sorry about your grandma."

They trade sympathy in slow smiles at each other. Liza stares at Mai. How come Mai is all of a sudden terrifyingly good at knowing the right thing to say? Who would have thought her special brand of brutal candour would be needed right now?

No one Liza knows has ever died, except her opa, her grandfather on her dad's side. But she doesn't really remember it or him.

They sit there for a while in a heavy, contemplative silence. Suddenly, Olivia gets up and walks away. Liza wonders if something's up, but a few minutes later, she's back with all kinds of chocolate clutched in her hands. She plonks down on the lounger and gives them a sheepish smile. "I've never known a single person who died or ever had anything like this happen. But I thought maybe chocolate might help? I know it's not even midday, but..." She shrugs.

Mai shrugs and takes a bag. "Yeah, but I'm pretty sure this is one of those occasions that calls for chocolate for breakfast."

They laugh and take a packet, opening them up and passing it around. Olivia hands Tam an open packet of Kit Kat. "Well, we're all hoping for good news. And if you need anything, ask."

"Thanks," Tam mutters, her voice thick again. She pops a piece in her mouth, as if to stem more sobs.

They pass the chocolate around, talking every now and then, but mostly just quietly being there for Tam. When they're done, Mai suddenly clambers to her feet.

Olivia squints up at her. "Where are you going?"

"Got an ankle appointment in town. Dad organised it through some doctor friend. I might be off these stupid things when I get back," she says with a grin, tucking them under her armpits. "Dad says they might just give me some kind of walking stick."

"Do you need help getting there? I could come with."

"Nah, Reception booked me a taxi. It's going to be easy. I might be a few hours, though." She turns to Tam, frowning. "Sorry to leave right now."

"I'm okay," Tam tells her.

"She has us," Olivia says.

"See you guys later." She limps away.

Liza turns back to their shrunken group. Tam looks more peaceful now, as if the initial shock has settled. "What do you want to do now?"

Tam shrugs. "I really don't know."

"Do you want a swim or a walk?"

Tam shrugs again. Then she tips her head back and wipes the sheen of sweat from her face. "I can't think. Why does it have to be so hot?"

"I know." Liza sighs. "Humidity makes everything harder."

Olivia picks up their rubbish. "Why don't we go back to the room? Hang in the air conditioning and watch some TV?"

Tam nods slowly. "Yeah, let's do that."

* * *

After ten minutes of the air con blasting, the room is downright chilly. Liza shivers slightly as she changes out of her running singlet. On the porch, she can hear the low tones of Tam talking to her dad on the phone.

The bathroom door opens, and Olivia comes out. She sits on the edge of a bed, pulls her knees to her chest and hugs them, as if she's cold too.

"I feel *really* awful about before." Olivia stares down at her feet. Her toenails are painted a deep blue. "I should have checked on Tam. I just thought maybe she was having a fight with that boyfriend or something. I didn't realise it would be something so serious." She shrugs. "But even if it wasn't, I should have still checked on her. That was really shitty."

Liza watches Olivia as she stares downward, frowning, caught up in her guilt. She feels bad for Olivia. Not because she regrets not helping Tam. She should a little. But because she gets the feeling no one could ever be harder on Olivia than she is on herself.

She's just trying to figure out what to say when Tam comes back in. She tosses her phone onto a bed and flops down next to it.

"How's your Dad?" Liza asks.

Tam shrugs and runs a finger back and forth over the patterned spread. "Couldn't get him. He's probably in the orchards. I'll try later. I just talked to Matt for a minute."

Before anyone can say anything else, the cabin door opens, and Mai shuffles in. "Surprise!" she says, holding up a high-tech looking walking stick. The bandage on her ankle has been downgraded to one of those stretchy support elastics. "Check me out!"

"Yay!" Olivia claps loudly.

Mai holds up her hand to stop them. "But I've got something even better." Her eyes are alight. Liza wonders for a moment if she even remembers the mood she left behind.

"What?" Olivia sounds more suspicious than excited.

Mai just grins and holds out her hand in front of the door. "Ta da!" she cries.

At first, the shadow that steps inside the door is just that: a backlit shadow, reduced to outline by the fierce afternoon sun. Then, as it steps into the cool, darkened room, it turns into...Kit.

Liza's jaw drops. Before she can say it, Olivia's already gasping, "What are you doing here?"

Kit grins. "Hi!" Then she dumps her bag and goes straight over to her cousin, flopping on the bed and engulfing her in a huge hug. "You okay? I'm so, so sorry, Tam."

Tam starts to cry again. But she smiles through her tears and yanks at a strand of Kit's dirty-blonde hair. "How the hell did you get here?"

Kit laughs. "You're not going to believe it." She jumps up from the bed. "I'll tell you once I say hi to these beautiful creatures."

Kit skips over to Olivia, who is still standing agape between the two beds where she jumped and froze when Kit came in. Kit grabs her by the shoulders and shakes her. "Hi!"

Olivia grabs Kit's face and squeezes it like an old Italian nonna, grinning. Then she gives Kit a smacking kiss on the cheek.

Kit turns to Liza, her blue eyes shining. Still shocked into silence, Liza slowly finds her feet. And when she's finally upright, she engulfs Kit in a ferocious hug.

"Lizey," Kit whispers from somewhere deep inside their hug. "You good?"

"I'm good," Liza mutters, squeezing Kit's small frame. She lets her go and stares at her. "What the hell are you *doing here?*"

CHAPTER 35

Olivia, Kata, Thailand

Olivia trails behind the others as they weave their way down the narrow street. Tam is up front, phone in hand, navigating. She's hunting for the side street harbouring the restaurant she wants them to go to tonight.

They've already been on a couple of these culinary mystery tours with Tam so far as she searches out places she's read about. And even today, in her misery, Tam flat out refuses to eat in any of the crowded places all along the beach strip. Says she hates their toned-down Thai flavours and their side serves of fries for the unadventurous tourists. She wants *real* Thai food.

Tonight Tam's seeking out another place she's read about on her foodie blogs. Olivia doesn't mind the hunt, though. The end result is usually worth it, even if the walk is long and the places don't look like much when she gets there. She's learned that appearances can be deceiving when it comes to restaurants here.

Mai's walking beside Tam, poring over the map. Behind them, Liza and Kit follow. Kit's arm is thrown around Liza's waist, conjoining them like bestie Siamese twins. Olivia still cannot compute the fact that Kit is here. It's so strange and awesome.

Mai turns and whistles. She points down a small lane wending its way uphill. You can't go anywhere away from the beach road without hitting a steep ascent, Olivia and her calves have quickly learned. She obediently follows, watching Kit and Liza. They look so different from each other from behind, Kit with her messy blonde hair and Liza with her cascade of dark curls. They're so different from the front too. Staring at them, a feeling she can't place ripples through her. She sighs. This whole week has been packed with unfamiliar feelings and diabolical overthinking. It's both confusing and boring.

She follows them along the steep path and into a garden shaded by the wide sprawl of a wax-leafed tree. The restaurant looks like an open garage with a busy kitchen inside. A series of tables and chairs are spread out under the trees. Waiters dart between tables, taking orders and running food while tinny Thai music whines from a set of speakers dangling from a branch.

They sit at one of the few vacant tables. Menus are instantly slapped down on the worn laminate. Olivia picks one up, turning it around in her hands. One side has a small section in English. She puts it down without reading it, though. Thinking isn't high on her list of capabilities today.

"So, Kit, how did your mum afford your ticket?" Liza settles into a seat opposite Olivia.

Kit passes a menu to Tam and laughs. "You're not going to believe this. Remember those scratchies she's addicted to?"

"Of course I do. I bought her some for Christmas last year." Liza's jaw drops. "She won? Like more than five dollars?"

Kit cackles. "Yup. She won *ten thousand* dollars."

"No way!" Tam leans forward, blinking. "Go Annie!"

"I know, right? So she rings me up and she's like, 'Okay, you're going to Thailand to meet the girls.' Of course I was all 'what are you talking about?' and 'no way.' I wanted her to her spend her money on something for herself. But she kept going on and on about how I'd missed my big holiday with you guys and that it was a rite of passage and that she has plenty of money for all of us to have a treat, blah blah. Chloe's getting a bond on a flat." She rolls her eyes. "Which means she's moving out, thank God. Anyway, and then your dad rang, Tam, and told us how you guys were worried about Bill."

Tam nods, her chin propped in her hand.

"And then she *really* insisted. Said I needed to come and hang out with you."

Tam presses her shoulder against Kit's. "I'm glad you did."

"I know. It's so insane. Though Mum's probably spent more than ten thousand dollars in her life buying those things."

"I didn't think anyone ever won big," Liza says.

"Nah, sometimes they do." Mai leans forward, folding her arms on the table. "When we were doing statistics, Mr Bacash showed us this old video from the news when this guy won like a hundred thousand bucks or something. He was this really down-on-his-luck old dude, and when they got him to re-enact buying and winning the ticket for the cameras, he won *more* money. How crazy is that?"

Kit shakes her head. "No way."

"Yes way. He just started weeping right there on the spot. It was so cute. Anyway," she says, shimmying her shoulders and pointing at Kit. "How amazing am I for keeping this visit a secret?"

"How long have you known she was coming?" Mai's got a point. Olivia is stunned that she kept her mouth shut on this one.

"A few days. Kit emailed me. It was nearly impossible not to act all excited and give it away."

Olivia catches Tam's eye, and they burst out laughing. So does Liza.

"What?" Mai looks between them all, frowning. "What?"

Tam leans forward, and rests her hand on Mai's wrist. "Mai, you're always excited."

"What's so bad about that?"

"Nothing," Olivia says through a giggle.

"Anyway, I kept it a secret. I'm amazing," Mai sings loudly, flinging out her hands.

Olivia laughs at her blatant self-congratulations. "Yes you are." She turns to Kit. "So how long are you staying?"

"Just a week. I'm staying here, and then I'm going with Tam to Bangkok for a couple of days. I didn't exactly give my jobs much notice, and I want to keep them. When do you go to China?"

"Same day these guys fly home. Like, an hour or two before their flight."

"You're going to China?" Liza asks.

"Shanghai. Just to see Dad for Christmas."

Liza just nods and looks away quickly.

Olivia blushes, though she has no idea why, and looks down, inspecting a torn fingernail so she doesn't have to meet anyone's eye. Why does she have to feel so awkward still?

"It's just you and me on the flight home, lady." Mai grins at Liza and then turns to Tam, flapping the menu in her direction. "Hey, what are we eating here Ms Master Chef?"

Tam is already scrutinising the menu. "It's supposed to have incredible noodle dishes. We can either order our own or share?"

“Let’s share,” Olivia says quickly, happy to put her dinner choice in someone else’s hands. Then she doesn’t have to think. “You guys decide.” She drops her menu and immediately fades out of the decision-making.

It’s been such a weird day. Everything went sideways. She still feels like such an asshole for not going after Tam. Still, she would never have expected Liza to come at them the way she did. But there was something about it being Liza that made it even more confronting. She was *ferocious*. It was unnerving and also kind of amazing. Kit arriving out of the blue is also kind of unsettling. Olivia isn’t exactly sure why, though. Maybe it’s just the unexpectedness of it all. Whatever it is has left Olivia feeling weird and edgy.

She rests her cheek on her hand and listens to the others joke with the young waiter, wishing she knew why she feels this way.

* * *

The bass thumps in Olivia’s chest, making her feel slightly nauseous. She tries to ignore it as she sips her cocktail, a lurid green thing Mai brought back from the bar before she flitted off to socialise. It’s not really helping with the nausea much.

They are in a tiny bar in a laneway off the beach road. It’s crammed with the town’s small but clearly raucous gay community and a throng of tourists. It’s steaming and loud, and the atmosphere would probably be infectiously joyous any other night if Olivia weren’t in the mood she is in right now.

“It’s only fair,” Mai had insisted as she held up the rainbow-coloured flier someone has just thrust at her. “We’ve dragged Liza to all kinds of straight places, now it’s our turn to go to one of hers.”

“Um, that’s okay, *really*.” Liza looked completely dubious, like a gay bar had no part in her plan for the night. Or even her week. But it was too late, Mai was already asking the guy in the bright red singlet who handed her the flier where they would find the place. Olivia smiled half-affectionately and half-impatiently. She knew this whole expedition was less about Liza, really, and more about Mai and her constant need to be wild and whacky and adventurous. Here’s something else she can Instagram the hell out of.

So here they are. And Olivia wishes they weren't. Mai and Liza are over at the opposite wall with a bunch of Swedish girls Mai started chatting to about half a minute after they got here. Olivia and Kit are perched at the end of the bar with their drinks. Kit's telling her about her new housemate, and Olivia's trying her best to listen, nodding in what she hopes are the right places. She just can't seem to focus on anything tonight.

While Kit talks, Olivia sips her sickeningly sweet drink and watches Mai talk while Liza and a girl with a short blonde bob listen. Liza's wearing that blue kimono top they bought that first day in Florence. It's the first time Olivia's seen her in it. It looks great against her skin, which is even darker after a few days here.

Every now and then, the blonde girl turns to Liza and asks her something, as if trying to draw her into the conversation. But Liza doesn't say much. She just nods, gives short answers, and gives her that shy Liza smile.

Olivia knows now that Liza's not really that shy, though. She's quiet, and she's more likely to only contribute to a group conversation if she's prompted. But it's not really *shyness*. It just reads that way. If you ask her something directly, she'll look you in the eye and answer straight away. And when she's talking one-on-one, she can even be chatty.

Maybe Liza's just not in the mood for this night. Olivia can definitely sympathise with that. All she wants to do is go to the bungalow and sleep. But she can't. Tam's gone back there to talk to her sick family friend, and Olivia doesn't want to disturb her. So she's forcing herself to stay here with this obnoxious house music and these fractured conversations. She guiltily tunes back into Kit's chatter. When she's done with her story about something that happened at her work, Kit leans in. "Hey, so tell me exactly what happened when you saw Will again?"

Olivia's just about to tell her when Liza squeezes through the crowd and joins them. She doesn't say anything, though, just stands there, like she's taking social shelter.

"Hey!" Kit grins slyly, like she knows exactly what Liza is doing. "Not into her?"

“Nah.” Liza gives her a genuinely bashful half smile and focuses on the ground as she sips her drink.

Kit wraps an arm around her waist. “Want me to pretend to be your girlfriend?”

“I’m alright. They’re all really nice. I said I’d get Mai a drink. You guys want anything?”

Kit contemplates the last of the green sludge. “No thanks. I think these things are actually more sugar high than alcohol buzz.” She yawns. “And I’m too tired from the plane to drink.”

Liza meets Olivia’s eye for the first time. “Drink?”

“I’m good.”

Kit grabs Liza’s hand as she turns for the bar. “Dance with me later?”

“Of course. We all will.” She looks at Olivia again, smiling her invitation.

And Olivia can’t help smiling back at her. “Maybe.”

CHAPTER 36

Kit, Kata, Thailand

Kit rests her elbows on the wet tiles and kicks her legs gently in the water. It's only early, but already she can feel the stickiness of the day descending on them.

"This Lewis guy doesn't have a thing for you, does he?"

Kit frowns at her cousin. "What? No." She bites her lip. He doesn't, does he? He doesn't *act* like it. He just seems like a good friend. Brotherly. Like someone who looks out for her. They have fun together. She tells Tam that much.

Tam nods slowly. "Guys always have this protective thing with you, don't they? I guess it's because you're cute and small." She laughs. "They never think that about me."

Kit wrinkles her nose. "I don't *want* guys to feel protective of me. I can look after myself."

Tam chuckles. "Sometimes."

Kit pouts at her, miffed. But she knows she can't be mad, really. This getting-her-crap-together thing is only new.

Tam leans on the edge of the pool next to her, her pale, freckled arms folded in front of her. "You know, I'm thinking maybe I'll come home when you do."

Kit stops kicking and frowns. "What? Why?"

"Because." Tam rests her chin on her arms. "Because of Bill leaving. And I'm worried about leaving Dad alone. It must be weird for him."

"He's not alone, Tam. Aunt Anita's there. And Matt's working with him at the orchards, isn't he?"

"I know, but—"

Kit stares at her. "But what? Yeah, I'm sure he's sad and worried and everything, but what can you really do about that? It just...*is*. You can't change it."

Tam sighs. "I know."

Kit nudges her cousin. "And what about these cooking classes? You can't give them up. You've already paid, and you've been hanging out for them all year."

Tam turns and rests her cheek on her arm. "I guess I just feel bad about being away so long, with everything that has happened this year."

"Tam, he *wants* you to do this. I bet if you told him you wanted to come home, he'd tell you to stay and not to worry about him."

Tam nods, but Kit's not convinced. It's impossible to persuade Tam of anything she doesn't want to be persuaded of.

Finally, Tam says. "It's hard to get out of the habit of thinking I have to look after him. And out of the habit of worrying about him."

"I know." Kit nudges her shoulder. "But you have to."

Tam's eyes tear up. "I think I'm just homesick. I think I've been homesick most of the time. This trip has been amazing, but I just want home and Dad. I miss it all the time."

"That's not really surprising. Remember when you used to come stay with us in Melbourne? You were *always* homesick. Even if your dad was with you." Kit snickers. "Then you'd just get homesick for the dogs."

Tam lets out a small chuckle. "True. Anyway, I don't know. I'm just thinking about it."

"It will all be there in a few weeks' time. So for whatever my opinion's worth, I think you should finish the trip," Kit tells her. Then she decides to change the subject. Tam's so damn stubborn that she knows there's not really any point in pushing it more. "So, what's happening with Matt?"

"I don't know. I mean, we talk all the time, and he's not dating anyone else, but it's confusing. I can't really tell where we're at. If that was a one-off for him or more."

"Sounds like you just need to ask him flat out."

Kit likes Matt. She's hung out with him a couple of times. He and Tam are perfect for each other. She can imagine them marrying, having kids, and buying their own place somewhere on the peninsula. They're both that kind of people. Settlers. They seem like they belong to that place.

Tam turns to her and grins. "I probably should ask. But I'm scared." Then she flicks some water at her. "Anyway, it's so good to see you. I'm really, really glad you came."

Kit smiles at her cousin. Fierce, honest and awesome Tam. She's glad to see her too. In so many ways, she makes up for having Chloe as a sister.

Tam pushes away from the wall and sculls slowly backward across the pool. "Is it really weird that we're swimming in a pool when there's a whole ocean across the road?"

Kit shrugs. "Probably." She dives under the water, kicking through the cold, clean water, incredibly happy she's not in Melbourne getting ready for yet another shift at work. She swims lazily to the end of the pool and gazes around the courtyard with its lush, exotic garden and vibrant flowers. The air smells so different here, smoky and fragrant. She loves being somewhere so different from anything she's ever seen or experienced. She sighs. Five more months, she reminds herself. Just one five-month slog, and then she'll have enough saved to do more of this.

She hasn't told anyone about her overseas plans yet. She doesn't know why, exactly. Maybe she's scared they'll think the idea is dumb or that it's just another half-baked plan that won't work out. She'll have to tell them at some point. But for now, she's holding it close like a small, treasured seed of possibility.

CHAPTER 37

Liza, Kata, Thailand

Kit loops her arm through Liza's. "So you've decided?"

Liza nods and kicks at a lump of seaweed that has washed up onto the beach. "I think I'd already decided before I left. Subconsciously, anyway. You know, I had this conversation with Olivia about it back in Florence, and I was talking about it like I had this decision to make. But then I realised it was actually already made. I don't want to race anymore."

"Then don't."

Liza smiles. She loves the way Kit sees things so simply. Not for the first time, she wishes hard that Kit will find the thing that makes her happy too. Aside from making other people feel good.

And quitting running *is* simple, she realises, when you strip it back of things like guilt and obligation and all those things that keep you doing something when you don't want to do it anymore. Just don't do it. Everyone will get used to it. They'll have to.

"Hey, speaking of Olivia, is she alright?" Kit asks suddenly. "She's been kind of quiet."

Thrown, Liza shrugs. "Don't know. I guess so."

"Mm," is all Kit says. They skirt around a gaggle of kids digging a deep crater around a lumpy sandcastle. "I can't believe Will's being such a prick. I think it's really thrown her. She seems distracted."

Liza just nods. Because she can't exactly tell Kit that she has no idea because she and Olivia haven't really been talking to each other much since they slept together. It's totally uncharted territory, this feeling of wanting to keep something from Kit. Liza's always told her everything. But not this. She can't. It's too close and too weird. And she childishly wants to keep it between her and Olivia. Because maybe that's the only thing keeping it a little special for her. So she won't have to turn it from an incredible night into an embarrassing drunken mistake. Something public, available for comment or gossip. Not that Kit *would* gossip, but still.

And what makes her feel even worse is the vague flickers of relief that Kit hasn't been here this whole time. Because she knows for certain, somehow, that nothing would have happened between her and Olivia if Kit had been here the whole time, buffering their growing friendship. Every time she feels that sneaking, guilt-making feeling, she strikes it back.

"So has everyone been getting along?" Kit asks.

Liza squints out across the water to where people are riding jet skis across the crests of waves and shrugs again. "Yeah, mostly. It was a bit weird at first, not knowing each other that well. But we're pretty good now." She doesn't say anything about snapping at Olivia and Mai the other day. Why bother? That whole miserable little morning after Tam got the news has actually made them feel closer. At least it feels that way to Liza.

Kit smiles. "Good. You know, I was thinking about it a lot when you guys first left. I was really worried. I kept trying to figure out if any of you wouldn't like each other."

Liza grins. "Nope. All good."

"Good." Kit moves closer to the water, kicking her feet in the wet sand. "So, meet any more nice gay ladies since Portugal?"

"No." And it's not a lie. Because as far as she knows Olivia's straight as hell. Except when red wine makes her not.

"Boo. Any *not* nice girls?"

"Ha ha, *no*. Any more questions, Mum?"

"Sorry, I just want to know everything, that's all. I missed you all."

"I know." She grabs Kit around her waist and squeezes her tight.

* * *

Olivia, Kata, Thailand

Olivia doesn't figure out what it is making her feel so damn off until the next day at the beach. It takes a while, though. For the first half of the day, all she knows is she feels unprecedentedly shitty. And now, sitting on the beach in the early afternoon, the feeling has shifted to good old-fashioned angst.

She watches Liza and Kit wander towards them, deep in chat, and wonders if Liza has told Kit. They *are* best friends. Do best friend disclosure rules trump the "what happened in London" holiday rules? Olivia has no idea. She does know that with Kit's arrival there has been a resurgence in weirdness about what happened between.

And weirdly, it's partly because she misses Liza. She'd subconsciously decided that in Thailand, she and Liza would settle back into that easy, warm dynamic they'd created before they slept together. But they've barely had a moment together. Kit's arrival hasn't allowed it.

It's funny. If Olivia had been posed the idea that she'd feel jealous of anything, she'd have thought it would be about having to share Kit with Liza. Because that's something she's never had to do. The two friendships have always been so separate that there's never been need to negotiate these uncertain terrains of possession. But Olivia's realising it's actually the other way around. A tiny part of her is disgruntled at having to suddenly give up Liza to Kit.

She tries to push these thoughts away, tired of her own pettiness and misery. Instead, she concentrates on tuning into the conversation in their little beach camp. Kit and Liza are back, and Mai's jabbing at Liza's belly, bared in her dark orange bikini. "Did you get that ridiculous stomach *just* from running? Because if that's the case, I'm hitting the streets the minute I get this off." She wriggles her bandaged foot.

"Me too," Tam says, looking self-consciously between her own slightly rounded belly and Liza's disgustingly toned one.

Liza laughs and lies back on her sun lounge. "It's not just running. We had to do a heap of conditioning and weight work. Sit-ups, lifts, everything."

"Damn." Mai sips her coconut juice and sighs. "Oh well. Guess I better not run then. Phew."

Kit sits down on the beach bed with Liza. "I got all obsessed and jealous with Lizey's abs once. I asked her to show me how to do some exercises to get them. I nearly died!"

Liza laughs and pats Kit's leg. "Yeah, you refused to walk to school the next day, you were so sore."

Olivia watches as Liza holds her phone up and begins to narrate all her trip photos for Kit. As she speaks, she glances at Olivia, and then looks away just as quickly.

What does that mean? Olivia picks up her tablet and tries to read instead of giving over to these constant thoughts about the riddle of Liza. But she can't focus. When Olivia looks at Liza, something quickens in her and all she hears is noise. She doesn't know what to make of these rogue reactions, but they're becoming harder to ignore. She surreptitiously examines her. She isn't beautiful or even classically pretty. But then she *is*. You just have to look at her for longer than most people would bother to give a plain-on-first-look face. Then you realise she's actually quite striking. It's a slow burn, but it's worth it.

Olivia sucks in a breath. A blush washes over her cheeks. Jesus, what is she *doing?* So much for trying not to think about this. Instead, it's on a tortuous loop. Embarrassed, she stares out at the beach. It's more packed than usual today. Children cluster near the rocks, all intent on some miniature fantasyland they have created that the adult eye cannot fathom. Local women traipse slowly down the beach hawking sarongs and fans to tourists. Leathery old men spray tanning oil over themselves. Impossibly skinny women in barely-there bikinis hold the hands of their boyfriends, chiding them in languages she cannot understand.

Kit suddenly squeals and breaks into laughter. "Olivia!"

Olivia jumps. "What?"

Kit is peering at Liza's phone, still giggling. "That's too funny."

"What is?" Olivia sits up.

Liza takes the phone from Kit and comes over to her. Grinning, she leans down and places the screen in front of Olivia's face. "I forgot about this," she says with a laugh.

Olivia doesn't remember the photo being taken, even though the scene is familiar. It's from Italy, right at the beginning of their Cinque de Terre walk. They stopped for gelato before they began. She's standing in front of ocean, a dripping pink ice cream clutched in her hand, pulling a stupid face. Her hair is blowing across her crossed eyes, and her stained-pink tongue is sticking out. Olivia laughs reluctantly. It's awful. She snatches the phone out of Liza's hand and gives her a playful glare. "This better not be on any social media."

Liza laughs and shakes her head. "It's not. I promise."

Liza goes to take the phone back, but Olivia holds it away, still staring. "I don't even remember you taking it. Why didn't you show me?"

Liza clasps the wrist holding the phone. "Because I knew you'd tell me to delete it." She grins at her, playful, her brown eyes shining.

"True. I probably would have."

Liza beams knowingly at her. And with that smile, something in Olivia's chest thumps. It's so insistent that she knows it's telling her something very important. It's telling her something she's already supposed to know about the sincerity of that "I know you" smile Liza is giving her. It's telling her she should pay attention to the way it seems to say "*I like* knowing these things about you." About how it's especially and only for her. And it's telling Olivia she likes it. More than likes it.

Liza gives her one more teasing smile, plucks the phone out of her hand and saunters back to Kit. Olivia shuts her eyes, squeezes them tight against the overwhelming, seasick sense of inevitability. It's a sensation that forces her to realise, like advice from the bluntest but kindest of friends, that this is not just about sometimes being into girls. This thump in her chest is very specifically about being into Liza. Sickeningly so. And she has just been letting herself avoid those feelings.

It's not new, either, she realises. Her consciousness has just chosen not to pay attention. But now she can't ignore it. She sneaks another look at Liza from behind her iPad, watching as she points at something on her screen and laughs. And Olivia stops breathing for a moment. She's such a fucking idiot. How did she manage to convince herself that she's anything but completely into this girl? This girl who manages to be so beautifully constant and so deliciously surprising at the same time? She lets the breath out slowly. Yep, she is nothing other than smitten, and she's the dope who didn't see it coming. Not at all. Not one little bit.

She drops her tablet onto her stomach and stares out at the restless blue water. Now what the hell is she going to do about it?

CHAPTER 38

Tam, Kata, Thailand

Tam strolls into the bungalow and kicks off her sandals. She tosses the plastic bag full of weird and wonderful snacks she's found at the market onto the bed and takes a gulp from her water bottle. It's *hot* out there.

Kit's on Tam's laptop, chatting away.

"Who are you talking to?" She flops on the bed next to her.

Kit waves a hand at her as if to tell her to shut up. Then she says. "Thanks, Matt. Great to see you."

Tam is instantly alert. It's not *her* Matt, is it? She goes to grab the laptop and swing it around, but Kit slaps her hand away and says. "Okay, so Uncle Pete, she's here now. Tell her she has to stay, okay?"

Tam sits up, mouth open. "What the hell, Kit?"

Kit just grins and jabs a finger at her. "I may not be able to convince you of anything, you stubborn wench. But I am *not* above dobbing. You should know that. Welcome to your intervention." She turns the computer around. And there, on the screen, is her dad, looking as uncomfortable as hell, but there. When he sees Tam, his face breaks into that easy grin of his.

"Tamo."

"Dad," she breathes. She is overwhelmed with a sense of relief just to be looking at him.

"So what's this crap about you coming home early?"

Kit squeals, jumping off the bed. "And I'm *out*." She bolts for the door.

Tam goes to give her a filthy look, but she knows it won't be that convincing.

* * *

Liza, Kata, Thailand

Liza lies on her back and blinks into the semidarkness. She's too restless and full of thoughts to relax. And this room is too crammed with people and their sleeping sounds and movements. It's hard to carve a mental space for herself in this quiet din. She's been lying here for an hour, and she's no closer to sleep than she was when Tam flicked the last lamp out.

Giving up completely, she clambers out of bed, slips on her shoes, and pads outside. The air is less humid now, and she can hear the music and the traffic up on the road where all the clubs are.

"Hey."

She jumps and spins around. Olivia is curled up on one of the wooden chairs outside the bungalow.

Liza gives her a nervous smile. She hasn't been alone with Olivia in days. "I can't sleep," she whispers.

"Me either." Olivia chews on her lip. She looks kind of tense and worried. Maybe Kit was right. Maybe this Will thing is really bothering her.

"You want to go for a walk, maybe?" Olivia suddenly asks.

Liza ignores the tremor in her stomach and nods. "Sure."

They cross the road in silence and head, on some mutual automatic pilot, for the beach. The soft, dry sand seeps between Liza's sandals and the soles of her feet. All over the beach, dark figures in pairs or groups move up and down the stretch of sand, little more than moving shadows in the darkness and distance.

They stop on the crest, where the sand is still dry, and sit. Liza presses her palms on it, against the day's remaining warmth. She doesn't say anything. She's not quite sure what to say. So she sifts her fingers through the sand and glances slyly at Olivia. She's got her arms wrapped around her legs and her chin on her knees. The breeze whips her long hair across her cheek. She tucks it behind her ear and frowns. Liza's never seen her look so tense.

"You okay?"

Olivia smiles slowly, staring out at the black water. "I guess." She suddenly presses a hand on Liza's arm. "Hey, I wanted to say I'm so sorry. About snapping at you in London. I still feel awful for being like that. To you."

Liza just stares, shocked into silence by this sudden physical contact.

Olivia rewraps her arms around her legs, hugging them against her. "When I said I needed a break, I didn't really mean I wanted space from you. I was just in a world of confusion, I guess." She presses her lips into a thin line. "I'd just been out with Will, and it did *not* go well. At all. And then there was what happened with us confusing the hell out of me..." She falters for a moment and turns to face the water.

Liza blinks, but doesn't say anything. She had no idea that what happened between them had affected Olivia that much. And because she suddenly desperately wants to know why, she doesn't speak. Doesn't want to destroy the possibility that Olivia might say so with her own clumsy words.

Olivia turns and gives her a weak smile. "And then there was the fact that seeing Will reminded me how our problem had always been me not feeling the same for him as he did for me. There was sleeping with you—with a girl—and I really liked it. And I guess maybe I was trying to figure out if these things were, like, mutually exclusive or not, you know?"

Liza nods blindly. A surge of hope, of possibility, rises in her. But she checks herself. Even if Olivia is having some kind of girl-liking revelation, she might not necessarily be having them about *her*. Maybe Liza just happened to be there.

"And it kind of freaked me out. And then, when you came to see me at the hotel, it was all kind of hitting me. Total information overload, I guess." Olivia lets go of her legs and sits back a little, flicking her hair out of her face. "It doesn't freak me out, you know. Being with a girl. It freaks me out that maybe it's a *thing*. Because if so, how did I not already know it was a thing?" She holds up her hands. "I mean, I feel like such a dumb ass. Because if it *is* a thing, it's taken me way too long to figure it out."

Liza bristles. She shakes her head. "Sheez, Olivia, will you just let up on yourself?"

Olivia gives her a startled look.

"Are your parents like, *really* pushy or something?"

Olivia shakes her head slowly. "No. Not at all, actually. I mean, they're happy if I do well, but they're not intense or anything. Why?"

"Because you're *so* hard on yourself. About everything. About screwing up your exams, about not keeping up with the news, about not realising these things about yourself or your relationships." Liza shakes her head, staring at her. "Why do you do that? Put so much pressure on yourself to get everything right?"

Olivia blinks. "I didn't know I did."

"You kind of do," she tells her gently. "In fact, you totally do."

Olivia stares out at the water, clearly giving it some thought. Finally, she shrugs. "Maybe it's got a bit to do with my family. They're all so goddamned talented. Even Anna, my sister. I feel pretty flaky compared to them."

Liza shakes her head and smiles at her. "You're not a flaky person. Trust me. And you've got to be nicer to yourself. We're *eighteen*, Olivia. I'm pretty sure we're not supposed to have everything sorted by now."

Olivia just draws slow circles in the sand and shrugs.

"You know, it took me six years of sprinting around a track for thirty hours a week to work out I didn't want to do it anymore. I also thought I should let some girl treat me like crap for months because I thought it was the only way I was ever going to have a relationship. But I'm not sitting here beating myself up about it. I'm just accepting it as something I needed to figure out. And now I'm moving on. I highly recommend it." She smiles gently at her.

Olivia just looks at her for a minute, her face unreadable. Finally, she nods slowly and stares down at her hands.

Not sure what to say now, Liza looks out at the shifting ocean. The waves sound louder now than they do in the day, thick and bassy.

"Hey, remember that last night in London? When we were at the pub?"

Liza stiffens. "Yeah?" she says slowly.

"Can I ask you something?"

"I guess."

"Were you weirded out when I was talking to that guy? I saw you looking at us."

Liza lets out the breath she's holding and gives her a cringing smile. "Was I that obvious?"

"I just looked over, and I saw your face. You looked, well, less than happy."

Liza's cheeks start to burn. She cringes, positive Olivia will be able to see how red it is, even in the semidarkness. "I'm so sorry."

"What for?"

She shrugs helplessly. "I'm *trying* to be cool."

Feeling Olivia's stare on her, she knits her fingers together into a tight knot and stares out at the water, completely embarrassed. But she had to say it. It's becoming harder to hide behind this awkward guise of friendship. And even harder now Olivia has asked that question. Besides, she thinks, they only have a few days left. She can figure out a way to survive them and then, you know, avoid Olivia for the rest of her life.

Olivia stares for what feels like forever. "Really?"

Does this girl really have no idea how lovely she is? How smart and wry and infinitely crushable? She sighs, fully reconciled to her own humiliation. "Really."

There's another long silence. Then Olivia turns her head a little toward her. "You don't have to be cool."

Liza's pulse quickens. Swallowing hard, she brings herself to look at Olivia.

Olivia's smile is shy. "I don't *want* you to be cool. Actually," she says slowly, her eyes fearful. "Maybe I kind of hoped you weren't cool about it."

Liza lets out a slow breath. A radiance settles on this moment. And even though she knows that this is Olivia granting her permission, that if she were to kiss her right now, that Olivia would kiss her back, she doesn't. Instead, she stands, brushing the sand from the back of her legs. Then she turns and takes Olivia's hand and pulls her up with her.

Maybe it's just because Liza still needs to test this thing a little before she leaps. Maybe it's because one more step and she'll be way past smitten. And she needs to know Olivia is definitely with her if she's to going to go there. But maybe it's also to savour it. This moment. To just wait here, giddy, on the brink of something. It's exhilarating. They walk slowly and silently towards the water, as if they're both too scared to break this moment with words.

Olivia's fingers weave between hers as they walk, making something more intimate, and ridding Liza of the last shreds of doubt. When they reach the water, they pause. Waves chase each other onto the wet sand, glinting silver where the moon's rays dance off them. Right now, the world is made up only of a shifting mass of inky black water, the dark shapes of islands in the distance, and Olivia's fingers threaded between hers.

Olivia kicks off her shoes. "Come on." She steps into the rushing water, pulling Liza behind her. Liza hurriedly kicks off her own sandals and follows her in. Right now, she'd follow this girl anywhere.

The water swirling around her legs is tropical warm, like tepid bathwater. Liza longs for that brisk chill of the beaches back home. It's hard to feel refreshed in the heat of the day. But right now, it's perfect. They wade out slowly, following that inexorable pull of the ocean. Before they reach the spot where the waves break, foamy and rushing, Liza tugs Olivia's hand. "Undertow," she warns.

"I know." Olivia steps closer, and Liza can see her face clearly in the moonlight now. She's smiling. She loves the way Olivia smiles at her. She feels discovered by that smile. Olivia's arms wind around her waist, and suddenly she can't wait a second longer. She slowly loops her arms around Olivia's neck and kisses her. And Olivia kisses her right back. They linger in it as music pounds from one of the beach clubs and some girls scream excitedly somewhere out on the road. It's a languid but hungry clutch, one she never wants to leave.

Finally, they retreat and just stare at each other a while. Liza breathes slowly and tries to absorb the impossible loveliness of this moment and this girl. Olivia's smile turns wry as they stand there, arms wrapped around each other, waltzing involuntarily with and against the restless current.

"This is so bad B-movie," she says. "Isn't it?"

"What is?" Liza's voice comes out all stammering.

Olivia chuckles. "This. Us." She lifts her arms and wraps them loosely around Liza's neck. "Kissing in the ocean by moonlight," she says in this soap opera voice. "On a tropical island, no less."

"I think it's a peninsula, actually." Liza grins.

"Pedant."

Liza swallows hard, staring at her. "But I think it's kind of amazing, too," she confesses, blushing. "It's nothing I pictured happening tonight."

Olivia's smile is bashful. "Me too, obviously. On both counts."

There's a thrill through her blood as Olivia's arms wind tighter around her waist. She stares at Liza, and her smile turns mischievous as they move slowly backward into deeper water. Even in the dark, Liza can see the playful glint in her eye.

"What?" is all she manages to ask before a wave pounds into her, breaking over her back in a thunderous rush of noise and foam. Olivia clings to her front, sheltering from its force, as if it will help, and it's all Liza can do to stay upright as it slams into her. When it's passed and she's dripping and breathless, she shoves Olivia backward into the swirling water and makes a break for the shore. Olivia is just behind her, spluttering and laughing.

"Sorry, just thought I'd give you the full cheesy romance treatment," Olivia gasps as she catches up with her and clutches her dripping hand.

They flop on the dry sand further up the beach, their heads pressed together and their fingers entwined. As she stares up at the misshapen half-moon, Liza feels electric and calm at the same time, a surprisingly incredible cocktail of feelings.

Olivia squeezes her fingers. "I'm so glad I came on this trip."

And Liza smiles because she knows what Olivia really means is she's glad she came on this trip *with her.* That this happened. She rolls onto her side, rests her cheek on her hand, and smiles down at her.

Olivia doesn't smile back, but her expression softens as she runs the back of her hand over Liza's cheek.

"Why do you like me?" Liza can't help herself. She needs to know.

Olivia contemplates her for a moment and then shrugs. "Because you're sweet and smart and I love talking to you. And you're also kind of...quietly mighty." She nods as she says it, as if satisfied with finding the right words.

Liza smiles, enchanted.

"I tried *not* to like you."

"Why?"

She shrugs again and rolls onto her back. "I don't know. I guess because I didn't think it made sense at first. To who I thought I was."

Liza nods. She gets it. "I tried not to like you either."

"Why?"

"Because I thought I shouldn't like you." She smiles, tracing her finger over Olivia's wrist. "But it was too hard not to."

"Yeah, because I'm so irresistible," she says, sarcastic. Then she just stares at her a moment. "So there's all those reasons why I like you. And then there's the fact that apparently I just find you really, really hot." She shrugs comically, as if to say she has no control over that part.

Liza laughs. And because she couldn't stop herself if she tried, she shuffles closer and presses her lips to Olivia's again. And Olivia's arms are around her instantly, pulling her toward her. Giving up any pretence of restraint, Liza climbs right over her, straddling her legs. And their kisses immediately deepen, all salty slowness and warm breath. Liza sinks onto her, feeling the clammy press of their wet skin and clothes. She drops her head and kisses Olivia's neck, tasting even more seawater slick there. Olivia inhales heavily and runs her hands up and down Liza's back.

They kiss for what feels like hours, in a slow roll across the sand, first one on top and then the other. Occasionally Liza hears people walk by, talking, but they must give them a wide berth, because she never sees them. Eventually, they find themselves lying side-by-side, legs wrapped over each other's, their kisses becoming more ferocious and exploring, their hips straining. Finally, Olivia pulls away and presses her hand against Liza's sternum. "We have to stop."

Liza frowns. "We do?"

Olivia nods and then breaks her own rules by kissing Liza again. She runs a hand along her side, grinning. "I am not going to be one of those gross Australian tourists who shags on a public beach. That's disgusting." She bites her lip, but it doesn't stem her smile. "But soon, I'm not going to be able to stop myself."

Liza laughs, delighted and relieved. "Well, in that case, I'll take your abstention as a compliment."

"Do." Olivia runs her finger along Liza's bottom lip. "Definitely do."

"But we do need to stop," Liza agrees. She sits up and brushes sand from her arms. "Because I'm not about to get sand all up in my business just for you anyway."

Olivia laughs as she stands. Liza grins. She likes that she can make Olivia laugh. They walk back up the beach slowly, hand in hand. Liza almost can't believe how good she feels right now. She finds herself constantly looking at Olivia, as if to check nothing has changed. But every time Olivia is looking back at her, and they just smile at each other.

Maybe this is it. This is what it feels like when a girl actually likes you.

When they're close to the bungalow, Olivia grabs Liza's hand, stopping her in her tracks. "Why do you like *me?*" she asks in a whisper.

Liza smiles and takes her other hand as well. She's about to answer when a toilet flushes and a door closes inside. Olivia presses her finger to Liza's lip until the sound of footfalls cease. Then she replaces it with her mouth. When they finally break the kiss, Olivia buries her face in Liza's neck and lets out a tiny, mournful moan.

"I know," Liza whispers, running her hand through Olivia's long hair. She doesn't want this night to end either.

Eventually, Olivia pushes her away, but it's almost as if it's more to tell herself than Liza. Then she clasps her cheeks between her hands, kisses her, and gives her a slow, sweet smile. "G'night."

"Good night," Liza whispers, kissing her one last time before she follows her inside and flops down in her single rollaway bed, still reeling from this night.

CHAPTER 39

Olivia, Kata, Thailand

Olivia slides reluctantly into waking. The first thing she notices is the whirring rush of air conditioning, and the slight smell of damp that pervades the bungalow at all times. They have to sleep with the air con on even though it turns the air so frigid she has to bury herself under the doona to sleep. If they switch it off, the air thickens again within minutes, and it becomes too hot and muggy for them all to sleep in this small space. It's better to freeze, they've decided.

The next thing she registers is the quiet muttering of Mai next to her, dreaming hard. Olivia smiles. Of course Mai even talks in her sleep.

A tap is turned on in the bathroom. She rolls over, wrapping her arms around her pillow and opening her eyes slowly, making slow acquaintance with waking. On the other bed, two figures are buried under the sheets, reduced to just two piles of tousled hair, red and blonde. The rollaway at the end of the bed is empty. It must be Liza in the bathroom.

Liza. Olivia inhales involuntarily and presses her face into the pillow. Last night on the beach was ten kinds of amazing. And so surprisingly *right*. Yep, this new repertoire of sensations she feels in her stomach when she thinks about last night tells her that this thing is perfectly, immaculately right.

She still can't believe she made last night happen. She's not sure she's ever been so brave in her life. Wanted to be so forward and brave. In fact, it might be the first time she's ever gone after something she wants.

She blinks into the shaft of sunshine shooting through a gap in the blinds and considers this brand-new knowledge. In fact, it might be one of the first times she's ever really *known* what she wanted. Everything else lately—dating Will, applying for law, even going on this trip after Kit pulled out—she has just let happen. Because she thought she *should* want these things. It feels like a strange, bold, brave new world to be chasing something with such certainty.

Sure, maybe she made it so Liza would have to be the one to kiss her, but Olivia did let Liza know the shape of her feelings. Because she actually *knew* the shape of her feelings. And now, for the first time in her life, she understands how magical it can be when two people figure out they feel the same thing for each other.

The bathroom door opens and closes somewhere behind her, and her brain goes into rapid shutdown. Footsteps pad past. Holding her breath, she watches Liza by the front door, yanking on her runners and taming her hair into a high ponytail. As she wraps the elastic around her curls, she shuffles from side to side, driving her feet all the way into her shoes.

Olivia watches this little pre-run ritual, safe in her cocoon of covers. When Liza turns to leave, she spots Olivia watching her, and her hand immediately catches the doorframe as she stops to meet Olivia's gaze. With a shy smile, Olivia clutches the sheets closer around her. A warmth radiates through her as they shyly re-examine each other. She's sure they're both looking for the same thing.

The smile Liza gives in return is sweet but electric. It lingers until she steps outside and becomes little more than a silhouette in the bright morning sun. When she jogs away, Olivia rolls over and buries her head under the pillow, happy and relieved. Last night is still there, safe and sound.

* * *

Kit, Kata, Thailand

They take a back road to the temple. The steeper the hill gets, the slower they walk and the quieter they all become. The trees thin out, giving way to lush greenery. The air thickens.

For one long steep stretch, Kit stares at her feet, using all her energy to breathe and walk. When the road finally flattens out a little, it's thinner and wearing at the edges. They stick to the shoulder in a single file, because every now and then a bike or car tears past at full speed.

Catching her breath before the next climb, Kit takes in their surroundings. The few houses up here are smaller and wooden and hemmed in by trees and flowering vines. A man sits on a wooden step eating a piece of fruit and reading a paper. A toddler stumbles around on the grass near him, clad in just a nappy. Neither of them pays the slightest bit of attention to them. Outside another house, Kit spots an old woman as she stops by her window, running a tea towel over a cup, and glances at them before going about her business. On the veranda are hundreds of fastidiously arranged flowering pots. Kit stares, fascinated.

Finally, the trees thin out and give way to a huge cleared area. And looming above them, just like in the brochure, is a giant, white, cross-legged Buddha. Kit stares at its benign countenance as it overlooks the hills and coast below.

"Hey!" It's Mai, waving as she limps toward them. She caught a cab up the hill. She tips her head back and squints at the statue as they join her. "Now I get why they call him Big Buddha."

Olivia nudges Mai. "You are hilarious."

"Let's go up." She points to where rows of tourists wind their way up a path to the foot of the statue from the car park on the other side.

The others trek up the last of the hill, walking sign-posted paths. Kit stays put, though. She doesn't see the point in getting any closer to this mammoth entity. He dominates the sky from here. Instead, she gives him one last look and turns her gaze back the way they came. In front of her stretches hills and islands and coast as far as she can see. She shakes her head, hardly able to fathom how beautiful it is here. The others like Thailand too, but they don't seem as taken as Kit is. That's probably because they've been spoilt by so many sensory riches this last month.

When she first picked Thailand, back when they were first planning this trip, she'd just thought of the beaches and clubs and resorts, places where they could indulge themselves in holidaying on the cheap, partying and sunbaking. She had no idea that what would capture her so fully would be the other things, the unfamiliar, sometimes dirty and chaotic but always fascinating things she's seen and smelled. Right now, all she wants to do is go back into those quiet, hilly streets and explore, feel that quiet awareness of those neighbourhoods.

She takes in the view and thinks of her mother back home. Kit knows Annie will never, not even with the money she won, do or see something like this. Already, she has tied herself firmly to one tiny corner of experience, of possibility, and is determined to stay there. And Kit realises how easily she might have done the same. How easily she could have found another boyfriend to add to a long line of boyfriends. She could have kept a string of shitty jobs too. In fact, she might have waited a couple of years and popped out a baby instead of a university degree, like her mum did with Chloe. Maybe if she were lucky, she'd take a long weekend in Queensland one day and talk about it as that one big trip.

But now, with just this tiny little taste, with this sensation of being somewhere so strange and so familiar at the same time, she knows she is utterly seduced. And as she stands there with the Andaman Sea, blue and glittering, rolling away in front of her, she knows she has made the right decision to go with Lewis next year. She doesn't want to live in a tiny universe like her mother has made for herself. She wants to see everything this world has to offer her. She wants to *want*.

She sucks in a deep breath of sea breeze and holds out her arms for a second, not caring how stupid she looks. She tips back her head and grins and just gives in to this feeling.

* * *

Liza, Kata, Thailand

She leans forward a little, adjusting her position on the seat. "Are you ready?"

The only response is the slide of arms around her waist.

"Excited?" she asks this time, clutching the handles, getting a feel for them.

"No." Olivia laughs and squeezes her. "I'm *terrified.*"

"Don't be." She leans to the side to offset a wave washing under them. Olivia squeals in her ear. Liza laughs. She can't help herself. They rock back and forth violently, but stay easily upright.

She grips the handles impatiently, wishing the others would hurry up. She's *so* ready for this. Tam's still helping Mai clamber on behind Kit, while the woman renting them the skis holds Mai's crutch for her on the beach. When Mai is on, Tam climbs astride her own jet ski.

Another wave breaks around them, pushing them around in a half circle. Olivia's grip tightens, and she yelps.

“It’s going to be okay, I *promise,*” Liza tells her. “Fun even.”

“It better be.” Olivia gives her leg a surreptitious squeeze. A small current jolts through Liza. And before Olivia can relinquish her grip on her leg, Liza grabs her fingers and grips them hard before dropping them as the others come closer.

“Ready?” Tam yells over the crash of waves and the motors.

Liza nods. Hell yes.

They take off in a collective roar of motors, skating over foamy crests of vivid blue water and dropping into the dips between waves. With each one, Liza’s stomach rises and falls independently of her body. She loves that sensation. Olivia, apparently, does not, given the vicelike grip of arms around Liza’s waist, and the bruising press of forehead on her spine. She smiles and wishes she could say something to comfort her, but she knows she’ll relax into it soon.

And she does. As they ski out onto smoother water, past the break, all Liza can hear is the roaring rush of air past her and the sound of Olivia’s screeches mellowing from terror to delight.

As soon as her grip loosens, Liza grins and accelerates.

CHAPTER 40

Tam, Kata, Thailand

Tam holds her face up to the surprisingly cool breeze and kicks her bare feet through the sand. Waves crash loudly onto the shore next to her. All around, people are gathered in tight clusters on the beach, drinking and partying.

The others are just ahead of her, by now familiar strutting shadows. Everyone is still on a high from the club. The only way they knew to experience the bittersweet finality of their last night of the trip was to dance it out. So they dressed up and trooped down to one of the zillions of beachfront bars. It didn't matter which. Tonight was about them, not the venue, even if the place they chose was uncomfortably steamy and overcrowded, and the drinks only stayed cold for minutes after purchase. It didn't matter that the music was a string of achingly familiar, tired dance anthems. Nothing mattered. The five of them were so deeply committed to enjoying themselves that it happened anyway. All those faults in the stars of their night were just things to be laughed at. Annoying things to be given a patronising, indulgent pat on the head and then ignored as they danced and laughed and talked crap, giddy on some sort of mutual holiday high.

It's the first time Tam can remember them all truly spending a night out *together* since they came on this trip. They've had their moments of solidarity, but there have always been other things, other people, or just their lack of familiarity causing them to split off. But tonight was different as they banded together, thick as thieves in their mission to ignore the fact that tomorrow this will be over. And maybe, just maybe, to celebrate the fact that they got through this thing together. No, Tam corrects herself, more than got through. They even had a good time mostly.

And Tam partied too. Because even in the face of everything that has happened on this trip— the lack of Kit, the homesickness, the news from Bill—she has loved it. And she, too, needed a night like tonight to pay a ridiculous but fun tribute to the experience. And to this band of girl misfits she has grown to truly like.

It's easier too since she spoke to her father yesterday and endured his vehement "there's no way you're coming back early" lecture. After talking to both him and later to Bill on the phone, she's found some kind of sad peace in the fact that no matter where she is, there is nothing she can do. That truth will be as heartbreakingly immutable at home as it is here. So why not stay? A calm resignation has stolen over her. She cannot control this. It will not be controlled. So she might as well not try.

Being with these people and in this place has a rapidly approaching use-by date, so she tries her best to focus on being here in this moment. She hurries along the sand, carrying her sandals. Mai and Kit are leading the pack with their drinks in large plastic cups. Mai's telling Kit a story about a hilarious miscommunication they had with a fruit seller at a market in Rome. Tam grins. She'd forgotten about that already. There have been so many funny, strange moments strung out over the last month. They'll all come back to her at some point, she knows, but it's impossible to hold them all at once.

"You're doing *what?*" Mai suddenly yells into the darkness, grabbing Kit's arm and shaking it. "Seriously?"

"What are you doing?" Liza asks, sounding worried.

Kit turns and kind of cringes. "I'm going travelling at the end of May with Lewis, and I'm going to work in an orphanage in Ukraine."

For a moment Tam just stares at her cousin. Then she smiles and shakes her head. That's one thing you can always rely on with Kit. Expect the unexpected.

But before anyone can say anything, Kit clenches her fists and frowns. "And no one is allowed to laugh or tell me it's a dumb idea or anything, because you guys are all going off to uni and Tam, you're going to do your cooking thing, and I have no idea what the hell I want to do except that maybe I want to do this." She folds her arms over her chest and glares, as if challenging them to suggest otherwise. Tam's never seen her cousin look so fierce.

Olivia grabs her hand. "Hey, Kit, no one is going to tell you it's dumb. *I* think it sounds really exciting."

"Me too," Liza tells her.

"Hell yes!" Mai throws an arm around Kit's neck. "It sounds awesome! And who's this Lewis guy?" She drags Kit along the beach, firing questions at her.

Tam doesn't hurry. They'll have plenty of time to talk about it on the bus trip tomorrow.

As she slowly trails after them in the moonlight, Tam spots Olivia reach over and grab Liza's hand. She lets it go just as quickly. Liza turns and smiles at her, nudging her with her shoulder.

That was definitely more than just friendly affection. Tam smiles to herself. This seems to be a night of surprises. But there was a moment, back in Italy, now that she thinks about it, when she fleetingly wondered if Liza might have a thing for Olivia. And she has been aware of them becoming closer since then. They seem to talk endlessly about their bookish things, but she had never really considered the possibility that if Liza did have a crush, it might be reciprocated.

She watches them as they walk quietly behind Mai and Kit and wonders how long it has been going on. She's happy for Liza. For both of them. She's not about to say anything, though. The sweet, furtive nature of that little show of affection tells her they're not sharing this thing yet.

As she strides along the sand, tired and a little drunk, her mind swings automatically to Matt. And she immediately feels the impatience and uncertainty that comes with that territory. When will she know what this thing with him is? She bites down hard on her lip. She already knows the answer to that question. It's like Kit said the other day: it will happen when she just *asks*. She just has to gather up enough brave to do it.

When she catches up to the others, they're sitting on the sand watching some kids set off firecrackers at the other end of the beach. They're pathetic things, fizzlers, shooting up only a few metres and crackling a little in a show of sparks before dying.

"I can't believe we're leaving tomorrow." Liza hugs her knees. "This has been so great. I wish I had longer like you, Tam."

"Me too," Olivia agrees. She turns to Kit. "How long will you go for?"

Kit shrugs. "As long as I can afford." She sounds excited and nervous.

Liza wraps an arm around Kit and rests her cheek on her shoulder. "I'm so excited for you."

Kit leans against her friend. "I don't even want to go home now. I could stay in Thailand forever."

"Not me," Mai announces. "I'm so ready to go home. I miss my friends."

"Thanks," Olivia retorts, throwing a piece of shell at Mai.

Mai ducks and giggles. "No offence to you guys, of course." She sips her drink. "No, I think we did well on this trip for a bunch of strangers travelling together."

"And thanks again," Olivia says.

"Except for us, of course," Mai says, throwing an arm around Olivia's neck. "But I think the teacher would have given us a sticker for playing nice in the schoolyard. It could have gone really badly."

Olivia laughs. "True."

Tam smiles. Trust it to be bigmouth Mai to acknowledge out loud that none of them were sure that this holiday was going to work out.

"You know, I never got one of those stickers," Olivia grumbles. "I don't know why. I was nice. I shared my playlunch."

"Maybe the teachers didn't want to be seen sucking up to the writer's daughter?" Kit suggests.

"Oh yeah," Olivia says glumly. "See? Another of my life sacrifices to my mother's brilliant career."

"Oh you poor, poor thing." Mai holds up her glass. "To us!"

"To us!" they all cry, even though no one but Kit has a drink left. Mai and Kit share around the last of their cocktails. They sip and laugh at their sad little toast and then lapse into a mutually dreamy silence.

And for a while, there are just the sounds of other people's parties, of crashing waves, and of the eternal hum of traffic on the beach road.

Liza suddenly speaks up. "Do you guys *feel* like adults now? I mean, we're supposed to be. We're eighteen, we've finished high school, we've travelled overseas now, and we're going to be at uni soon."

"And we can vote and drive," Olivia adds.

"And drink."

"But do you *feel* like an adult?"

"Sometimes," Mai says. "But most of the time, I feel like a dumb kid."

"Thank God," Olivia says. "Me too."

"Me three," Kit adds.

"Good," Liza says. "It's not just me, then."

They sit there on the sand and talk, as if reluctant to break with this night, with this buoyant, intimate mood they've found themselves in. Tam wraps her arms around her legs and looks up at the scatter of stars. She knows what Liza means. But this night also feels like they're all on the threshold of something, instead of just something ending. She's just not sure what it is, exactly. But it's a good feeling. She knows that much.

One by one, they all lie back on the sand, staring up at the star-flecked sky, and Tam listens to them talk about the first thing they'll do when they get home.

"I'm going to eat Vegemite toast," Liza tells them.

Olivia laughs. "You're such a cliché."

"So? I miss it. What are you going to do?"

Olivia lets out an extravagant sigh. "I'm going to lie sprawled across my big double bed in my nice, silent, dark room, and I'm going to sleep. Alone. Without anyone snoring or talking or turning on the light in the middle of the night."

"Oh yeah, that's going to be amazing," Mai says. "I'm not going to travel again until I'm rich enough to never have to stay in hostels."

"Spoilt brat," Olivia teases.

Tam smiles. She knows Mai will travel again, with or without her hotel rooms. But she also knows Mai has no idea yet how lucky she is to have done this. Tam though is pretty sure she now knows how lucky *she* is. She has nearly everything she wants. When she thinks of that awful time of her father's illness, she now has other things to hold it up against. She thinks of Dan, back in Slovenia, losing his dad so young. She thinks of Bill and his family, awaiting the inevitable up North. She thinks of those people huddled on the boat on the TV screen at a train station in Italy.

She looks around at the other girls, trading jibes and laughing. They're all so lucky.

"What about you, Tam?" Liza asks, pulling her back in momentarily.

"I don't know," she says vaguely, rubbing the sand from her legs. She knows what she'd *want* to do. She just doesn't know if it's possible.

That's it.

She gathers up the sense of possibility this night has given her and stands, checking her watch. He'll still be up. "I'll be back, guys." She ignores their questions, steels herself, and dashes across the road. She lets herself into the bungalow and goes straight for her computer.

When he finally materialises on her screen, she lets herself breathe again. "Hey," he says, like he saw her this morning.

She doesn't return the greeting. Instead she asks, "are we together?"

"Uh, you know you're on another continent, right?"

She doesn't even smile. "You know what I mean."

He reaches out for his cup and takes a slow sip of his tea instead of answering.

She feels her face flush. "I mean...in the romantic sense of together." She swallows hard, her face turning even redder.

He doesn't say anything. Just stares into his cup.

Terrified now, she starts to talk. Fast. "Because the last couple of weeks have been really scary and hard, and I'm scared nothing's going to be the same at home, either." She takes another breath and pushes it out. "And before I left, we slept together."

He smiles gently at her. "I know. I was there."

"But I have no idea what it meant." She folds her arms over her chest. "I mean, I have no idea if it means anything to you. It did to me," she adds in a whisper. She bites down hard on her bottom lip, mostly to stop herself from crying. "And I need to know if you really do like me, or if that was just a thing, because I need to know if there's something good waiting for me when I get back."

He puts his cup down and stares at her, his brown eyes keen and calm as ever. He shakes his head and smiles. "Tam, I keep trying to tell you every time you ask me if I'm with anyone else. I'm only looking at you. I'm waiting for *you*."

Something tingles through her, but she takes her time with this information, breathing slowly in and out. Then she nods, matter of fact. "Good."

He grins.

"Now," she says. "Tell me about the orchards. When do the pickers arrive?"

He just shakes his head, grins, and then does as he's told.

And when she's done talking to him, she ignores the pull of her tiredness and walks back to the beach to join the girls.

CHAPTER 41

Liza, Phuket, Thailand

Liza folds herself into her seat and fidgets with the zipper on her bag, frowning. Mai is hunkered down next to her, in deep consultation with her phone. All around them sunburned, dishevelled tourists mill around the departure gate, waiting for their flight. Liza checks the time. They still have an hour until boarding.

It's been a day of goodbyes. First they farewelled their beachside home and Nisha, the sweet, harried landlady. Then they delivered Tam and Kit to the bus station, where they hugged and laughed and shouted goodbyes as the girls boarded a gaudy pink bus for their trip northward. Then the three of them caught a taxi to the airport, where they delivered Olivia to the gate where she will catch her flight to Shanghai. And that was the moment when the end of this trip began to feel uncomfortably real for Liza. Now she's sitting here waiting for her own flight, a tight knot of something un-nameable and sharp taking up all the space in her stomach.

The last goodbye, with Olivia, was awkward and stilted. It had to be. Because Mai was there, and she doesn't know about them. Then, how could she? Not even Liza knows anything certain about them yet. Not about what's going to happen now, anyway. She only knows what has been between them so far, something lovely and awesome and kind of breathtaking. For Liza, anyway.

But since that night on the beach, they've barely had more than a moment to steal alone. There was that one sweet minute yesterday morning in the bungalow when Mai and Tam were in the pool and Kit went into the bathroom. The second they found themselves alone, Olivia darted over to her. She leaned over Liza where she sat on the couch and dropped several quick kisses on her, her palms pressed hard against Liza's cheeks. Then, as the toilet flushed, she grinned and ducked away, and Liza was left breathless and smitten and wanting. That moment also confirmed something Liza was already fairly certain about. Like her, Olivia isn't ready to share this. Not yet. And that's fine with her.

Except it meant they couldn't say goodbye properly just now.

Mai dominated the farewells, of course. She had no reason to think it needed to be any other way. Liza and Olivia did little more than exchange a brief hug and tense smiles as they parted. Olivia handed her a book too. "To read on the plane," she told her, placing it in Liza's embarrassingly shaky hands and smiling. "In case you don't have one. I didn't want you to panic."

Liza laughed shyly. Then the moment was stolen back by Mai and her hugs and her *I'll miss you*s and her cute but frustrating departure drama. And Liza had to just stand there and watch, not allowed to indulge in even a fraction of Mai's extravagant show of feeling.

And as they strolled back to find their own gate, that thing in Liza's stomach started to harden and hurt. She kept her eyes to the ground and prayed Mai would keep prattling about the date she's set up with Campbell back home so that she could stay safely in this mortifying, tearful silence.

It's not leaving Olivia, exactly, that's causing these epic angst levels. She's only going to Shanghai for a week. It's the not knowing. Not knowing how what has happened will figure in the broader picture of their lives. Olivia's given her no reason to think it ends now, but she's not given her any concrete hope of a foreseeable future either. And Liza would like to have just enough confidence to be certain that what happened between them feels real enough to carry over to home, for Olivia to want to acknowledge it beyond the realm of this holiday. But that messy, mute experience of Alika won't grant her the confidence to find that level of faith on her own.

So she sits and stews, about to get on what feels like an interminable flight, carrying this load of uncertainty. And she's just not sure she can do that.

So, before she can talk herself out of the flash of the idea brewing in her brain, she turns to Mai. "Hey, I'll be back. I forgot to get water."

Mai just nods. She's still deep inside her phone. As Liza stands, she suddenly lifts her head. "Can you grab me some gum?"

"Uh, sure." Liza drops her bag onto the seat and makes a break for it.

* * *

Olivia, Phuket, Thailand

Olivia yawns and stares at the digital sign above the gate. They'll be boarding soon. Once she's on her flight, she plans on some serious napping.

An elderly couple march over to the seats in front of her. They slowly sort out their array of hand luggage and finally settle in. The woman rests her handbag in her lap and proceeds to examine Olivia carefully.

Olivia gives her a brief, polite smile and looks away. She has no idea if the stare is one of those "look at that nice young lady travelling on her own" ones or one of those tsk-tsking "youth of today" stares. Either way, she's totally unwilling to engage and find out. So she fervently ignores it and pretends to sort through her carry-on bag instead. She busily shuffles her earphones and toiletries and wallet around even though she already organised it this morning, and prays the woman finds something more interesting to stare at.

What she doesn't expect is for something more interesting to turn up in the form of Liza. One moment Olivia's re-folding her travel scarf and tucking it in her bag and the next she's staring, open-mouthed, at the panting figure in front of her.

Before she can say a word, Liza drops down onto the seat next to her and asks, "What happens now?"

Olivia doesn't respond, silenced both by this surprise appearance and by the eyes of the old lady. She can feel them boring curiously into her.

"Come here," she says huskily, grabbing Liza's wrist and leading her away from prying eyes. Liza obediently follows, breathing heavily.

As they cross the busy passage to an empty departure gate, Olivia grins. "Did you just do a full Hollywood sprint through the airport to get back here?"

Liza laughs bashfully. "Maybe." Her face turns a shade pinker.

Olivia leads her behind a wall near the empty gate, where they're shielded from the relentless coming and going. It feels like the entire world is scurrying to get somewhere. "Are you okay?"

Liza chews at the side of her lip and nods slowly. The rise and fall of her shoulders slows as her breath steadies. "I just wanted to... I don't know. We never talked about this or what happens after, you know?"

Olivia nods. "We didn't." They couldn't really. There was never a moment.

"Do we..." Liza stares at Olivia, her lips pressed together. Finally, she speaks again. "I mean, can I call you? After we get back? I just..."

Happiness and relief steal through Olivia. How did this girl sneak up on her? So unexpectedly? So entirely? She drops her bag onto the carpet and wraps an arm around Liza's neck, pulling her into a fierce embrace. "Liza, of course you can call," she whispers into her hair. "You *better* call."

As Olivia says the words, the tension in Liza's embrace disappears. Her breath slows against Olivia's neck. They hold on to each other in a long, full silence. Suddenly Liza snickers. "I mean, I thought I could maybe cyber stalk you while you're in Shanghai, but the Chinese government make it bit hard."

Olivia laughs and pulls away. She leans against the wall and smooths a finger along Liza's arm. "This, with us, it doesn't change for me just because we're going home, you know."

"It doesn't?"

"No." She looks up shyly and smiles. "I want go on a date with you."

And Liza's sweet, smitten smile is her reward. "A date?"

"Yeah, a date."

"Okay." Liza nods slowly. "But I'm not really sure I know how to take someone on a date."

Olivia grabs Liza's hand and laughs, completely charmed by this small confession of ineptitude. "It's not exactly rocket science," she teases.

Liza blushes. "I know."

Olivia presses a hand against her pink cheek. "Then I'll take you on one."

"And show me how it's done?"

"Yep." Olivia laughs again, but then turns serious. "You know, I wanted to talk to you. It's just been hard with everyone around and these last crazy couple of days."

"I know. It has. And I got a little freaked." Liza lets out a little breathy laugh. "Which is why I did that embarrassing little dash across the airport."

"Did you take out any little old ladies on your way?"

Liza shrugs. "It's possible." Then she gives Olivia one of those small, secret smiles of hers. One where the bridge of her nose wrinkles. It makes Olivia want to kiss it. Kiss her.

But Liza gets in first. She leans in slowly, pressing her lips against Olivia's. Overwhelmed by this sudden, delicious assault, Olivia wraps her arms around Liza's neck. They kiss long and hard, happily folded into their own little world by the dimly-lit departure gate.

They remain in this heady cling until one of the relentless announcements on the airport PA system mentions Bangkok, and Olivia is forced to pay attention. She drags herself away and peeks around the edge of their hiding place behind the pillar. Everyone at her gate is slowly gathering their things and lining up to board. It's time.

She frowns and turns back to Liza, pressing her palms against her stomach. "I have to go in a minute." She leans in and drops a fresh kiss on her, though, not ready just yet to depart this little limbo they have made for themselves.

Liza is not ready either, apparently. She nods and gathers her into another tight embrace. Olivia pushes her face into that spot between Liza's neck and shoulder and just gives in for a minute to a silent bout of missing her.

After a long silence, Liza whispers in her ear. "Because you're beautiful and funny and smart. But mostly because you're not embarrassed to admit your favourite book is still a kids' book and that you'd rather eat mixed lollies for dinner than vegetables."

"Huh?"

"That's why I like you. I didn't get to tell you."

Olivia grins and grips her tighter. She breathes deep, inhaling Liza's scent, the one she discovered that night in London when they first kissed.

"I'll see you soon, okay?" Liza whispers, pulling away.

Olivia nods. "See you in eight days." Then she smiles. "Oh yeah, and in the meantime..."

"What?"

"Which one of us is going to tell Kit?"

Liza laughs, her eyes shining. "Good question." She shrugs and squeezes Olivia's hands. "I will, I guess."

"I was hoping you'd say that."

"I'm sure you'll hear from her three minutes later."

"Yeah, I'll prepare myself for squealing messages."

"Well, I guess she'll be kind of surprised. Her besties hooking up."

"Of course she will." Olivia laughs. "*I'm* surprised."

Liza picks up Olivia's bag, places it in her hands, and presses a final kiss on her. Then she sighs. "I better go. I told Mai I was just going to get some water."

As they move back into the crowd, Olivia tugs gently on her sleeve. "Hey Lize."

"Yeah?"

"Read the book I gave you."

"I will." Liza gives her one last smile, waves shyly, and turns on her heel. Olivia watches her jog lightly away, her dark curls bouncing against her back.

And she can't help smiling.

* * *

Liza, en route to Melbourne

Wedged into her window seat, unable to sleep, Liza finally pulls out the book. The plane's engines hum loudly in the night as Mai dozes next to her, a snoring pile of eye mask, scarf and blanket. Liza idly flicks through the pages, wondering if she has the attention span for reading right now. Maybe she'd be better off finding some, easy fluffy movie on the entertainment system. She stops turning pages at the sight of some handwriting at the top of a page flipping by. Curious, she turns back to it.

She reads the message written in neat blue pen and smiles, clasping the book tightly.

Chapter six already, huh? I hope you like it. I miss Thailand already. It had red curry, the ocean, and you. Three of my current favourite things. O. xoxo

CHAPTER 42

Tam, Hobart, Australia

Two weeks later.

She has no idea how she managed it, but somehow Tam is the first in line. She pulls her carry-on higher on her shoulder, every ounce of her being focused on covering the last stretch of tarmac between her and her dad and Matt. Behind her she can feel the other passengers stacked up like a wall of impatience.

As the flight attendant shoves the door open, she can see the squat, white building that is the small airport and the streaked glass windows of the arrivals area. Her heart quickens. So close.

The moment the woman steps aside, smiling dutifully and wishing her a safe onward journey, Tam is off like a shot. But the moment she steps out onto the steel steps that will take her down to the tarmac, the world forces her into a brief, involuntary stop. The sun beats down on her face as a brisk wind rushes in from the coast, cooling it immediately. It whips across the tarmac, lifting her hair from her shoulders and forcing her to grip the railing. She takes a deep breath, inhaling that achingly familiar blend of salty sea air and eucalyptus.

Home.

CHAPTER 43

Five months later.

Lizey!

I'm in Ukraine. Can you believe it? I can't. Not one bit. Mostly because I'd never even heard of this place until a few months ago. I keep looking out the window of the hostel at Lviv and laughing because it's so weird to be in a place you've never even had a mental picture of, if you know what I mean? This all of a sudden feels very, very real, which is amazing and scary at the same time.

The hostel we're staying at is in the middle of the old city. We take the train to the town where the orphanage is on Thursday. First, we'll explore a bit. Tonight we're going to the bars with some cool Polish students. Lewis says we're too scruffy to get into the clubs. Only models and their boyfriends allowed, basically. And I forgot my little black dress and my stilettos. Too bad.

Anyway, I better get ready to go out. I just wanted to say hi and that I love you and I miss you. Give Olivia a squeeze for me—not too big an ask, I know (-;

Love love love, Kit

* * *

Liza, Melbourne, Australia

Liza smiles at her phone. It's been three days since they saw her off at the airport, and she misses her like mad already. She hopes Kit has an incredible time. She's worked so hard for this trip.

She slides the phone into the back pocket of her jeans, clutches her pile of books tighter, and gazes down the tree-lined avenue that runs between the old and new parts of the campus. And she stands there in the sunshine until finally, she spots her among the crowd of students, her honey brown hair catching the sunlight and turning it amber as she walks.

She watches Olivia's eyes search the path ahead, her bottom lip caught between her teeth. When she spots Liza, her face softens into a smile and her step quickens.

And as she waits for Olivia to get to her, Liza remembers Tam's teasing question in her email last night.

So, are you "feeling" life now, like you wanted to?

Yes, she is.

###

About Emily O'Beirne

Thirteen-year-old Emily woke up one morning with a sudden itch to write her first novel. All day, she sat through her classes, feverishly scribbling away (her rare silence probably a cherished respite for her teachers). And by the time the last bell rang, she had penned fifteen handwritten pages of angsty drivel, replete with blood-red sunsets, moody saxophone music playing somewhere far off in the night, and abandoned whiskey bottles rolling across tables. Needless to say, that singular literary accomplishment is buried in a box somewhere, ready for her later amusement.

From Melbourne, Australia, Emily was recently granted her PhD. She works part-time in academia, where she hates marking papers but loves working with her students. She also loves where she lives but travels as much as possible and tends to harbour crushes on cities more than on people.

CONNECT WITH EMILY:

Website: www.emilyobeirne.com
Twitter: www.twitter.com/emilyobwrites

Other Books from Ylva Publishing

A Story of Now

A Story of Now Series – Book #1

Emily O'Beirne

ISBN: 978-3-95533-345-4
Length: 367 pages (128,000 words)

Nineteen-year-old Claire knows she needs a life. And new friends. Too sassy for her own good, she doesn't make friends easily anymore. And she has no clue where to start on the whole life front. At first, Robbie and Mia seem the least likely people to help her find it. But in a turbulent time, Claire finds new friends, a new self, and, with the warm, brilliant Mia, a whole new set of feelings.

Fragile

Eve Francis

ISBN: 978-3-95533-482-6
Length: 300 pages (103,000 words)

College graduate Carly Rogers is forced to live back at home with her mother and sister until she finds a real job. Life isn't shaping up as expected, but meeting Ashley begins to change that. After many late night talks and the start of a book club, the two women begin a romance. When a past medical condition threatens Ashley, Carly wonders if their future together will always be this fragile.

The Space Between

Michelle L. Teichman

ISBN: 978-3-95533-581-3
Length: 280 pages (92,000 words)

Life is easy for Harper, the most popular girl in her grade, until she meets Sarah, a friendless loner who only cares about art. Inexplicably, Harper can't stop thinking about her. Unsure of her feelings for Harper, Sarah is afraid to act on what her heart is telling her. She can't believe Harper feels the same. Can Harper and Sarah find a way to be together, or will fear keep them apart forever?

The Light of the World

Ellen Simpson

ISBN: 978-3-95533-507-6
Length: 357 pages (107,000 words)

Confronted with a mystery upon her grandmother's death, Eva delves into the rich and complicated history of a woman who hid far more than a long-lost-love from the world. Darkness is lurking behind every corner, and someone is looking for the key to her grandmother's secrets; the light of the world.

Coming from Ylva Publishing

www.ylva-publishing.com

Flinging It

G Benson

Frazer, head midwife at a hospital in Perth, Australia, is trying to make her corner of the world a little better by starting up a programme for at-risk parents. Not everyone is excited about her ideas. Surrounded by red tape, she finally has to team up with Cora, a social worker who is married to Frazer's boss. Cora is starting to think her marriage is beyond saving, even if she wants to. Feeling smothered by a domineering spouse, she grabs hold of the programme and the distraction Frazer offers with both hands. Soon the two women get a little too close and find themselves in a situation they never dreamed themselves capable of: an affair.

As the two fall deeper, both are torn between their taboo romance and their morals. But walking away from each other may not be as simple as they thought.

Not-So-Straight Sue

Girl Meets Girl Series – Book #2

Cheyenne Blue

Lawyer Sue Brent buried her queerness deep within, until a disastrous date forces her to confront the truth. She returns to her native Australia and an outback law practice. When Sue's friend, Moni, arrives to work as an outback doctor, Sue sees a new path to happiness with her. But Sue's first love, Denise, appears begging a favor, and Sue and Moni's burgeoning relationship is put to the test.

Points of Departure

ISBN: 978-3-95533-698-1

Also available as e-book.

Published by Ylva Publishing, legal entity of Ylva Verlag, e.Kfr.

Ylva Verlag, e.Kfr.
Owner: Astrid Ohletz
Am Kirschgarten 2
65830 Kriftel
Germany

www.ylva-publishing.com

First edition: 2016

Credits
Edited by Astrid Ohletz and Michelle Aguilar

Printed in Poland
by Amazon Fulfillment
Poland Sp. z o.o., Wrocław

56273756R00162